SOMEBODY
ELSE'S SKY

JESSICA
HAWKINS

© 2017 JESSICA HAWKINS
www.JESSICAHAWKINS.net

Editing by Elizabeth London Editing
Beta by Underline This Editing
Proofreading by Tamara Mataya Editing
Cover Design © R.B.A. Designs
Cover Photo by Perrywinkle Photography
Cover Model: Chase Williams

SOMEBODY ELSE'S SKY

ISBN: 0-9988155-0-0
ISBN-13: 978-0-9988155-0-3

TITLES BY
JESSICA HAWKINS
LEARN MORE AT JESSICAHAWKINS.NET

SLIP OF THE TONGUE
THE FIRST TASTE
YOURS TO BARE

SOMETHING IN THE WAY SERIES
SOMETHING IN THE WAY
SOMEBODY ELSE'S SKY
MOVE THE STARS
LAKE + MANNING

THE CITYSCAPE SERIES
COME UNDONE
COME ALIVE
COME TOGETHER

EXPLICITLY YOURS SERIES
POSSESSION
DOMINATION
PROVOCATION
OBSESSION

PREFACE

LAKE, 1995
PRESENT DAY

Gripping a bouquet of peach and cream garden roses, I peeked around the hotel's archway. Friends and family quietly filtered onto a perfectly manicured lawn, murmuring as they took their seats for the ceremony.

The sun began to set over the Pacific Ocean, fiery orange dipping into cool blue. This morning's cloud cover had given way to an unblemished sky. With everything happening around us, it should've been easy to avoid looking at Manning, but that always had been, and always would be, impossible for me. My gaze lifted above the crowd and down the petal-scattered aisle. Manning stood under the sheer curtains of a gazebo on the edge of a cliff, his back to me as he spoke to the best man. The first time I saw Manning on that construction site, he'd been larger than life. Today, he was so much more. He commanded attention without trying. His shoulders stretched a bespoke suit, and his hands sat loosely in his pockets as if it were any other day.

He turned his head, giving me the pleasure of his profile. Strong jaw, full mouth, thick, black, recently trimmed hair. Even with the scar on his lip and the new, slight curve of his nose, he looked refined, the sum of all my dreams come to life.

Henry spoke to Manning with the air of a father figure, his hand on Manning's shoulder. Manning just listened and rubbed his sinfully smooth jaw as he stared at the ground. Henry paused, as if waiting for an answer or acknowledgement, and his smile faded. He looked to the back of the decorated lawn, through the arches hiding the bridal party. He looked at me. Maybe Manning wasn't as calm as I thought. Maybe he was having second thoughts.

I, on the other hand, had only one thought.

Mine.

1

MANNING, 1994
FOURTEEN MONTHS EARLIER

With my back against a concrete wall, I stared out at the jail yard and flicked ash from my cigarette. If I could look at anything other than electric fencing, concrete, sand, and sweaty men, I would. In ten months, I'd memorized this view. California desert stretched far enough to make the mountains seem an unobtainable freedom, June heat turning the horizon into a watery mirage.

It was still better than staring at the underbelly of a top bunk. I'd be doing that later, but not for much longer. I'd gotten some good news the week before.

"You wouldn't believe this bitch," Wills said, clutching a handwritten letter as he paced a strip of dead grass, the bottoms of his orange pants dragging.

"She's threatening not to bring Kaya for the rest of my sentence."

"So?" I asked through my next drag.

"Cecelia's going to keep my baby girl from me? Fuck that."

"She said the same thing last month. And the month before."

"This time it's for real. I can just tell." He ran his hands back and forth over his buzzed scalp, crinkling the paper. "She does this just to screw with me."

We'd had this same conversation at least twice a month since I'd arrived. The first time my cellmate had gotten a letter and gone off the handle, I'd told him not to call his girl a bitch. That'd gotten me a riot of laughs from the guys in cells around us. The time after that, I'd asked why, if he'd cared so much about his 'baby girl,' he'd held up a gas station at gunpoint, knowing where it could land him?

That time, the laughter never came. "Providing for my family," he'd said, getting in my face, his chest inflated. "Think you're better than me, pretty boy?"

Wills was small but built. I had almost half a foot on him and most of the other guys, too. Only a few matched me in height. When I'd arrived, I'd been skinny compared to them but after ten months of lifting and a prison job in construction, I'd bulked up.

Wills'd shoved his hands into my chest, but I hadn't budged except to raise my eyebrows. He'd backed off, schooling me loudly enough for everyone to hear. "Don't tell me how to take care of my daughter. Respect."

Respect. Number one rule in the yard. People my size got more passes than most, but that alone didn't earn me respect. I had to command it. I couldn't take any shit.

Wills used my cigarette to light his. He pointed to a spot on the page, but his hand shook so badly, I wouldn't've been able to read it if I'd cared enough to try. "Right here," he said, butt dangling from the corner of his mouth. "'You won't see Kaya again until she's eighteen,'" he read aloud. "'By then she'll probably be two kids deep because of you, and you won't even be there to experience it.'" Wills looked up at me. "How fucked is that?"

"Fucked," I agreed.

"Cecelia was the only woman I ever loved." He aimed his beady eyes at me, and they flashed with excitement. "Too bad she turned out to be such a *cunt.*"

I wiped sweat from my temple with my sleeve. "Fuck off, Wills."

"Aw, come on, Sutter. Don't be such a pussy. Just once, I'd like to hear you rail against that blonde bitch of yours."

I had to let his shit-talking roll off my back or it'd get me into trouble, and now that I could almost taste freedom, I had to watch my temper. Instead of beating his ass, I got him where it hurt by ripping the cigarette out of his hand and flicking it into the dirt.

He scrambled after it, popping it right back into his mouth. "Asshole."

The guys talked a lot of shit about who they'd fucked, how, and the ways they'd been screwed over by the women in their lives, and no matter how hard I tried to ignore it, my mind always went to the same place—my sister, my aunt, my mom. Lake and Tiffany. I never spoke of them in there. The guys could be brutal. Sinister. Especially from where they stood, behind bars, already ensnared by the law.

I took my last hit of nicotine right on schedule and tossed the butt. With the hem of my shirt, I cleaned my face of dust and sweat as I went to sit outside the visitor's room.

I waited thirty minutes to hear my name. "Sutter," CO Jameson called. "Your blonde's here."

I'd stopped keeping track of time, but I always knew the first and last Friday of each month thanks to "my blonde." Not only had she scheduled work to have those days off, but she drove three hours each way to be here, and that was about as much as anyone had done for me lately. Maybe since I'd left my aunt's at eighteen.

When I entered the visiting room, Tiffany stood from a bench and smoothed her hands over a short, plaid skirt. I wove through the tables to her and bent for a quick kiss.

She put her arms around my neck. "How are you?" she asked in my ear.

"Same."

"Same's good."

As we hugged, her short top rode up a
expose her lower back. I pulled away so my
wouldn't go where it shouldn't and took th
across from her. "Did Grimes call you?"

"Two more months." She slid a few ba
M&M's from the vending machine across the
and kept one for herself. "I can't believe he was r
Are you relieved?"

When my public defender had presented my
bargain, he'd said I was likely to get out early for go
behavior. I'd been skeptical, but it turned out I'd o
have to serve half of my two-year sentence.
Overcrowding helped moved the process along.
There were men shoulder-to-shoulder at every
cafeteria table. Out in the yard while we worked,
someone was always shoveling or pouring concrete
nearby. If I wasn't careful, they'd forklift my ass. To
shower, I waited in line forty minutes to stand under a
spigot for sixty seconds. Our cells were close enough
to hear guys spanking it. That'd all work in my favor,
though, as long as I kept to myself the next couple
months.

"I won't be relieved until I'm breathing air
outside this shithole," I said.

The air conditioner hummed to life. I'd've been
grateful if it actually cooled the room a few degrees,
but it just added another layer of noise to everyone's
conversations. "Did everything go okay with the new
guy they put in your cell?" she asked.

7

That depended on her definition of *okay*. Considering she wasn't locked up in here, it was likely different than mine. "It's fine."

She narrowed her eyes. "I don't believe you. Did someone figure out he was, you know . . ." She lowered her voice. "A snitch?"

Wills and I had been assigned a new cellmate last month. Once it got out he'd ratted on a rival gang member for a lesser sentence, it hadn't taken long for word to spread to the wrong people. "They put it together last week," I said. "Wasn't any chance they wouldn't."

"And?"

"And nothing." I didn't see any point in worrying her.

She put an M&M in her mouth, chewing absentmindedly, then sat up a little straighter, as if she'd come to a decision about something. "Did they beat him up?"

"Well . . . yeah."

"How bad? You can tell me. You don't have to protect me like you would *some* girls."

Far as I knew, none of the guys in here were worried about scarring their girlfriends. Tiffany wasn't exactly innocent, but she'd lived a pretty sheltered life. I rubbed my jaw. "Pretty bad."

"Were you there?"

I shifted in my seat. I'd been working across the yard but close enough to see it go down. If I could've intervened, I would've, but from day one I'd had a plan, and that was to keep my head down and stay out of trouble.

An inmate a few tables away grabbed his kid's arm. I glanced at CO Jameson, who was already heading over.

"What happened?" Tiffany asked, sneaking glances as the female guard handled a man twice her size. She escorted him out more nicely than I would've. "You can tell me, Manning. You should talk about it. It's not healthy to keep it inside."

I didn't know about all that, but truth was, watching a defenseless man get the shit beat out of him had stuck with me. A man I'd talked to, had shared a cell with, and there wasn't anything I could do about it. "Slock," I said. "He's been in the infirmary a week."

"Slock?"

It was a common enough weapon in here. Tiffany really didn't know shit about this stuff if she'd never heard the term. "Lock in a sock."

"Like the kind I used on my high school locker?"

"Exactly." I demonstrated winding up a sock, pausing to gauge her reaction. She worried her lip between her teeth but nodded me on. "Then you swing it," I said. "He lost an eye."

She sucked in a breath. "Could that happen to you?" she asked. "You're a big guy."

She wasn't even going to comment on the eyeball? I almost laughed. She got points for that. I could think of a few people I'd never burden that image with, but I didn't want to go there, so I kept talking. "Nobody's too big to go down," I answered. "But you don't need to worry about me. I don't get involved with anyone's business. It's not like you see in the movies. I leave them alone, they leave me alone, and if I do come up against something, I stand my ground."

"Like that fight a few months ago? Over the M&M's . . ."

"It wasn't a fight, and it wasn't about candy. That fucker stole cigarettes and orange soda from my bunk." I kept my head down, but there were some things I couldn't let slide. We had limited access to the commissary store—I couldn't just replace what he'd stolen. And I couldn't let it go. Not in here. *Respect*, Wills would say. So far, it was the only altercation I'd shared with Tiffany.

"You punched a guy over candy and cigarettes," Tiffany said.

I had to smile at how ridiculous it sounded. "You make it seem like we're a bunch of toddlers."

Her posture relaxed a little. "Well, then I probably shouldn't show you what I brought. None of it's suitable for children." She picked up some books from the bench and stacked them on the table. "They're from a thrift store," she added quickly, "so don't wig out on me. They were cheap. You like that author, right?"

I flipped through the one on top, *Fear and Loathing in Las Vegas*, grateful to have something good to read. Books were the one thing I'd even consider trading cigarettes for. "Yeah."

"The clerk recommended the other ones. He said if you like Hunter S. Thompson to try Tom Wolfe and . . ." She checked the spine of *Slaughterhouse-Five*. "Kurt Vonnegut. I read a little of it. It was weird, but I remember you telling me about that cockroach book, and probably not much is weirder than that."

This time, I did laugh, the rumble in my chest a foreign feeling. A good one. "These are perfect. *But . . .*" I pulled the next in the pile in front of me—a Webster's dictionary that looked heavy enough to knock out Wills. "How'd you get this in here?" I asked. "And what's it for, protection?" I curled it like a weight, but it was surprisingly light.

"Open it, but not all the way."

I snuck a look under the cover. The first half of the book was intact, but she'd cut a square in the center, about two-thirds of the way in, stuffed it full of loose cigarettes, then lined the rest with books of stamps. I rarely sent outgoing letters, but guys like Wills could send two a day and postage wasn't cheap. "Tiffany."

The air conditioner cut out. "I know, I know."

I'd told her plenty of times not to waste her money on me. She sold clothing on commission, so her paycheck depended on her hustle, and I kept telling her to put extra money in the bank. But she did stuff like this each visit, bringing me things I could use or sell, greasing the guards, adding to my commissary account. "How much did this cost you?"

"A couple Esprit tops with my Nordstrom discount." She lifted her hair off her neck, resettling it over her shoulders. My eyes automatically dropped to her chest. "Don't worry about it. The guards like me."

"Is that how you get by them in those outfits?" I asked. She dressed to the nines for every visit, from her earrings to her shoes. At first I'd asked her to stop. The guys gave me shit for it, and according to visitation regulations, she wasn't supposed to dress sexy. Somehow, she always managed to get by with a little cleavage or leg or midriff or something.

"What's wrong with my outfit?" she asked. "You don't like it?"

"You look good." Today, her white t-shirt was tight enough that I could see the outline of her bra. It was definitely padded, her tits big and round, inviting my hands to curve around them, my cock to slide between them. I licked my lips. "Too good."

"Well, I won't apologize for that."

The clock behind my head ticked on, a reminder that time was limited. I forced my eyes back to the contraband in front of me. Nothing killed the threat of a boner like a musty dictionary. "You know you can bring stamps in, right?" I teased her. "Don't need to get all cagey about it."

"It's more fun this way. Speaking of *fun*." She slipped a *Playboy* from the bottom of the pile. I was one of the lucky bastards whose girlfriend brought him porn and probably the only guy who didn't care about it.

I took the magazine. A naked blonde I recognized from MTV looked back at me from the cover. Her knowing blue eyes and smile-smirk were familiar. "She looks a little like you," I said. "Maybe in a few years."

She vaulted forward to see better as I checked for the centerfold. "Jenny McCarthy?" she asked. "I think her boobs are fake. Do you like that?"

"No." I closed it. "Thanks, but I told you, I don't read these."

"And I told you, I don't believe you. But if that's true, just trade it for whatever you need. But," she lowered her voice to a breathy whisper, "not before you check pages eighteen and nineteen. *Don't* trade it until you do that."

"What'll I find on pages eighteen and nineteen?" I asked, watching her fingers twist her hair into one, big golden curl.

She smiled with her lips closed, like she had a secret, and I knew what I'd find on pages eighteen and nineteen—or more like stuck between them. The female correctional officer on duty, Jameson, was all right, so I peeked inside at two Polaroids of Tiffany in black lingerie. As I followed the lines of her curves, my balls tightened. This, the possibility of one day having it, got me off way more than glossy chicks I didn't know. "Who took these?"

"Sarah. She did it for her boyfriend, too."

"You know CO Ludwig might 'confiscate these,'" I said. He'd cleaned me out of cigarettes, porno, and chewing tobacco during the last shakedown, and that fucker would delight in violating any inmate by taking his girl's photos.

"So you'll have them until he does." She shrugged. "He's pathetic. That fat idiot has to take them because unlike you, he has nobody to give him any."

I didn't like the idea of it, but Tiffany took it in stride. She knew how little control I had in here. I didn't know many girls who wouldn't freak out about a "fat idiot" drooling over their photo. Behind the Polaroids, she'd folded up a page torn from a magazine. I opened it. Tiffany smiled brightly on the page in khakis and a navy polo, her arms crossed as she leaned her shoulder against a man wearing the same outfit.

"My second catalogue," she said. "It's for this company that sells uniforms. I know the clothing is hideous, but I wanted you to see—"

"I don't care what you're wearing." I smoothed out the creases. "You look happy. Even prettier than Jenny what's-her-name."

She nudged my leg with her foot. "Thank you."

"Any more news from that agent lady?"

Her blue eyes lit up. "I have a go-see for a swimsuit company this weekend. My agent thinks I'll get it. They're looking for a beach babe."

"You're a beach babe if I ever saw one."

"I need this job, Manning. I can't wait to quit Nordstrom. My manager has been so obnoxious this week. She made me vacuum the fitting rooms twice in one day. As if anyone could tell the difference."

Outside this space, I would've stopped her there. I couldn't fake interest in overpriced clothing, the women Tiffany constantly had to compliment, or sales floor brawls over commission. But my life was about routines now, and this was part of ours. Hearing about her day-to-day life, it wasn't much, but it was something I looked forward to anyway.

Tiffany'd gotten a modeling agent after I'd been locked up, and almost right away, she'd been in a catalogue. Paid pretty well, too, though she'd blown most of the money already. "It's just temporary," I reminded her.

"I know. I'll feel better after I pick up my paycheck." She put her hands in her lap. "Which is something I wanted to talk about. I've been thinking."

"Yeah?" I sat back in my seat. "What about?"

"I've been saving a little each pay period like you said."

Before this, I'd been pretty good about setting extra money aside. It was all gone now, mostly on fines and restitution, but I'd been going over savings accounts and compound interest with Tiffany during our visits. Apparently, her dad had tried and given up, but I figured she had to see the light sooner or later. Maybe she finally had. "Good," I said.

"And, well, things have been really tense at home, so I might . . . I might try to get my own place."

"Can you afford the rent?"

"I can if I cut back shopping at the store. I just save so much with the discount."

"Not more than you'd save if you didn't buy anything," I pointed out.

She considered that a second. "I never thought of it that way. Anyway, what do you think? About the apartment?"

As long as Tiffany lived at home, she'd be under her dad's thumb. I didn't see how that had helped her up to this point. "I like the idea."

"Really?" she asked. "My dad says I can't afford it."

"Well, that's because he hasn't seen you try. Prove him wrong. Get a roommate if you need to. Move inland. Stop eating out. You can do it if you set your mind to it."

"You really think so? Because I've looked into it, and I *do* think I can do it, but when he said that, I started to doubt myself."

"I know you can make it happen," I said. "You just have to stay focused."

"Okay. I will." Her smile fell into a frown when she checked the clock over my head. "I have to go in a minute. If I don't run the errands Mom gave me for tonight, I'll be dead meat."

"What's tonight?" I asked.

"Oh, it's . . ." She glanced away.

She always looked left when she was exaggerating or stretching the truth. Wherever she had to be tonight, she didn't want to tell me. I couldn't think of any reason why that might be except one—another guy. We'd never really made things official, her and I—she called me her boyfriend, but I suspected she hadn't gone almost a year waiting for me. Nor did I expect her to. We'd never slept together, so it seemed like a fair arrangement.

Tiffany came around more often than anyone. Every couple months, Henry, the officer who'd looked out for me after Maddy's death, drove my aunt almost four hours to Blythe for a visit, but they couldn't make it out as much as they wanted to.

Tiff was consistent and affectionate, reminding me she cared, touching me the way nobody had in almost a year. I wouldn't be happy to hear she was seeing another guy tonight, but I wouldn't make her talk about it. I opened my hand across the table, and she put hers in it. "You don't have to tell me. But everything's all right?"

"I'm just stressed with work and my dad and hearing about USC nonstop—it's her birthday. That's why I can't stay long. Mom ordered this fancy cake, and I have to go pick it up."

Her.

I tensed. Tiffany hadn't even said her name, but I knew. It was an interruption to our routine. Tiffany rarely brought up her sister, and when she did, I shut down the conversation. I wanted to know everything, but Lake belonged outside these dismal walls, away from this dusty town off the freeway, and far from my mind. So I knew nothing. I never asked about her, and except in moments of extreme weakness, never thought about her, either. Just the mention of her felt like a sucker punch. "It's today?" I asked. "Her birthday?"

"As if every other day isn't about Lake, now we have to throw her a stupid party." She fidgeted with one of the paperbacks' creased covers, folding up the corner. "It's obnoxious."

"What's the date today?" I asked her.

"Why do you care?"

I took a breath. "Never mind."

Ten months. That was how long I'd gone without a fix. Lake's letters came every couple weeks. I'd opened the first one, but that was it. I'd known right then that if I was going to make it through this, I couldn't think of her. Couldn't be inside her head that way, and she definitely couldn't be inside mine.

A year from today, she'd be eighteen, but that didn't matter anymore, not when I'd turned into *this*. Standing in that courtroom last August, hearing Lake's voice in the same moment I was falsely charged with burglary, I'd turned and seen something no man ever should. One way or another, the pain and confusion on her face all led back to me. I'd exposed her to this life and chipped away some of her innocence, and I'd never forgive myself for it. I wouldn't make that mistake twice.

I hoped that Lake never thought of me, never worried about me. That I was far from her mind. At the same time, it killed me that I might be.

Fuck. She didn't belong in here. I pushed thoughts of Lake out of my mind and focused on Tiffany. She'd been loyal and deserved my attention. Not only for sticking by me, but for stepping up when I'd needed her. After my sentencing, Tiffany had taken my lease to Dexter Grimes, who'd told her there was no way to break it without a fee. She'd set her mind to it anyway and had convinced the landlord to reduce it. All I'd lost was a couple hundred bucks and last-month's rent. Then, she'd sold my furniture and car. Part of that money went to student loans that hadn't amounted to anything, and the rest went to the victim or my commissary.

My chest tightened just thinking about. Having Lake on my mind again, I already needed another cigarette. If I could smoke two at a time, I probably would. Nothing brought me pure pleasure like smoking. Tiff's visits were a highlight of my stay. Cigarettes, though, they made life in here worth living.

I turned in my seat to check the clock. Five more minutes.

I started when Tiffany touched the back of my neck, her finger slipping down my skin, under the edge of my collar. "Is this new?"

"Young lady," a voice came over the intercom. Ludwig. I hadn't even seen him come in. "You want to touch a man in this room, go right ahead—just make sure he ain't in orange. First and final warning."

Tiffany took her hand back as I sat forward again. Ludwig was the only man in the room not wearing prison scrubs. "Don't do that," I said under my breath. "They'll restrict us to non-contact visits."

"Sorry. What is it?"

I rubbed the back of my neck, the hairs on end where her fingers had been. "Tattoo."

"But of what? All I saw was a thin line."

I wasn't sure how she'd seen anything at all. It was simple, black tracings on the back of my right shoulder. "It's nothing. Dumb. One of the lifers used to be a tattoo artist and I was bored."

The ghost of her fingers lingered. It felt good to be touched. Tiffany wasn't scared, didn't hesitate, just reached out and did it. As if it were normal.

As if I wasn't a convicted felon.

"Don't go getting my name in ink or anything," she said, smiling a little. "A friend of mine's boyfriend did that inside. Now they're broken up."

"You breaking up with me?" I asked.

"No way."

"Who of your friends has a boyfriend inside?"

"You don't know her. Anyway, he's out now."

"Time's up," Jameson called.

Tiffany stood, tugging down her skirt in a way that was almost cute, a little self-conscious. To me,

Tiffany and Lake were complete opposites, but they looked alike to the rest of the world. Sometimes, I'd catch glimpses of Lake in her sister. An expression she'd made before, a gesture, the way she pronounced a word. Blonde hair, blue eyes, smooth skin. It made forgetting Lake even harder and left me worrying about Tiffany driving up here alone, being around the facility when I was incapacitated.

"You really shouldn't wear that stuff around here," I told her.

"I want to look good for you."

"Yeah, well, you look good to the other guys, too." I stood. "They see you in that skirt and I get shit for it."

She cocked a hip, leaning her thigh against the edge of the metal table. "Really?" she asked excitedly. "I heard it gives you street cred to have a hot girlfriend."

"Where'd you hear that?"

"I've been asking around. Reading some stuff."

Truth was, at some point, I'd started to look forward to seeing what she'd wear—it was a sweet kind of torture—but the guys baited me with it all the time. "I've got the best-looking girl in the joint," I said. "They go crazy over you."

She tucked her chin into her shoulder, her cheeks reddening. "That's so sweet—"

"It's not a good thing." I shook my head. "If you heard what these guys said . . . what they called women . . . there's nothing sweet about it."

21

"You sound like my dad. He hates that I come here. He thinks it's dangerous. I told him—it's a *prison*. Everyone's already locked up. It's probably the safest place I could be."

Charles was right to be concerned. They'd called Tiffany and other women lots of things. Bitch, sexy, walking pussy. It was true what I'd said—I got it worse than most because Tiffany was ten times better looking than their visitors, but that wasn't the only reason. The guys knew it was the only thing that got to me. After Tiffany's first visit, a few weeks following the arraignment, one of the guys had gone as far as to mimic bending her over the cafeteria table. Stressed from getting shoved into this new life, I'd flown off the handle and sent him to the infirmary. I'd almost caught more charges. Rumor had spread about how fast I'd put him down, but I'd also shown them exactly how to get to me.

Now, I kept it inside. It was counterintuitive to take a calming breath when they called her names, but it wouldn't do anybody any good if I got myself in more trouble. I stopped giving a fuck. In here, women were bitches, even though we'd give our left nuts for a few hours alone with one. In here, justification was a rampant disease. Men killed and stole for their families. For their brothers. For their bitches. Out of respect. Or a debt to pay. Everyone was guilty of something.

Even me.

2

MANNING

The days after Tiffany's visits usually dragged, but this time was worse. She'd caught me off guard when she'd broken unspoken protocol and mentioned Lake. My self-control got slippery. Her name was everywhere. I saw it in books, heard it on the news. A guard had an upcoming vacation to *Lake* Tahoe. An inmate's daughter was starring in a school production of Swan *Lake*.

I went to the library to distract myself. Since I'd been twelve credits short of a criminal justice degree before all this, I helped with some of the guys' cases and they paid for that. But combing through legal books reminded me of my early days in prison, when I'd done nothing but try to understand how I'd gotten here, so my mind drifted to that night in the truck with Lake. It was the first time I'd thought of it in weeks. I left the library to work in the yard, mixing and placing concrete in hundred-degree weather until I thought I'd pass out from the heat. All that for fifty cents an hour, half of which went to the victim's compensation fund, but at least I'd been forced to learn a lot on the job. More than I would've jumping from crew to crew like I'd been.

A few nights after Tiffany's visit, following a full day's work, I went to my cell for lights out.

Wills sat on his bunk, short legs dangling over my bed as he sniffed the air like a rat. "You still got that jackbook?"

"No." I'd traded my porn for Cup Noodles and cigarettes.

"How about we swap—pictures of my girl for yours?"

"Not unless you want to take a trip to the infirmary."

Tiffany's Polaroids and catalogue tear-out were hidden in my legal paperwork with my letters. Just to make sure he hadn't fucked with me, I went and squatted in front of my locker, opening my files to check that everything was there.

"I've been looking at the same titties for months," he pleaded. "I need new material."

Lake's name found me again, her pretty scrawl tempting me from the corner of each of her envelopes. If I could get one message to her, it would be to stop sending the letters. She needed to know they made things worse for me. I was strong enough not to read them, but I couldn't bring myself to trash them like I should. The smart thing would've been burning each letter as it'd arrived. Having them here was dangerous. The guys, they couldn't know about Lake. They didn't need that kind of lethal ammunition against me.

I stood up. My body ached, my muscles fatigued from a rough few days outside, but hard labor kept me sane. Focused.

Wills picked up his feet as I ducked to sit on my bed with the letters, and he belched a familiar tune. "It's the theme song from *Growing Pains*," he said. "You know that show with the curly-haired kid?"

Maybe Madison had watched it; I couldn't remember. I'd never talked to Wills about my sister, though. Or anyone in here for that matter. I lay back with an arm behind my head, staring at the underside of Wills' bunk. The springs glinted from the fluorescent lights, winking at me like stars. I could be back at the camp pool with Lake if I'd just let myself go there. Her curious hand inching across the pavement toward mine. Even with my eyes on the sky, I'd heard her shallow breathing, sensed her nervousness. I'd wanted to find out exactly what thoughts ran through her head, what had made her come looking for me. What had prompted a quiet, almost shy girl like her to check out *Lolita* from the library and then tell me about it. I was pretty sure she'd talked herself into everything she'd done that

25

night. Asking me questions about Madison. About myself. Leaning in to try and kiss me.

She was seventeen now.

I pushed the thought away. Her age didn't matter. She could've been twenty-four like me, but I'd still be a convict with a "suspicious" background as my lawyer had put it. A minimum-wage construction worker. The son of a murderer.

"You think it'll affect my daughter, me being gone the first few years of her life?" Wills got in a philosophical mood some nights. "Like babies just know that shit? Or you think they're as dumb as they look, all *goo-goo ga-ga*?"

It made me think of Madison as a baby. I was six when she was born. I'd been an okay brother. I could've been better. Looking back, after her death, there were some things I regretted. I'd stay out after my baseball games instead of coming home for dinner. I'd hide her annoying flute, even though she needed to practice for a recital. I hadn't considered that my little sister might not always be around to kick out of my room or tease for watching cartoons.

"I think babies know," I said.

"But how?" He sounded sad.

"Just do. It's biological or something. Like how they just love you without having to be told or taught."

The bunk squeaked as he shifted. "Deep," Wills said. "You know what I heard today? Avocado is a fruit. How messed up is that?"

"What'd you think it was?"

"I don't know. A vegetable, I guess. I never thought about it."

Avocado sounded like the most luxurious thing in the world right then. On sourdough bread with turkey and ham, sliced cheese and mayo? I'd trade a pack for a bite of the Lake Special. I lay there, imagining Lake layering meat with the precision of a surgeon. Even if the sandwich hadn't been so good, I would've enjoyed it just because of the care she'd put into it. Why? What'd made her want to feed me? What'd given her the courage to come over to the wall that day I'd found her bracelet?

I forced my eyes open. It was as if finding out Lake's birthday had busted some kind of dam in me. I couldn't keep her off my mind. I picked up the top envelope from the stack, turning it over in front of my face, and ran a fingertip along the corner, over my name in her neat, girlish handwriting. A mix of cursive and print, smooth but broken.

"What're you doing down there?" Wills asked. "Jerking off to your blonde?"

"Fuck you."

"Fine, geez. I did it the other afternoon just knowing she was in the building."

I *was* thinking about my blonde, and it made my chest burn. I grabbed more letters, sorting through them for the only one I'd actually opened. The first I'd ever gotten and had attempted to read. I unfolded the lined paper that had been ripped out of a spiral-

27

bound notebook and words jumped off the page at me.

So sorry . . . my fault . . . can't live this way, knowing I did this . . .

I gritted my teeth, looking away. I didn't want to read this. Couldn't. I still had two months in here and if I let her in now, it'd make things so much fucking harder. Why did she send them? What good did it do? I turned the page over to the last few lines.

I'll come visit every chance I get. Don't be mad at me. I'll make this up to you.

I almost crumpled the page, my hand shook so bad. There was no mention of anything in the letter other than what she'd done. How sorry she was. All the ways it hurt. That wasn't the life I wanted for her, and she knew it. I could still feel her between my legs on the horse, laughing into the wind, gripping my forearms even though she had to know I'd never let her fall.

Since I'd gotten here, I'd been in two fistfights, had faced down a man with a shiv, and had been verbally abused by CO's. But reading about her guilt over that night was harder than any of that. I found her most recent letter, the one I'd picked up last week, and stuck my finger under the flap, easing it open.

Wills started on some rant about tonight's mystery meat and how he'd probably have diarrhea in the middle of the night. That small motherfucker had a weak constitution. One thing I'd learned in prison was that I could eat anything and still, sometimes, try to bargain for more. I tuned Wills out.

Dear Manning,

I had to make a hard decision this week. I wasn't going to be a camp counselor again. I thought it would be too hard without you, but I think I'm going to do it. I love it up there and I want to see the kids. I hope it doesn't upset you. I'll make it up to you by riding a horse, but since I can't imagine being up there with anyone other than you, I'll do it by myself.

I swallowed and almost stopped reading. Selfishly, it did upset me. I wanted to be back there, in the woods where the air was fresh and cool, with no worries. Just her.

My dad and I had a fight. He wants me to join the track team next year so I can put it on my college apps. I said no. I don't run for him or for USC. I run for myself. Some days it feels like the only thing I can do. By the way, my infection is gone. I hope you weren't worried. I know you worry.

There will be a scar. Val says it's cool, at least.

My gut tightened, my hand instinctively balling up the envelope. What had infected her, scarred her? Who was Val? Was that a man or a woman's name? *Fuck.*

I skimmed to the end of the letter.

Please write me back. Please add me to your visitor's list. I miss . . . everything.

Love,

Lake

PS My birthday is in less than two weeks. I'll be seventeen (but you know that).

29

I dropped my hand, clutching the page. *Love, Lake*. The words were tiny daggers dipped in sweetness and plunged into my heart. I'd never approve her as a visitor, that was for damn sure. She was a minor and couldn't come alone anyway.

Next to me on the mattress were the answers to my questions, but the first and last letter told me all I needed to know. I wasn't strong enough to handle being in Lake's head. When she hurt, I did more than hurt—I felt like shit. Like a real criminal for letting things get this far. But hearing she was doing better without me around, yeah, *that* made me feel like shit, too.

I closed my eyes. She was going to camp. Getting back on the horse. Running for herself. She was better, stronger, growing up, and if I were still in the picture, that wouldn't've been the case. The evidence was clear—in a matter of weeks, I'd turned her perfect life upside down. She was getting it right-side up again, like I'd always known she would. That didn't mean it didn't hurt, knowing she was moving on, but as long as she was happy, being away from her was the right thing.

I must've drifted. When I came to, the lights in the cells and hallway had dimmed. The jail was still, quiet, and that only happened at the dead of night. I gathered up the letters to put them away when I noticed the other one I'd been avoiding. It wasn't from Lake, but it'd be easier to read since I didn't really give a shit what it said.

I ripped open the envelope, probably taking off some of the letter itself, and held it out to the bit of light coming into the cell.

Did you get my last few letters, Son?

I've been calling, but they say I'm still not approved to visit. Your mom, either.

I was planning to drive out there. I didn't want to go into all this over a letter, but what else can I do? It's like a parasite inside me, and I can't move on with my life until I get it out.

Weak, pathetic piece of shit. My dad's chicken-scratch filled up three whole goddamn pages, front and back. I'd read his first letter with my eyebrows drawn, certain it'd gotten to the wrong "son."

Apparently, he'd been released from Pelican Bay and had been looking for me ever since. If he'd reached out to Henry or my aunt, they hadn't mentioned it, because we all had an understanding— we didn't talk about my dad. It wasn't until I'd been locked up that Dad had been able to find me. His letters were so fucking pitiful, sometimes they even made for a good laugh.

I skimmed the words so I could trash it as fast as possible.

Rehabilitate myself . . .

In a program . . .

Bad things.

Your sister.

Innocence.

My attention snagged on Madison's name. I held the letter closer to my face, squinting to read.

Your sister lived in her own world. Madison could occupy herself for hours. Sometimes I just couldn't stand not knowing what was in her head. It drew me to her . . . and it infuriated me. My counselor says her innocence and simplicity "defied" the chaos in my head. I would ask her what she was thinking, but she kept me out on purpose to torture me. To tempt me. She matured too fast. One minute she was my innocent little girl, and overnight she started to change. You don't know what it's like to watch a girl become a woman.

The priest says I can be forgiven, but I have to ask for it, so here I am, asking. First, I should explain.

My father, your grandpa, started molesting me when I was seven or eight. The first time I touched your sister, it was an accident.

The floor bottomed out. I sucked in a breath as I shot up to a sitting position, knocking my head on the top bunk. *No no no.* This wasn't happening.

I made confession to the Lord. It's not enough. I want your forgiveness, too.

My teeth ground together to the point of pain.

Your mother took it hard, but she's decided to stand by me . . .

The dankness of the cell began to close in, suffocating me. I put my head between my knees, holding my ears as the room spun. My quiet, thoughtful sister who'd once cried herself to sleep because we'd caught a mouse in a trap. Who wouldn't harm an insect. It had to be wrong. A sick joke by a sick motherfucker. My dad had always been off, had demons.

I got up and paced the cell. I hadn't known any of this, but I *had* known he was wrong in the head. That he'd beaten each of us up at some point. And I hadn't stopped him.

My brain pounded, swelling in my head. My eyes burned. My heart blistered, setting fire to my chest, face, and scalp. That fuck. That stupid fuck. It wasn't enough to kill Madison, he'd had to ruin her, too. Steal her innocence from right under my nose. Maddy's and my bedrooms had shared a wall. How could I not have known? I wanted to scream, howl, feel the cold, steel bars of my cell breaking apart by my hands. I want to get loose so I could wring his neck and drain the life from his body.

I leaned my back against a wall and pinched the inside corners of my eyes. Like a sponge, hot water came out. I hadn't shed a tear since Madison's death nine years ago, not even during her funeral.

Because I didn't cry. I didn't breakdown. I got stronger. I made sure it didn't happen to anyone else I loved. I protected.

This, though, this was different. I'd lived under the same roof as a monster. Madison had never said a thing to me. She'd been a shy kid, and now I knew— she must've been a scared one. She'd never try to spite or manipulate my dad. That wasn't her. His belief that she had, that she'd tempted him, was one of a coward. And he wanted *forgiveness*? He hadn't changed a bit.

I slid down the wall, sitting with my head between my knees and my hair in my fists. This was the end of the line for me, a second death for Maddy. Any goodness I might've thought there was in this world, my dad had just weeded it right out. And there wasn't a thing I could do about it, barred in an eight-by-six cell, trapped with nothing but my father's sins and the encroaching memories of Lake, the seventeen-year-old girl I needed to forget—now more than ever.

3
MANNING

Playing cards were dealt, checked, folded, swiped off the table in front of me. Three of clubs. Ten of diamonds. The queen of hearts blinked at me, morphing into a jack of spades. I rubbed the corner of my eyes and tried to focus. I couldn't lose this game.

I didn't normally gamble—I could go to SHU for it, and that'd be getting off easy. I didn't want to owe anyone anything in here, least of all money. Lately, I needed more and more ways to burn off my nervous energy, though. Working outdoors eight hours wasn't cutting it. I hadn't slept more than three hours a night since reading my dad's letter earlier in the week.

Some men shouted at the fight on TV, then at each other.

I slid three brown M&M's into the middle of the table. "Raise."

Officer Ludwig sauntered into the room belly first. "Hey," he said, circling the couch to block the TV. "Settle down."

It was the worst thing he could say. *Shut the fuck up* would've been better. At least that was man to man. *Settle down* was for disruptive elementary kids.

Ludwig turned his back to leave the room.

"Sorry, Lovedicks," one of the guys watching TV said.

He looked back, his jiggly jaw tense. "It's *Ludwig.*"

"That's what we said." Wills spoke from next to me. It was what nobody said. We all called him Lovedicks behind his back. He sometimes took it up the ass from inmates, even though *he* had access to outside pussy.

I glared at Wills for getting involved. "Don't be an idiot."

Like a predator picking up a scent, Ludwig prowled toward our table, hand on his holster. "You girls gambling?"

Sweat dripped down my temples. I wiped it away with my sleeve. "No, sir."

"Just enjoying some Go Fish and chocolate," Hendricks said from across the table, adding a lisp that made the guys snicker.

"You think I'm dumb?" the CO asked. "Can't tell a game of poker when I see one?"

"You wouldn't know a real game of poker if it *poked* you in the eye," Puentes said. He'd been transferred here for having his men on the outside kill a guard in his home. "Like Hendricks's dick did to you last night."

The mocking only ticked Lovedicks off more. He hated that we all knew his taste for cock, but it didn't bother him enough to stop. He jabbed his baton into Hendricks's shoulder. "He's dreaming if he said that."

"So I guess that white stuff in the corner of ya mouth is mayo," Wills said.

Lovedicks slammed his baton on our table, scattering M&M's. "Shut up, or I'll call lights-out early."

The guys never learned. They just liked to start shit, even though the guards always won—no matter their size, disposition, or rank on the ladder. My knee bounced under the table. It wasn't nerves—I had a good hand. It was the fact that it was always a million fucking degrees in this place.

CO Jameson came into the room, her brown ponytail swinging like a horse's mane. "Everything okay in here?"

Lovedicks retreated to lean against the nearest wall, but he kept his eyes on us.

Jameson scanned the room and met my eyes. "You good, Sutter? Sweating through your scrubs there."

"Fine. Just hot." Jameson was the only guard I sometimes talked to. She was my age, still wanted to help around here. I hoped she'd wise up and get out of this place soon, just not before I did.

"Go Fish, *cabrón*," Puentes hurried me along.

"Trout." I matched Puentes's bet with the code word for *call*. *Goldfish* meant *money*, *Betta* was *all in*, and *chum* signaled you were out.

"You ever get on top?" Wills asked Lovedicks but continued before he could respond, "Nah, never mind. You're not the type."

"Why, you interested?" Lovedicks asked. "I wouldn't shove my baton up your ass, even if you begged."

Wills stood up, his temples going veiny. "Beg? *Me*? You think I got to beg for anything? I don't beg for shit, lardass."

"Sit your ass down, con," Lovedicks said.

"Yeah, sit the *fuck* down," I said, "and trout or chum so I can wipe the floor with your ass, get my goldfish, and go to sleep."

"Sutter's gotta go jerk it to his blondes," Lovedicks said.

I ignored him, motioning for Wills to play his hand or fold.

"Blondes?" Wills asked. "He got more than one?"

"Yeah, you haven't seen the other one?" Lovedicks asked. "Blonde, sweet-looking thing, barely-legal pussy. She's come by a couple times, trying to sneak in and see him."

Every muscle in my body locked up. I didn't even think her name, didn't picture her so they couldn't read my thoughts. She'd come around? Looking for me? I didn't want her within a hundred miles of this place. The card under my thumb creased down the middle.

"*Tsk, tsk*," Wills said to me. "You been holding out on us, Sutter?"

My pulse pounded against my temples. *She's seventeen. Seventeen.* I would've told them that to shut them up except that it'd only make things worse. These idiots would have no problem beating off to a seventeen-year-old and some of them were probably pedophiles like my dad.

Pedophile.

It was the first time I'd associated him with the word. What made me different from him? From them? I'd put my hands on Lake when she was sixteen, and I'd wanted to do a hell of a lot more than that. Her face flashed across my mind, and I squeezed my eyes shut, trying to erase her from this shithole.

"Legs for miles," Lovedicks continued. "Blonde hair past her tits. Just like Manning's girl, but younger. Sweeter."

"Shut—" I wheezed, my chest too tight. "Shut the fuck up."

"What're you gonna do, make me? You can't do shit." Lovedicks rounded the table, prodding the middle of my back with his baton. "Pussy that good can't be off limits. The little bitch is straight from heaven."

My hands shook so hard imagining Lake in the same room as Ludwig, I dropped my cards. She was too good to be talked about that way. "Stop." I wasn't sure if I was commanding myself or him. "Stop."

Jameson had moved away to watch the fight, but she looked over. "Let up, CO."

"Don't you know?" Wills said. "Manning don't like pussy. He's a closet fag."

"Come on, Sutter," Hendricks said. "Plenty of us were in your shoes once. Trust me, the sooner you give in, the sooner we'll get you loosened up."

Wills knew I'd never turn, but some days, out of boredom, he went on benders, trying to get me to explode. "I told you a thousand times—my girl's off limits."

"I'm not talking about your girl," Lovedicks said. "Talking about the other one. What's it, her little sister? When's the last time you saw her? Skinny little thing, but I'll bet she didn't have any tits back when you knew her."

Time slowed. The fluorescent lights above flooded the room, turning the walls that'd held me inside for months blindingly white. *Words, not truths. They want you to crack. Words meant to instigate.* That was what I told myself when the guys dug in, but still, I found myself standing, my rage too big to sit on.

"You ever tasted that sweet, young cunt?" he asked.

My self-control slipped. Images that'd haunted me for days flooded in. My dad alone in the house with Madison. Lake stripping off her shirt in the lake. I hadn't told her to stop, because I'd liked it. I'd been weak. Lake floating on her back, all breasts, pink mouth, and hair. Who knew how many nights I'd slept in the room next to Madison's while *he'd* been in there?

"You should've seen her crying and begging the guards to let her in," Ludwig went on. "She nearly got on her knees. Maybe if she had, they would've—"

When I grabbed one end of the baton, Ludwig's mouth and eyes popped open. Instinctively, he pulled back, but I was stronger. I yanked it away from him and vaulted toward him. This wasn't some girl they were talking about—it was Lake, my Lake who'd never be mine, an angel who'd never look over the likes of me. I saw red, and my dad's revolting face, and then I saw black, nothing but rage. I threw the baton, and it hit a wall with a sickening thud. I'd kill this sick fuck with my bare hands.

"Holy shit," someone said.

"Stand down, inmate," Jameson called.

I had Ludwig by the neck. "You like little girls?" I slammed him up against the wall. "You think you're untouchable?" I squeezed with all my strength. People pulled at my shoulders but my grip tightened and tightened, Ludwig's blubbery face flushing purple as his eyes bulged out of their sockets.

Any will to fight drained out of him. There was just fear there, and it spurred me on. He deserved to be shitting himself for calling her what he had, for being a monster, for thinking he could get away with it, for having the nerve to ask forgiveness.

People tried to get between us, to drag me to the ground. I'd wanted to be like Ludwig once—to serve and protect those who couldn't do it for themselves, but My dad was a pussy and a coward and I came from him. I could be just as menacing.

I let Ludwig go only to smash my fist into his face, jerk his chin forward again and clock him right in the nose so the back of his head hit the wall.

A riot had begun behind me and in a matter of seconds, I was on the floor, covering my head as a baton landed on my bicep, my hip and back. Ludwig sank down against the wall, wheezing, trying to communicate to the other guards, bloodied . . . but alive.

Steel-toed boots socked me right in the gut, then my face. The back of my skull cracked against the same wall I'd just had Ludwig up against and it all went black.

4

LAKE

Summer ended how it'd begun. School started Monday, and we spent our last weekend of freedom the same way we had our first one and many in between.

The plan went something like this—go to a hotel pool and work on our tans. Once security kicked us out, go to the beach or hang at the mall food court or shop for used CDs. Go home, shower, hitch rides to house parties and look for beer. The beer wasn't for me, I didn't drink, but if I wasn't reading, running or volunteering, I had to be doing something. Anything, as long as I didn't have time to think.

A year had passed without Manning, and it'd been the worst of my life. So far, 1994 had been a letdown. Kurt Cobain had died, not just died but killed himself. It'd put a lot of us in a funk, from my classmates to my teachers, and Tiffany especially. She'd been a little different ever since. After she'd helped break Manning's lease, she'd started talking about getting her own place, but it wasn't until Cobain's death in April that she stopped relying on modeling, got an interview at Nordstrom, and began seriously looking at apartments.

Now, we were headed toward 1995, and the ache of losing Manning wasn't as sharp, but it'd spread and seeped throughout my body like thick, machine-gun-black tar. The throb lived inside me. I'd thought of one thing with the onset of summer—Manning. Leather car seats gummy from the heat, and wet, salty hair sticking to my arms. I'd lived through an entire week in Big Bear. Campfire-and-pine-needle air took me back to him that night we'd walked to the pool, hedging our words, keeping just enough distance under a painfully beautiful sky. How was it possible to look up and see the same immovable stars I had a year before when so much had changed?

It'd been a particularly bad summer, but it was over now and Manning was coming home soon. Nobody would tell me exactly when. Dexter had said maybe as soon as September, which was now, but that he'd call when he had a date. Manning never answered my letters, and Tiffany didn't volunteer much when I was around. "It's not appropriate for someone your age," she'd say about her visits with Manning, and my dad would agree. She didn't really think that, I was sure. It was as if the information gave her power over me.

Tonight, my friends were on phase three of the plan to get drunk. We'd been unsuccessful all afternoon. Sun-soaked and sandy, Val and I flip-flopped into a classmate's house in Laguna Beach, dragging our feet on the beige stone flooring. We'd come with Vickie and Mona, but they had a crush on the same guy and scattered to find him. Everyone showed off tanned arms and legs in tank tops, shorts, and dresses. The kids at my school took sunbathing more seriously than final exams. Even I had stopped slathering on the sunscreen. I looked better with a tan . . . not that I had anyone to look good for.

Val channeled Drew Barrymore tonight in dark lipstick and wild, curly blonde hair. She'd unbuttoned her red blouse a little too far, her cleavage buoying a necklace with a black cross. She called it her *Poison Ivy* look, because she was always referencing her life back to movies, music, or books. Next to her, I must've looked angelic in a baby-blue, short fuzzy sweater.

"I wish my name started with a 'B,'" Val said. "Everything good starts with a 'B.' Booze, boys, books." She stopped at a stereo and showed me a CD case. "Buckley-comma-Jeff."

"Beavis," I added.

"And Butt-Head."

Val got me. The *me* I hadn't known I was before her. Starting school last September had been a struggle. I'd wanted to give up. I'd played the scene over and over in my head, Manning being led away in cuffs because of me. The only thing I'd thought about was writing to him or trying to find a way to visit him. I'd been depressed and lonely when I'd met Val, who'd just moved to Orange County from Seattle with her mom.

"Did you know your sister's here?" Val asked, nodding through a doorway.

Tiffany sat on a kitchen countertop surrounded by boys I recognized from her grade. Most of them were in college now, not all of them, though. She still hadn't signed up for classes even though she kept saying she would. "No, but I'm not surprised."

"Five bucks says she's telling them about her big, bad prison boyfriend."

My heart seized and then released, an automatic reaction to anything Manning. "Now you're just tossing out 'B' words."

"I can think of a couple more."

Val and Tiffany didn't get along. Neither had Val and I at first. The principal had asked me to show her around campus her first day, and I would've rather stuck my head in a garbage bin after lunch, but as always, I'd done what was expected.

"Is this place a lot different than Seattle?" I asked Val between the math and science buildings.

"What kind of a question is that?" she shot back. "Seattle has music, art, and culture on every corner. This place is as new and shiny as a polished turd."

I gaped at her. "What?"

"Plus there's the whole rain versus sun thing." I must've looked pretty disturbed, because she added, "Well, don't cry about it."

I had cried in the bathroom twenty minutes earlier, and also during first period, and because of that, I really couldn't have cared less about this new girl and her attitude. "Like I'd cry over an insult my five-year-old cousin could've come up with. You don't need a tour. The campus is small. Good luck."

I walked the length of the math building before she caught up to me. "Sheesh. The principal promised you'd make me feel welcome."

"I'm sure he can assign you to someone else. I'm not in the mood for this."

"Then why'd you agree to it?"

I picked up my stride, but so did she. "Because I'm trying for Student of the Month this year."

"It's only September."

"If they pick me early, I won't have to hear about not getting it all year from my dad."

"Oh. Well, if it makes you feel any better, my dad's dating someone five years older than me."

I wasn't sure why that should make me feel better, but I got the feeling she needed to say it. "Sorry."

"Is that why you were crying? Your dad? By the way, you seriously need some, like, cucumbers or something. Your eyes are really puffy."

I hugged my binder to my chest and turned a corner toward the amphitheater to show her where next week's pep rally would be. "Yeah. I guess."

It turned out I hadn't needed to show her the way to the amphitheater. We'd gone to the rally together. I learned that Val's idea of a good time was Vietnamese food with eighties romantic comedies, and if her mom was out for the night, a glass of rosé. I hadn't really known what I'd considered a good time but it wasn't any of those things—until Val.

"There's my girl." A familiar, deep voice boomed over the living room crowd. "Move aside, assholes. Let the ladies through."

Corbin and his sun-bleached hair stood inches taller than anyone else. Even if he weren't waving both hands overhead, I would've spotted him easily.

The crowd parted for Val and me. "Welcome home," I told him. His nose was pink and peeling, but he was bronze everywhere else. "How was vacation?"

"My brothers and I tore up the shores of Hawaii. It's unrecognizable now." He nodded at Val, then looked down her blouse. "What up, V? Nice, ah, necklace."

"Thanks. Are you the keg master or what?"

"No, but I can be." Corbin filled three beers. I didn't want one, but I'd learned if I didn't carry a red cup around parties, everyone would try to force one on me. "So let's see this infamous scar," he said.

I extended my arm, showing the faint, pink circle of raised skin near the inside of my elbow. He ran a thumb over it and shook his head, *tsk*ing. "What the hell were you thinking, Kaplan? You can't just pick up a stray cat."

"It was a kitten, and it was in pain," I said. In retrospect, yes, it'd been stupid. We'd been on a class trip to Laguna Art Museum and out front, under a lawn sculpture, had been a little, mewling furball. With teeth. I'd had to go to the emergency room—right away—but Lam, named after the museum—was alive, healthy, and had been adopted out. That didn't change the fact that I'd gotten an earful from my dad about my weird new hobby.

It had started with the running, and the running had started with a need to burn off the things that ate me up inside. Guilt over what I'd done. Hurt that Manning had neither written me back nor asked to see me. At seven o'clock on a Saturday morning, I'd been jogging by the pier and had nearly stumbled over a beached dolphin. After I'd run to call animal control and waited until they'd arrived to guide it back into the ocean, the handler had told me, "You did good."

You did good.

It was the same thing Manning had said to me before they'd taken him away.

Since then, I'd been volunteering at an animal hospital a couple times a month.

"I'm going to look for some chow while you two 'catch up,'" Val said, air quotes and all.

She left us alone. Corbin opened one arm to me, and I hugged his middle as he moved us away from the keg. "I don't want you to go," I said, looking up at him.

"I really thought about staying," he said. "But it's where I want to be."

Corbin was headed for NYU in three days, but he and I were as close as ever. He'd been good to me the past year. According to the whole school, Corbin and I had been dating since camp. It wasn't true, but Corbin had been too focused on baseball, surfing, and NYU to date, and having Corbin as a rumored boyfriend was better than having guys ask me to school dances or for Friday night pizza or, God forbid, to the Fun Zone. I didn't date. Had no desire to. Had no room in my mind for boys when there was only one Manning.

Corbin rubbed the fuzzy back of my thin sweater. "You look good, Lake," he said. "Real good. You're a knockout."

According to my mom, my body had been changing all year, but I hadn't noticed until recently. Summer had been good to me. I'd finally grown into my limbs, clocking in at five-foot-eight, almost two inches taller than my mom and sister. I'd lost ten pounds in the weeks after Manning had gone away and had started running soon after. My bras got smaller around the back and bigger in the cups. I had real breasts now, not as big as my mom's and sister's, which was disappointing, but I had them. Men had stopped looking around me to see Tiffany and my mom. That kind of attention didn't seem worth all the fuss Tiffany made over it, but I figured I'd understand better once Manning was the one looking.

"Are you nervous for college?" I asked.

"Nah."

We stood a little too close to the boom box, and Corbin raised his voice to speak over Adam Duritz crooning "Round Here."

"What about you?" he asked. "You're a senior now. Lots of responsibility." Corbin tapped his Solo cup with mine. "How's it feel?"

"Overdue."

"Is that Corbin I hear?" Tiffany called from the next room.

Corbin and I exchanged a look. He put an arm around me and led me into the kitchen where Tiffany held court from a granite throne.

"I haven't seen a Swenson all summer," she said.

"We were gone most of it."

"Well, work keeps me busy anyway," she said gravely.

"Still at Nordstrom?"

"And doing some modeling. Between that and driving all day to see Manning twice a month, I hardly have time for anything else."

I looked into my cup. What I knew about her visits came from her conversations with other people. I didn't believe most of it. Supposedly, he'd wanted conjugal visits but wasn't allowed them. He held her hand while they talked. He shared all kinds of things about his past. I knew my sister. She'd say they'd had sex right there on the visitation table if she thought someone would believe it. Anything to shock people.

51

"Right." Corbin nodded, glancing around. Everybody in school knew about Manning thanks to Tiffany's big mouth, but Corbin was one of the only people who'd actually spoken to him.

I could ask for details now. Sometimes when I tried to get information, Tiffany shut down, but with other people around, she had a reason to blab.

Corbin beat me to it. "So he's still in the slammer then?"

Tiffany shifted. "Ow." She pulled up the outside of her thigh. Where her shorts stopped, her skin was red from the counter. "I've been up here too long. Help me down?"

Corbin knew better than to argue. He held her hand as she hopped off, her wedges thumping on the floor. She brushed off her hands and said, "He was supposed to get out for good behavior this month."

Was? Visions of Manning packing up his things, filling out paperwork, making living arrangements, calling me on the phone—it all disintegrated. "He's not anymore?"

"Her boyfriend's straight thug," someone said from behind us. "She told us all about him."

I shot a glare over my shoulder at the gangly kid from Tiffany's class who looked as though he'd spent the summer playing Nintendo in a basement.

"What happened?" Corbin asked. Even *he* perked up, leaning close, and in moments like these, I understood exactly why Tiffany continued to see Manning. He made for a good story.

"I don't know if I should say." Tiffany glanced at me from under her lashes and away. "It's upsetting."

"You told a stranger," I accused, gesturing at the guy behind me. He knew more about Manning than I did, which might've surprised me if this whole situation hadn't been backward from the start.

"He got in a . . . fight," she admitted.

Corbin shrugged. "There are fights all the time in prison."

"Not like this. He went after a *guard*, Corbin. And apparently, he almost killed him."

I sucked in a breath. A *guard*? That he almost killed? I could barely picture Manning fighting another inmate, much less someone of authority, someone in the uniform he wanted to wear. "I don't believe you," I said. "Manning isn't like that."

"How would you know? You haven't spoken to him in a year."

I pulled back, stung. Would a year in there change Manning? How could it not? Fundamentally, though, at his core, Manning was *good*. He didn't even belong in there.

"Did he get in trouble?" Nintendo kid asked.

"I don't know. I haven't spoken to him since it happened, but his lawyer said there'd be some kind of trial thing about a misdemeanor? If they decide it's assault, it would mean more time."

More time. It knocked the wind out of me, stealing my ability to do anything other than stay upright. *But Manning's good.* As tough as he looked, as built as he

53

was, he was a protector, not a fighter. Corbin took my free hand, maybe sensing my confusion. In moments like these, I wished someone knew the whole truth. I'd carried it on my shoulders so long. My only outlet was writing to Manning and even that had begun to feel painful and embarrassing as he continued to ignore me. Val and I talked about boys a lot, and I'd wanted to tell her what'd happened, but I could never convey the story the way it deserved to be told.

"Is he okay?" I asked.

"It took two guards to pull him off."

Corbin raised his cup to his mouth. "I believe it," he said before a sip. "He's a massive guy."

"But he's okay?" I asked.

"Yeah." She leaned her back against the counter. "I mean, Dexter wouldn't really get into the details. He said Manning had to be subdued, and they put him in solitary confinement."

"Subdued? Solitary confinement? Does that mean he's alone?" I asked. "When was this? What does subdued mean?" Plastic crackled under my grip and beer erupted over the sides of my drink, down my top.

Corbin lifted the cup out of my hand by its rim, setting it aside. "Jesus, Lake."

"I'll know more after I see him," Tiffany said. "It's been a couple months since our last visit."

That meant he'd potentially been isolated for some or all of that time. The wet spot on my top chilled my skin, and I shivered.

Corbin put a hand on my shoulder. "Let's clean you up."

"Why didn't you tell me any of this?" I asked Tiffany.

Tiffany shifted her eyes to me. "You know why. Dad doesn't want you to know. He says it's bad enough I brought a criminal around you."

I clenched my teeth. Manning wasn't a criminal, and even if he was, I'd known him first. She had some nerve acting as though *she'd* brought him around *me*. "You should've told me anyway."

"He thinks I'll *corrupt* you," she continued. "If only he knew the truth."

"What's the truth?" Corbin asked.

My blood ran cold. Ever since Tiffany had said she'd seen me get in the truck with Manning late at night, there was a line to our arguments I couldn't cross. So far, she hadn't said anything to Mom or Dad about it. Whether it was for my sake or Manning's, I wasn't sure, but I was grateful. I didn't trust my dad not to go to the police and try to make things worse for Manning.

So instead of fighting her, I closed my beer-sticky fingers into a fist around the mood ring I'd found in Manning's bag of personal items. Top-heavy and too big, the stone often slid to the inside of my hand. It was real, colossal, and a constant and welcome reminder of him—and of my guilt.

"The truth . . .?" Tiffany said, letting it hang in the air. "The *truth* is that Lake has a crush on my boyfriend."

My face flamed. "No I don't." It wasn't a lie. A crush was fun and exciting, butterflies, pink cheeks, lash-heavy glances. My feelings for Manning were crush*ing*. Late night sobs and black holes. Curled fists and fingernail crescents imprinted in my palms.

Regret.

Corbin snorted. "You're disturbed," he told her, leaving my side to swipe a dishtowel from the kitchen sink. He draped it over his arm, grabbed his drink, and pulled me away by my hand. "Come on, Lake."

"Where?" I asked. I tried to gauge his mood, unsure if I should tell him that what Tiffany had said wasn't true. He didn't seem bothered by it, though.

"Bathroom." He laced his fingers with mine as we cut through the party, his thumb rubbing the stone of my ring.

"Stop touching it."

He glanced over his shoulder at me. "You're weirdly superstitious about that thing. I've tried to tell you, it only detects your mood—it can't *ruin* it."

It did, though. I wasn't sure how to explain that to him. I hated the idea of anyone else touching Manning's ring.

Corbin released my hand when we reached the bathroom. "She's sick," he said to the people waiting in line, pushing me inside, not that anybody would stand up to him.

He locked the door, and I washed my hands. As I dried them, I looked from the ring to my face in the mirror. Did Manning still think of me in there? How did I look to him? Like I had back then, a young girl who'd made all the wrong choices? I'd been too timid when I should've been bold, too impulsive when I should've held back.

"What's wrong?" Corbin asked.

What was wrong? My chest throbbed all the time, a gaping wound waiting to be filled or bandaged or prodded. Manning was alone and possibly hurt and nobody knew when he'd be back. As if I could tell Corbin any of that. What was wrong was that I was in love with someone who might never be mine. Someone I hadn't seen in a year and whom I saw everywhere. I did double takes at the mall, in the supermarket—even, sometimes, at school. I'd felt his presence behind me as I'd ridden a horse by myself for the first time.

I worried I'd forget his face. I didn't know anymore the exact spot I came up to on his body because I'd grown. I'd changed on the outside and on the inside, too. Seventeen was worlds away from sixteen. Did he know that? Could he tell from my letters? Did he know that no matter how much I changed, where he was concerned, I was the same girl who'd looked up at him on a wall and fallen right in love?

Corbin's eyebrows knit together. "Here," he said when I didn't answer. He held out his beer. "Chug this."

I took the drink. I took it to fill a black hole that couldn't be filled. No matter what I put in there, it eventually seeped out. I took it to see what would happen. My friends were so obsessed with getting drunk. My parents talked about wine varietals and regions all the time. Val had a strange fascination with rosé. I downed the whole thing in one go.

"Damn," Corbin said, grinning. "I leave you for a couple months, and you turn into a verified alky."

I shook my head. "No. Not really."

He took the cup from me, wet the hand towel, and pressed it to my belly. With a squeeze, he soaked my top, sending a rivulet down my tummy. "Lift your arms," he said.

"Why?"

"You want to go home smelling like a brewery? Your dad'll kill you."

True. Vickie, Mona, and I were supposed to be having a sleepover. I raised my hands and he slipped off my sweater. He ran the stain under the faucet, averting his eyes until he finally snuck a glance at my bra.

I covered myself. "Don't look."

He smiled crookedly but returned to his task. "Why not?"

"Because."

"Relax. I've seen you in a bathing suit lots of times."

I frowned. "I wouldn't say *lots* of times. Maybe twice."

"Five times." He took my top out and laid it on the counter to dab it with the towel. "There's the one-piece you wore on the beach last summer and then again for boogie boarding the week of your birthday. Then you have the hot pink bikini with the rhinestones that you bought for that end-of-the-year pool party. You also have a blue Roxy one I've seen at the beach and when you came to watch me surf Thalia."

I studied his profile as he focused on drying the stain. His golden hair was so thick, it didn't even really fall when he bent his head. Somehow over the past year, he'd become my best friend. Val supported me just by being herself, by testing my boundaries, and making me laugh, but Corbin and I had a bond. He held up my top. "It's damp, but it's clean. Arms back up."

It took me a second to register. The beer was already starting to hit me. I lowered my hands and stood there. Letting him see me in my bra didn't feel as uncomfortable as I might've thought. What if? What if my life was easy and Corbin was 'the one'? What if Manning wasn't in the picture? Would I let Corbin's hands warm and comfort me?

His eyes roamed another second, then he stepped closer. "You good?"

"I'm great," I said. "Loose or something."

He gripped my sweater, wetting his lips. "Lake."

I smiled, wrinkling my nose at him. "Corbin."

"Can I kiss you?"

I was so surprised by the question that I blurted, "In the bathroom?"

He chuckled, then passed me my sweater. "Good point. Come on."

After I dressed, we left the bathroom, and I followed Corbin upstairs to a dimly lit room clouded with smoke. A few kids I didn't recognize lounged on overstuffed leather couches passing around a joint. The glare of the TV turned the smoke green and blue, pink and white.

Corbin nodded at one of the guys. "Move." He did, sloth-like as he rocked forward and off the cushions to give Corbin and me the couch.

MTV was on. The next music video started, the title "Soon" by My Bloody Valentine popping up in the corner. Corbin handed me a joint I hadn't even seen him light. "Smoke this."

It was the opposite of what Manning would do. He went out of his way to keep his vices from me. I remembered how he'd played with a cigarette on the wall, tapping it on his knee, sticking it behind his ear. Nothing took me back to him like the smell of cigarettes. This wasn't what Manning smoked, but maybe it would make me feel close to him anyway. I put the joint between my lips, sucked as deeply as possible—and coughed for a full two minutes while my eyes watered and my throat burned.

Corbin laughed. "Sorry. I should've warned you that might happen. I've been toking so long, I forgot what it's like in the beginning."

I'd never even had a cigarette, but here I was, smoking weed. I put both hands on the sofa as my environment sharpened then softened. The black leather cushions made it feel like we were in the back of a car. I sank into them. The music video began to spaz, flashing colors, images echoing like sound.

"You all right?" Corbin asked with a lopsided smile.

I blinked a few times. It wasn't unpleasant. The opposite, actually. I realized I was grinning. "I think so."

He sat up, took the blunt, and put it on the coffee table. Angling in front of me, he blocked the TV and kissed me. Lost in the new sensations, I didn't see it coming so I just sat there, stunned. I'd never been kissed, not even by Manning, not really. I had touched my lips to the corner of his, but that wasn't anything. This wasn't how I'd envisioned my first time. I didn't care that it was at a stranger's house or that we both had beer breath or that I was surrounded by stoners. I only cared that it wasn't Manning.

"Why?" I asked.

"Why what?"

I didn't know how to answer. I hadn't meant to say it aloud. I had no idea what I was even asking. Someone sparked a lighter over and over.

Corbin pressed his forehead against mine. "I've wanted to do that since I saw you eating cotton candy on the steps that night at the Fun Zone."

He was so close that his face doubled and I had to shut my eyes. Darkness began to swallow me up. I moved back against the arm of the couch, and Corbin took it as an invitation to lean on top of me. He slid his hands around my waist and pressed his face into the crook of my neck. My top stuck damply to my skin, but my chest prickled with warmth that spread down my tummy. The alcohol, the weed, the kiss worked fast, loosening my limbs, settling my thoughts.

I wasn't sure how long I'd been sitting there. The song had changed to something I recognized, but it sounded both distant and all-consuming, like it was playing in the next room and in my head.

"Lake?" Corbin murmured. "You there?"

"Mmm." Jesus, I felt good. I'd drunk the beer to fill a hole, but I didn't truly believe for a second it would work. I'd been wrong. This was nice. Even having Corbin on top of me was nice. Maybe it wasn't a betrayal. Maybe Manning wasn't real, just a figment of my imagination. This was a better state of mind, less painful, an absence of ache. To be tipsy and wanted, it was a heady feeling.

Maybe *this* was real.

Corbin kissed me again, wet and slimy, but not in a bad way. At some point, I'd closed my eyes. I fought the urge to apologize for having no idea what I was doing. Was my breath fresh enough? Where did I put my hands? He put his in my top, sliding them up my stomach to my bra. "Let's go somewhere," he said. He slipped a finger into the cup of my bra, and my skin exploded with goosebumps. "It's too crowded in here."

It would be so easy to fall into the dark behind my lids, to give in, but the voice talking to me wasn't Manning's deep bass that'd rumbled against my palms when I'd hugged him, or the soothing monotone I'd clung to while contorted in the back of a truck the night the cop had nearly caught us.

Reality came back to me in pieces. The burn of my lungs, the murmur of voices, music. I should've recognized the song sooner, but it wasn't until that moment that I did. I hadn't heard it since the night Manning had driven Tiffany and me to the fair—I'd been trying to find it since.

I opened my eyes and pushed Corbin off to look at the TV. "Black" by Pearl Jam. I had to write it down this time so I wouldn't forget, but I couldn't move. "I need to get up."

Corbin pulled back a little. "I know it's . . ." He lifted a corner of his mouth, showing me his white teeth. "I'm not sure how it's, like, possible, but I know."

His words floated through my brain, disconnected from each other. What was he talking about? "You know what?"

"You're so beautiful. You're the center of everyone's attention. But . . ."

"But?"

"You're still Lake. So innocent. So sweet. I know you're a virgin, but I swear it doesn't bother me."

I looked down and shook my head. Warmth receded from everywhere but my face. Corbin could have anyone. I wondered if he'd taken a girl's virginity before—I was sure he had, or that he'd at least had the opportunity. "It's not that."

"Don't be embarrassed. I can show you how."

It hadn't occurred to me to be embarrassed, not with Corbin anyway, and not about my virginity. I crossed my arms over my breasts. I didn't want this, and for some reason, I felt guilty about that. "I'm sorry, Corbin."

He sighed, kissed my forehead, and sat back. "All right. I've waited this long. I can keep waiting."

I squinted at him. "Why?"

"Don't you have any clue how I feel about you?"

"I—no . . ."

That wasn't true. I had some idea. Corbin hadn't asked me out since that night at camp when he'd walked me to my cabin, but Val had tried to warn me about the situation in her own weird way.

"Don't you think if Vada Sultenfuss had known Thomas J. was going to go back into the beehive for her, she would've told him not to?"

"Um. What?" I asked. *"Who?"*

She sighed, exasperated. *"My Girl, the movie. You're Corbin's best friend. You have to be careful or he'll get hurt."*

"You're going to college," I told Corbin.

"So?"

"There will be more girls than you can count."

"I've met a lot of girls, Lake. I still like you the most."

Somewhere in the room, someone wrestled with a bag of chips. *Crinkle, kssh. Pop.* The top of my scalp tingled. Corbin's eyes were naturally clear blue, but when they were bloodshot like now, it almost hurt to look at him. "You'll meet someone better at NYU."

"Better? What's not better about you?" he asked. "I bet you can't think of one thing that's wrong with you."

Everything, I wanted to say. Everything was wrong if Manning was gone, and now he'd be away even longer. I couldn't even see that he was okay or tell him I was sorry. He wasn't around to scold me for sitting on a couch smoking weed with a boy.

Crunch crunch crunch. The room smelled like Doritos. I covered my ears.

Corbin chuckled. "You're too high for this conversation."

Val walked by the doorway, skidded to a stop, and came in. She threw her hands up, a can of Cherry

Coke in one and a white Airheads in the other. "I've been looking for you guys everywhere!"

"We've been here," Corbin said.

"And in the bathroom," I said, which made Corbin and me giggle.

"Weirdos," Val said. She tore off a piece of taffy with her teeth and pointed the candy at me as she chewed. "Are you stoned, young lady?"

Corbin nodded to the joint. "Help yourself."

"Nah. I'm kinda over this place. I would've rather had that Meg Ryan movie marathon. *Sleepless in Seattle* for the main course, followed by *When Harry Met Sally* for dessert."

"Dude," Corbin said. "You have to see *Joe Versus the Volcano*."

"Dude, I already have, like five times. When you're stoned—"

"*Yes.*" Corbin waved his hands excitedly. "When you're stoned! Let's rent it from Blockbuster and go to Val's. I'll find someone sober to drive us."

She raised her Cherry Coke. "Find me a car, and I'm your girl. I only took a sip of that beer. It was flat and gross."

Corbin stood, and they both looked down at me. I took his hand when he offered it, and he pulled me up. Val led the way downstairs.

"Please don't touch my ring," I told Corbin for the millionth time.

He raised our intertwined hands to inspect it. "I don't know why you're so attached to something you found on the ground. You don't even know what the colors mean."

"Yes I do. I figured it out, but when you change the color, I don't know how to feel."

"*You* change the color of the ring. It doesn't change you." He sighed but dropped my hand and slung an arm around my shoulder instead. A couple people snickered as we passed. I could already hear the rumors about how Corbin and I had been alone in the bathroom and then gone upstairs to make out. I didn't care. They could think what they wanted. Only one person's opinion mattered to me, and Manning would know when he got out that I was still here. Waiting.

I'd wait as long as it took. I would save it all. For him.

5
MANNING

I woke up to the slide and slam of metal on metal. Concrete box. Ceiling crack that ran from one corner to the middle and forked. Mold in the toilet. Sweatshirt over my mouth and stuffed into my ears to block out the screamed obscenities and the assaulting smell of urine and feces.

Like every morning at three o'clock, a hand slid a tray of shriveled eggs through a slot in the metal door. "You're out today," a guard said and shut the hole.

That was it. Three words and the only ones besides *inmate*, *strip*, or *let's go* that'd been directed at me in a while. I was out? Of solitary? I looked at the wall where I'd chipped off paint each day. Seventy-four. Did I give a shit about what day of the week it was or how long I'd been in here? No, but I didn't have much more to do than track time, and I wasn't even sure I'd counted right since I hardly knew night from day and slept in shifts. I couldn't even keep track by breakfast, because some days, the staff never brought it.

Under the metal slab and thin mattress they called a bed was a shelf with three books, paper, and a golf pencil. I hadn't seen grass or the sun since I'd stuck my shovel in the dirt and gone inside for dinner the day of the fight. I hadn't smoked since then, either, and I'd paid the price for that with withdrawals. The only human contact I'd had in two and half months was a CO cuffing me to and from the showers or for an hour of rec alone in a bigger concrete box with a two-inch sliver of window.

I needed to shake a hand or be touched by someone other than the fuck-face CO who kept "forgetting" my meals when I was already underfed. Or the guard who'd stand in my cell and chuckle while reading my letters to Tiffany. If one had ever made it to her, I'd be shocked. It was punishment for what I'd done to Ludwig, even though I was pretty sure he disgusted the other guards, too. I hated them and this hellhole and the inmates on both sides of me who banged on the walls all hours of the day. They could scream endlessly and must've painted the walls in shit for how bad the smell got sometimes.

I took the prison-made sweatshirt off my face and sat up, blinking against the fluorescent light overhead. My knees ached from bending them to keep my feet from hanging off the bed. I shoveled the food fast, partly out of hunger, partly so I wouldn't have to taste it. The juice carton was expired but I drank it anyway, and then it was back to pacing the six-by-nine-foot cell or looking at a wall. More thinking. Every thought there was to have, I'd had it.

No two ways about it—I'd snapped. No warning, no build up, no attempt to talk myself down. One second I'd been playing cards, the next, my hands were around a man's throat. I'd sat in here watching the scene play out in my head like I'd been an observer rather than a participant. I could see it clearly, because I'd seen the same thing happen with my dad. He never made a decision to hit one of us. He just did it, no discernable reason, pattern, or threat. He'd hit me over dirty dishes as a kid and my mom while she was just watching TV.

The only break in my routine since entering the hole had been a trial in front of a judge. If they'd charged me with assault, it would've meant a lot more time in prison. CO Jameson had come to my rescue, testifying that I'd been provoked, physically and verbally, by Ludwig.

It wouldn't matter if CO Jameson had personally delivered me an ice cream sundae each day in here— the truth was, guards were pigs and I regretted the fact I'd ever wanted to be a member of law enforcement. I had no shot at ever becoming a cop now, and that was a blessing. Charles Kaplan had been right. Only people at the top had power, and I'd never go to the top. Not with my record or background. I'd been so green, asking Dexter what my past or family history had to do with me getting convicted of a crime I didn't commit.

Being in here had given me lots of time to replay that night in my head. Look at it from different angles. Could it have been some kind of set up? Who'd been around the fire the night I'd taken Vern's truck? Who'd had beef with me? Everyone at camp was a suspect. Had I trusted the wrong people? Vern the janitor was a local. The officer who'd pulled me over had been friendly, but who was he anyway? Bucky, the camp cook, had had a problem with me from the start—was it because I had a girl he'd never dream of scoring? Then there was the chick I'd gotten the mood ring off of. I didn't know any of them from a stranger.

The smells, the noise, the guards and meal times meant I couldn't sleep more than a few hours a night. My thoughts had warped and changed and wandered but they never, ever went the fuck away. Sometimes, they were reduced to simple things.

Food. They weren't feeding me enough.

Shelter. I had a roof over my head, four dank walls, a shitter, and one-hour-a-day access to a window too small to see out of.

Survival. I was angrier than I'd ever been, but I'd have to check my temper going forward, or I'd end up back in here. I'd already bloodied my knuckles on a wall a few times reliving the days before I'd been herded here.

Sex.

I hadn't fucked in over a year, and I was certain it was killing me from the inside out. I needed a raw, animalistic fuck, and the last person I'd touched and kissed and felt was Tiffany, so I'd fantasize about what I'd do to her if they let her in here for an hour. I'd take her from every angle, in every way a man could think of.

I'd jerk off and then the guilt would hit. Tiffany didn't deserve to be treated like that, even in my head. When my heart stopped pounding and my thoughts had cleared, it was just Lake. Her spun-gold hair, eyes like fresh mountain water on a summer afternoon, light shining from within. My fantasies about her were different. Over and over, I thought about the moment I'd see her again. How it would feel to hug her, to smell her strawberry-scented hair again. Did she use the same shampoo she had back then? Would she dress the same, look the same?

Sometimes, out of nowhere, I tasted watermelon. I'd be in the middle of the most disgusting meal of my life and the watermelon had my mouth tingling. It made everything worse. I'd rather eat chalky meatloaf than be reminded of what I'd never have again. Nothing seemed to erase it. It was sweet, harmless, youthful.

When I got worked up over Ludwig and the injustice of being where I was, I'd lie on the cell floor like I had on the concrete deck of the camp pool and force stars onto the mottled ceiling. It was my most cherished memory, both when I'd done it with Maddy and later with Lake. I'd close my eyes and get back on the horse, Lake clutching me out of a childish yet grown-up fear. There was that awkward and wonderful kiss she'd pressed on the corner of my mouth, a nothing kiss behind my ear, then near my lips for only a second and yet . . .

What if I'd just done it? Just taken her in the lake like she'd wanted to? In the truck? Maybe it wasn't romantic, but I'd have been good to her. Gentle. I'd have gotten to know all the curves and lines of her body for a night. I'd have pushed her shorts down and eased into her, my rough hands greedy for her softness. I'd have taken the one thing I'd wanted more than anything else in years—Lake.

And I would think about that, my heart rate settling, eyes closed, my head back against the concrete. In my mind, I'd be in the truck with Lake in my arms, hands wandering over the silky, downy hair at the very top of her thigh. I'd open her shorts, kiss the peaks of her breasts, bury my cock in her until I'd spent myself to the point I could no longer get hard.

Her innocence and simplicity defied the chaos in my head . . .

I'd open my eyes to the four walls around me and realize I'd come again, thinking of Lake, like the piece of shit I was for wanting to strip away more of her innocence than I already had. I would cry for her, for Maddy, for the monster I'd allowed to hurt my sister, for the monster I'd become. I'd never been or be anything else. It was in my blood. Thinking of Lake that way was wrong, but I'd done it, and not just once, and maybe I should've just given in to her watermelon kisses. Then I'd be in here for a real reason and at least I would've had those moments of bliss in my life.

After breakfast, I drifted in and out of sleep until a guard opened the door, cuffs in hand. "Let's go, inmate."

"Where are you taking me?"

"Bermuda. Don't forget your bathing suit, motherfucker."

Back in gen pop, Wills had moved to the bottom bunk and a man I didn't recognize sat on a bed across from ours. I went to my locker. Most of my letters were there but not all. Anything I'd had from commissary was gone. I looked from Wills to the new guy. "Where's my stuff?"

Wills got up. "Welcome back, asshole." He nodded across the cell. "That's Javier. He doesn't speak English."

I slammed the door shut. I had to let it go. Some of Lake's letters were out there, but I'd at least been smart enough to rip her return address off of them the night I'd been tempted to read them. I couldn't afford to let it get it to me. It wasn't her, just some words on a paper.

"Bad in the hole, ain't it?" Wills asked. "No time in there. Nothing. Three hots and a cot." Wills' shiny head reflected the too-bright overhead lights. "Lemme see, what'd you miss. . ." Wills said. "Warden cracking down, made the guards send Puentes to SHU for taking some high-profile chester off the count and now they're all pissing themselves thinking Puentes's men on the outside will retaliate . . ."

Wills was talking too much, too fast. A prisoner banged on the bars of a cell and others joined in, hollering. Javier shouted something at me in Spanish. "You mind shutting the fuck up?" I asked both of them. "And move your shit off my bed."

Wills raised his palms but got to work. "Just trying to catch you up."

"What day is it?"

"Let me check my agenda and get back to you."

"Go to hell. When's the next visitation?"

"Two days, but you've been gone months, brother. You think your girl will remember?"

Two-and-a-half months was a lifetime to a twenty-year-old. I ran my hand back and forth over my hair. It was getting down to my ears. I needed a cut, a fresh shave, and about thirty hours of sleep. But first, I needed to call Tiffany to let her know I was out.

Javier stared at me and made the sign of the cross.

"What's his problem?" I asked.

"I think he thinks this place is haunted. Something about the prison being built on a cemetery."

I went to look through the bars of the window. I needed to see something other than gray concrete. But then, I thought better of it, turning to lean my back against a wall so I could see the whole room. So I could see Wills.

"Why you looking at me like that?" he asked.

A guard came down our aisle, tapping his baton against bars and walls. My heart beat unnaturally hard. "You knew I'd lose my shit," I said to Wills. "You pushed me anyway."

"I had no idea you'd go that far. Swear on my life. Swear on Kaya's life."

"I don't believe you."

"You think I'd tell a lie on my daughter's life, you piece of shit?"

"Yeah, I do. You're the piece of shit here, not me."

Wills got quiet. That was a first. Normally, he'd step up, accuse me of being a pussy or of showing disrespect. "You would've killed Ludwig," he said. "Over nothing."

"It wasn't nothing."

"I saw it in your eyes, some kinda . . ." He hovered his hand over his face, up and down. "This blankness, man. We all saw it. He'd be dead if Jameson hadn't been there."

I knew the look he was talking about. Unfortunately, it'd been passed down. Now that it'd happened once, had I broken some kind of seal? Would it happen again? How careful did I need to be? I was suddenly exhausted. Maybe this was my nighttime, I wasn't sure. I'd lost track of when and how many hours I'd slept in isolation. My temples pounded with the heat and incessant noise. There was only one way to calm myself down quickly. "You better put a cigarette in my hand right fucking now, and I want a carton by the end of the day."

"A carton? Are you mental?"

"I don't know. Try me."

Wills looked at me like he didn't know me, like I hadn't been his cellmate the past year. And then he got me a cigarette. Yeah, well, fuck him. He seemed different to me, too.

In the cafeteria later, men stepped aside to let me get my food first. Some kid I didn't recognize gave me his seat at a table. I didn't take it. I sat alone with my back to the wall, watching inmates and guards.

A group of men passed me. "Respect," one of them said. That was what almost killing a CO had earned me. I forked green beans into my mouth, watching the guys until they sat. Wills kept his distance. Something had changed. I was one of the bigger guys in the prison, but that wasn't news. There were men in here who'd done more heinous things than nearly strangle a man to death. The difference now, I guessed, was that I'd gone blank in the face, as

Wills had put it. I was unpredictable. At any moment, I could snap for no reason. I could hurt someone.

The thing that got me through was the fact that I had a court date. That was a good thing. It was the first step to my release. I would've been fine to work and smoke and sleep until then, but when Friday came around, Tiffany showed.

I'd just smoked three cigarettes in a row and felt a little woozy after my extended break. I wasn't even sure I wanted to see her, but when I did, I was glad she'd come. She'd dressed up for me, even more than usual. Hair, makeup, a velvety red dress, heels, the whole nine.

Tiffany's mouth fell open as I approached. I leaned down to kiss her cheek, but she threw her arms around my neck and wouldn't let go.

"Enough, inmate," a guard called over the crowd.

She smelled of something sweet, some kind of berry, and she was soft. Everything had been so hard up until now, and she was so damn soft, but I couldn't bring myself to put my arms around her. I didn't know if she was still mine, if she ever really had been. After the past few months, nobody and nothing felt like it belonged to me. "Tiff."

"Oh my God," she whispered in my ear.

"Sutter." The CO had gotten out the bullhorn so everyone turned to us. "Don't make me come over there."

I pulled back. Tiffany put her face in her hands and burst into tears.

"Jesus." I wasn't sure what to do. Tiffany had never cried in the year we'd been having these visits. Panic hit me in the chest. So much could go wrong. Was it Lake? Had Tiffany met someone else? "What happened?"

She shook her head.

Helplessly, I stared down at her. I couldn't even comfort her without risking getting in trouble. I didn't know how else to console her.

"I'm sorry," she said, moving her hands to cover her mouth. Mascara had smudged at the outside corners of her eyes. "I'm so sorry, Manning."

"Why?"

"You look—you look . . ."

I hadn't bothered with a mirror since I'd gotten out of the hole. It'd been eleven weeks without sunlight, exercise, REM sleep, or decent portions of food. My nose had been broken by a boot in the fight, and I doubted Medical had bothered to set it straight. They'd barely stitched up my busted lip properly. I could only imagine how I looked.

When the guard wasn't looking, I wiped her eye makeup away. "I'm fine."

"What have they done to you?" she asked.

"Nothing. I'm fine."

"What was it like?"

"I can't talk about it." Based on our previous conversations, I was pretty sure she could handle at least the basics of what I'd been through—the fight, a slow descent into madness—but there wasn't any way of putting it into words. I'd done my best when I'd written to her, but even then, I couldn't help playing it down. "Did you get any of my letters?"

"Letters? No. I got nothing. Anything I heard came from Grimes and he made it sound like . . . he didn't say that . . ." Her eyes scanned my face.

Afraid she might cry again, I gestured at the table. "Sit. We're drawing attention."

She dropped heavily onto the bench, and I sat across from her. "You *have* to tell me what happened, Manning. Please."

"Tiff, the best thing you can do for me right now is talk. Just talk." I waited for her to launch into it, whatever I'd missed over the last five or so visits we hadn't gotten. Instead, she just sat and stared at me. I must've looked fuck-all bad. I couldn't give a good goddamn about that, but what was going through her mind? Was it enough to turn her off me for good? Enough for her to walk away? And then what? I'd be alone, which I basically was anyway. So who gave a fuck what she thought?

I didn't control her. She might up and go at any moment, move on with another man, take Lake with her, and what could I do?

"You going to break up with me because I don't look the same," I said, "just fucking do it. I'm not going to sit through an hour of a Dear John pity visit."

"No," she whispered. She bit her thumbnail, slumping in her seat. She looked at me with a rare kind of vulnerability that reminded me of a young girl. *Her* as a young girl. And I had to admit, I didn't want her to go. I was angry. I was scared. There was definitely something very wrong, and it didn't have to do with my appearance. "What then?" I asked.

A few more tears slid over her cheeks. She shook her head hard. "Nothing. Sorry."

"Not nothing. Just come out and say it."

"I can't. I don't even know what it is, I just—"

"I'm not in the mood to play games." I'd had enough of those for a lifetime, and my patience was shorter than ever. If there was something I needed to know, I didn't want to sit and dig for it an hour. "Just say it."

"I think . . ." She brushed at an invisible spot on the metal surface between us and avoided my eyes. "I don't know."

Whatever she had to say, it wasn't going to be good. "Goddamn it, Tiffany."

"Fine." She studied my face again like it was a math equation. "I think I, like, love you."

6

MANNING

My alone time with Tiffany had just begun, but the damn clock ticked on behind my head. I couldn't just relax in this shithole.

"I think I, like, love you."

I sat, staring dumbly at her, as it sank in. It was the last thing I'd expected her to say. We'd been technically dating over a year. For any other couple, the "I love yous" would've been dealt already. "You think *what?*"

She fidgeted in the silence that followed, looking around the room. She didn't seem happy about it, just uncomfortable. This was the Tiffany I'd come to know the past year. Her natural response when she was nervous or embarrassed was to lash out, but sometimes, with me, her youth and insecurity surfaced.

"I didn't plan it. I didn't even know I did until just now . . ."

"*Now?*" I asked. Couldn't she see I was different now? That the reasons to leave had only grown? My early release had been revoked, and I'd seen and done things I didn't know what to do with. I'd snapped.

She put her elbows on the table and cried again. "You don't have to say it back," she said, sniffling. "I just . . ." She peeked through her fingers at me. "I know you've been through a lot, and it hurts me. I want to kill that piece of shit Ludwig for—"

"Not the place to make death threats." I reached out and took her hand. "This is a prison. They might lock you up."

She offered me a watery little smile. "I'm angry."

Over the past thirteen months, I'd been plenty angry, but having someone get angry *for* me, cry for me, express emotions I couldn't . . . it made my frustration with the system feel justified. "Me too."

As if that'd flicked on a switch in her, she sat up straighter and inhaled. "Is there anything we can do about him? File a grievance, or maybe even a lawsuit—"

"It's done. I screwed up, and I paid the price. I'm lucky to be out. Some guys stay in solitary for years, lose their minds. I just want to leave it."

She nodded and pulled my hand to her chest, and my knuckles brushed the mound of her tits.

"Are you okay?" she asked. "I know you're strong, but are you?"

"I'm horny."

She half-laughed, half-shuddered, as if she was still forcing back tears. "Seriously? You spent over two months in a room by yourself and that's what you have to say?"

"What else would I say?"

"I wish we could . . . just a few minutes alone."

"What, in some trailer with a guard outside the door?"

She shrugged. "I would, if it were allowed."

"Yeah?" I squirmed in my seat. I wanted to hear her say it. I'd been in my head too much, gone untouched longer than a man should. I needed to know she wasn't scared to want me. "If what were allowed?"

She blushed a little, a slow smile spreading on her face. "Whatever. You know." She bit her bottom lip. "A conjugal visit."

I'd taught her that word her second time here. After what I'd been through, just hearing the word *conjugal* made me half-hard.

"What happened with that guard?" she asked. My erection died, which was for the best. "Why'd you get into it when you knew you'd lose?"

I didn't know how to put it into words, and I wasn't going to risk reliving those moments while I was outside a cage. In solitary, with nothing to do, I couldn't avoid eventually going down that path, but at least I'd taken it out on the walls instead of a person. "I don't want to talk about it."

"You should," she pressed.

I squeezed her hand, then released it to lean onto my forearms. "The only thing that'll help me right now is hearing about you."

She sighed a little. "Well, I came to tell you good news. I found an apartment."

"Yeah? Where?"

"It's a two-bedroom in Costa Mesa."

I raised my eyebrows. Costa Mesa was still Newport Beach and not so far from the water. "How can you afford that?"

"It was Dad's idea. He wanted me to stay close to them and work. It's less than fifteen minutes from Nordstrom."

"That wasn't my question."

"I thought about what you said, getting the roommate or moving inland, but I just . . . it's not me. I can't not be at the beach."

"So he's going to help you out," I concluded.

"He's co-signing the lease and he'll pay part of the rent." She rushed her words out. "Well, most of it, so I can, like, eat. I'm not sure why he's doing it. I guess maybe he just wants me out of the house. But I'm not going to say no." After a breath, she asked, "Are you disappointed? That I'm not doing it on my own?"

Charles Kaplan might've been a jerk, but I had a feeling he truly did want Tiffany close. She was his daughter, and he was a protective asshole, kind of like me. If she stayed in Newport, he could continue to watch her, control her. Not perfect, but it was a start. "No. It's a step in the right direction."

She looked over my head, maybe at the clock, or maybe just a nervous habit. "So I was thinking . . . when you get out . . ."

I waited. "Yeah?"

She took a deep breath. "You should stay with me."

"Stay with you?"

"Until you find your own place."

I glanced around the crowded room. A place to go when I got out? I hadn't expected it, but if I was honest, relief hit me first. I'd known a few guys who'd been released since I'd arrived here. They'd all had places to go. Girlfriends, wives, parents. I had my aunt and Henry in Los Angeles, but L.A. wasn't an option. Not only could parole prevent me from living outside county lines, but L.A. felt too much like a home I wanted to forget. It was lying in the grass with Maddy, pulling her out of the pool a minute too late, my mom's betrayal, and my dad's abuse. If I could burn my childhood house to the ground without consequences, I'd do it. "Yeah," I said. "Maybe. It's not a bad idea."

"Or you could just move in."

"You mean, like . . . I wouldn't look for my own place?"

"Yes, like, move in. And stay." She smiled a little. "Pick out furniture. Have a key."

What she was describing was a home, not a place to stay. Since I was fifteen, I'd been kind of floating through life. I'd stayed with my aunt to finish high school, then I'd gotten the hell out of Los Angeles, landing wherever there was work. After the pain of losing Maddy, I'd thought that was the best way. The only way. It could've been a result of my current circumstances, but it surprised me that staying in one place and making it my own sounded better than returning to a transient life. Next year would be the tenth anniversary of Madison's death. Ten years of staying detached from anything meaningful—at least until Lake and Tiffany had come along. Maybe I was getting to a place where I could accept a life in which Maddy didn't exist.

I was getting ahead of myself. Tiffany probably didn't understand what she was suggesting, but I knew moving in wouldn't be as simple as unpacking my things in her apartment. "I don't know if it's a good idea," I said. "For one, the rent's an issue."

"My dad's covering it, though."

"Your dad's not paying my rent."

"But you don't have a job or anything. Is there anything left of the money I got you for the truck?"

I flexed my hands on the table. After legal fees and fines, and breaking my lease, I only had a few hundred dollars saved. Then some bitch who'd wrongly fingered me in a line-up, who lived in an upper-class Big Bear neighborhood, was getting twenty-five of my cents every hour I killed myself outdoors. "Not much," I said. "And I can't imagine your dad ever wants to see my face again."

"Don't worry about him," she said. "I have time to work on him until you get out. He'll accept you once he knows we're serious."

We were serious. She'd told me she loved me. And Tiffany wasn't going to let her dad get in the way of that. I shouldn't have doubted that Tiffany would show up for me today. She hadn't missed a visit yet, and she was probably getting shit from her dad about it all the time.

Did I love her back? Over the last year, I'd come to care about her more than I would've guessed. There still was, and always would be, a cavity in my chest. Lake's goodness had been the only thing so far to lessen the ache of that wound. Coming here, I'd had to numb myself even more—for survival. Dropping my guard, even for a second, had landed me in the SHU and fuck if I was ever going back there. But it occurred to me that somehow, Tiffany had gotten through to me.

"All these guys in here," I said, "most of them have someone on the outside holding them up. You've been that for me." I didn't have the brain power to mince words. I needed a cigarette. "I appreciate you. I think about you when we're apart, and I miss you. But I'm not going to tell you I love you just to say it."

She frowned. It was as good as admitting I didn't love her. Part of me worried she'd take that and leave, and the other part worried she wouldn't. At this point, trying to get love from the most important man in her life was part of her identity.

"I didn't tell you so you'd say it back," she said. "I never planned to say it. I'm not even sure how I feel about it. Love is weird. Like, I know my dad loves me, but sometimes I think to myself, 'my dad hates me.'"

Jesus Christ. I wasn't even sure where to start with that. "He doesn't—"

"I know he doesn't hate me," she said, waving her hand. "But he is disappointed in me, and I feel like I can't do anything right. When I try, I mess it up, or it isn't good enough."

It frustrated me to hear her talk that way—and that she was right. The truth was, Tiffany had everything going for her. She had the potential to succeed if she'd let go of this thing with her dad. "You need to see yourself outside your dad's eyes," I told her. "You've said to me before that you don't have the skills to do anything other than model, but that's just plain bullshit. You're smart and crafty and you're goddamn tenacious. That's a rare quality, Tiff. That'll get you far."

Tiffany looked taken aback, and I realized I'd raised my voice. Good. I hoped she'd heard me. She *did* have some qualities I hadn't come across too much in my life. For one, I'd just told her I didn't love her, and she'd barely batted an eyelash. For a sheltered Newport Beach girl, she was tougher than she looked.

"And let's get one thing straight," I added. "I'm not going to pretend I love you because I care too much about you to lie, but that doesn't mean I'm withholding it to punish you like your dad. Got it?"

She nodded, slowly at first, and then a little harder. "I understand. It's like I do things to get him to notice, and . . . that's wrong. Once I move out, and he's not around all the time, I can start focusing on what *I* want."

"Yeah." I felt a strange sense of pride, like I'd gotten through to her a little bit. "You still want me to move in? Or you want to be on your own a while?"

"I want you there. I mean, geez. Can't you see how good you are for me?"

For some reason, that dislodged something in my chest. *Good.* I wasn't good, but I wanted to be better. Better than the man who'd attacked a guard. Better than one who repeated his dad's mistakes.

"You were in that place for over two months," Tiffany continued, "but that counted toward your sentence. Grimes told me if you have no more incidents, you might still be eligible for early release."

I rubbed my jaw. I knew that, but I'd been so concerned about the fact that I was no longer getting out early, I hadn't paid much attention to the fact that I could get it back—but only if I stayed on track. "It's not as simple as just going home with you, though. I'll be on parole when I get out. They'll want to interview you. I'll be subjected to random searches. I could have a PO who's a dick and makes my life hell. You didn't sign up for all that."

"You think I would've visited just anyone every month for a year?" She opened her hands in front of her and counted off her fingers. "I went to your landlord, broke your lease, sold your stuff to help pay your fees. I got a job, and I've been working hard. You don't know since I haven't seen you, but I'm up for a promotion to assistant manager. For you. To show you I can be better."

Better. It was what both of us wanted. We had work to do, and somehow, lifting her up had forced me to up my game as well. I knew Tiffany had been trying, but she'd be twenty-one soon. I'd assumed that was part of it, getting older, maturing. I hadn't considered it might all be for me. "Why?" I asked.

"Why what?" She sounded exasperated.

"Why me?" As soon as I said it, I realized I'd been wanting to know since her first visit, but pointing it out to her would've only driven her away, and I'd needed someone then. "Why'd you go sort things with my landlord and take care of my shit and why do you still come around?"

She swallowed audibly, pulling her hands into her lap. "Because it's nice to feel needed."

The question was, who needed whom? "I didn't mean that the way it came out," I said. "I'm not sure who would've done it if you hadn't. I'm glad you did. I'm glad you're here."

"I know." Her expression eased. She *did* know. It was one of the things I'd always liked about her. Sometimes, her confidence wavered, but I liked that she faked it anyway.

"I'm just not sure I understand why."

"I don't think I know."

"And I think you do." I could see the wheels in her brain turning, but I let her off that hook to put her on another. "Have you fucked around?"

Right on cue, the CO got on his bullhorn. "Start wrapping up."

I'd heard the same question asked in here before by other inmates. There were stories, lots of them, about men accusing their girls of awful things.

Tiffany didn't react, which wasn't typical from what I'd seen or been told. "No," she said simply.

I wanted to believe her, but it seemed unlikely. I looked her in the eye. "I'd understand if you had, just tell me the truth. If I come out of here with you, it's a clean slate for us."

"I don't want a clean slate," she said. "You were good to me. I don't want to wipe that away. I haven't been with anyone else."

"But you could've been."

"Of course." She adjusted the sleeve of her dress. "I thought about it lots of times. I've had opportunities."

"I know you have."

"I guess you won't believe me, but I'm not a cheater. I think it's really low."

"Why wouldn't I believe you?"

"Maybe you think I'm, you know, slutty." She said it without flinching, straight up. "And, okay, I've been with some guys before you, but that doesn't make me a liar."

Well, she'd put me in my place, and she was right. "Okay, then tell me what you were thinking about just before this. Why me?"

Again, her eyes shifted, went a little distant. She was avoiding answering, like it was hard for her to say. "Look," she said. "I'm not proud of it, but at the courthouse, when Dexter gave me that bag of your things, the keys to your place and your truck, I was pissed. I didn't understand why, of all people, you thought I would know what to do with it. But the real reason I got mad was because I was scared. Nobody had ever just . . . trusted me that much. Your life was in that bag. I didn't know where to start. I was sure I'd mess it up."

I could've hugged her right then. It might've been the most honest thing I'd ever heard her say. She was scared. Did she think she was alone in that? All of us were just doing our best. "You didn't," I said. "You came through."

"I wanted to give it all to my dad to take care of. He's good at that kind of stuff. He probably would've gotten you out of the lease altogether." She spread her hands on the table as if she were inspecting her nail polish. I could see her thinking, though. "But then I remembered how good you'd been to me that night we had spaghetti at camp. You'd arranged that nice dinner for me, and you made me feel, I don't know . . . like I mattered to you. So even though I wanted to walk away, I decided to figure it out."

That night at camp felt like a lifetime ago. It made me think of Bucky, and how I'd wanted to wring that bastard's throat, even back then. Tiffany put on a good show, but I'd pretty much had her number from day one. If I'd been the first man to make her feel special for who she really was, then maybe it wasn't so farfetched that she was still sitting here.

That didn't mean she didn't deserve to be warned about what she'd be getting into with me. If anything, I owed her that.

The family at the table next to us stood and hugged. Time was up. "I'm not the same person I was back then."

"Yes, you are."

I wasn't. I'd seen more. I knew more. None of it good. Moving in with Tiffany would mean relying on her. Trusting her. I hadn't done that since I'd left my aunt's at eighteen. I had to know Tiffany wasn't going to scare easily. "You know what I thought about when I was alone too long?"

"What?" she asked.

"Fucking. Not in a nice way." I paused to check her reaction. She went a little pink but didn't back

95

down. "I come out of here, I'm not going to be able play Country Club Man like your dad. I'm not going to golf, and brunch, and go sailing or whatever the hell it is your friends do. It's going to be hard. I'm doing what I have to do for the basics—shelter, food, work."

She nodded. "I can help."

"I'm giving you an out." I'd had nothing before this, but at least I'd had a future. Now all I had was a past and a record. "You should take it."

"The more you tell me to, the less I want to."

Sounded about right. Tiffany looked hopeful. Maybe even happy. She was sitting here because of how I'd made her feel one night thirteen months ago. She'd done all right for herself since then, too, so she could be the girl I expected her to be. I hadn't done much right lately, but this—this felt good. Tiffany had been pretty lost when I'd met her, and now, she was making an effort. I'd helped someone, and after feeling as though my presence had made things worse for a lot of people, it made me want to keep trying. To get out of here. I could no longer join the police force and improve people's lives like I'd wanted to, but Tiffany, at least, I could help.

It was the first time I could remember feeling like I had any real power over my situation. She'd asked if I was disappointed in her, and I wasn't.

"Will you let Gary know I'm out of solitary?" I asked, getting up. "I gotta talk to him about something."

Her eyebrows scrunched. "What?"

"Work." It was partly true. If I didn't have to worry about a place to live, it meant I could focus on the next most important thing—money. On my old crew, a few of the guys I'd worked with had had been ex-cons. Gary might know people in construction. But since I'd gone into isolation, some questions had grown bigger in my mind. How had I gotten here at all? Was there more to my arrest than bad timing? Had anyone else been involved? As the director at camp, Gary would know more than most.

"I already called him. He's coming next week." She cocked her head. "You're not going to try and move in with *him*, are you?"

"I barely know him," I said. Gary had been to see me several times, and I considered him a good friend, but that was easy to do when you didn't have much else. I wasn't about to ask him to go through all the shit that came with housing a criminal. "He didn't offer anyway."

"Oh. Good," she said. "Because my place, it won't be much, but I know we can make it our own. We can make it a home."

Home. I hadn't had a home since Maddy'd died. I didn't even know the meaning of the word anymore.

But I still needed a place to live, and I could live with Tiffany for a while.

7

LAKE, 1995

AP History had never been so tedious, and that was saying a lot. The secondhand on the clock above the door moved about as fast as Progress, the class pet everyone called a turtle but was actually a tortoise. Mr. Caws was so monotone, he could dull anything, even the ache in my heart some days. But not today. Today, my chest hurt implacably, unyieldingly . . . and for good reason.

Vickie leaned over to my desk and whispered, "Let's go to Starbucks after school. I want to try that new Frappuccino thing."

"I can't."

"Dairy Queen?"

"I asked you Monday if you could take me home today." I fisted my pencil at both ends, fighting the urge to snap it. "You said you could."

"Well, sure. I thought you meant hang out. I'm not, like, your chauffeur."

"I know, but I really need to go straight home."

She shifted her eyes to check the front of the classroom. Mr. Caws droned on with his back to us, so she continued, "How come?"

"We're having a family dinner tonight."

"So? You already do that weekly. Why is today important?"

Why was today important? She honestly had no clue about anything. I mean, I hadn't actually *mentioned* today to her or anyone else for that matter. It felt too personal, too raw. Not something I could just bring up randomly in everyday conversation. Even the thought of it made my heart pound. I kept my eyes on the teacher. "We're having company."

Vickie gasped. "Is today—"

Mr. Caws stopped talking to look at us. "Girls," he warned.

"Sorry, Mr. Caws," we both replied.

He turned his back to write on the whiteboard.

"Tiffany's boyfriend gets out of jail this week, right?" Vickie whispered.

Tick tock. Tick tock. I swear, time hadn't progressed. The clock had to be broken.

By now, Tiffany would be on her way to pick up Manning. I wanted it to be me. I wished I wasn't too afraid to cut school. I wished I had my license. I wished Tiffany hadn't caught me getting into Manning's truck and found both a reason to be suspicious and leverage over me. "He's not her boyfriend," I said.

"Sure seems like it the way she talks about him."

"Well, he's not. Tiffany's delusional." She exaggerated about everything. She only had him because he was trapped. I knew Manning wouldn't forget me, even though he hadn't bothered to write me back. The way he'd touched me—even just for a few seconds—I could feel it in his hands. He wanted me. He cherished me. That didn't go away just because of some time apart.

If anything, that desire got stronger.

Tick tock. Tick tock. There were still five whole minutes until school ended. Four hours until Manning would be at our doorstep. Dinner was Mom's idea, one Dad had called "fucking dumb" right in front of me, which meant he'd been really angry. He'd eventually caved. Not to Tiffany but to Mom. In the time Manning had been away, Tiffany had managed to convince Mom he was innocent without revealing the truth about Manning and me. Dad didn't buy it. Manning had walked into *our* home uninvited, why wouldn't he walk into someone else's? But Mom wouldn't hear it. The man had been incarcerated for a crime he didn't commit, and he had no family to come home to but us. He deserved a home-cooked meal.

Tiffany thought so, too, even though she had her own place and could cook him a meal in her own kitchen, not that she knew how. Dad was outnumbered, even without my vote.

For the hundredth time today, I ran through all the things I planned to do as soon as the bell rang.

Go for a long run to calm my nerves.

Help Mom make the best food Manning would ever put in his mouth.

Make myself beautiful. Truly beautiful.

All of that would keep me busy until Manning got to the house. I needed to be *doing*, not sitting here *thinking*. I hadn't done anything good for Manning in too long. I'd only gotten him into trouble, damaged his life, his future. I wanted to serve him something wonderful, like the time I'd made him the Lake Special, my monster sandwich.

I had to show Manning I wasn't a kid anymore. That I wouldn't make any more mistakes. I was older, wiser, and my boobs were bigger. He couldn't miss that.

Mr. Caws checked the clock. "We still have five minutes."

God. What, was time going backward?

"Let's do some quiet reading," he said.

Time in 1995 was weird. It'd been killing me in all kinds of different ways ever since Tiffany had finally spilled the beans—Manning was coming home today, January twenty-third. Just like that, a year and five months into his sentence, Manning would be out.

Time had come to a screeching halt right then and there and had been creeping along ever since.

December had passed like normal, but January was almost over, and we still hadn't heard from USC. My dad's panic made me panic. It wasn't standard for packets to come before March, but Dad didn't see any reason I shouldn't get accepted early. Lots of my friends had heard from schools all over the country. Mona's mom had shown up in the middle of English and dropped a fat envelope on her daughter's desk. Vinny Horton was a scrawny, bespectacled nerd, but he'd put his fist right through a wall when he'd found out the quarterback had been accepted to Stanford on a football scholarship while Vinny had been waitlisted. College was everyone's world. It was *my* world. Every day that passed without a packet in the mailbox, I was letting my dad down.

And now, today, time was failing me again. I wasn't sure I could stand to sit here two more minutes, much less wait a full four hours to see Manning. Knowing he was coming was the best kind of torture. I packed up my Jansport and stared at the clock.

Vickie tapped the eraser of her pencil against her desk. "Most schools have a Sadie Hawkins dance for Valentine's. Why don't we?"

Mr. Caws looked up. "Girls. Don't make me tell you again."

Vickie opened her spiral-bound notepad and scribbled with the concentration of a doctor performing surgery. She tore the page out fast, the only way to do it in a quiet classroom, but Mr. Caws still looked up. Vickie put her hands in her lap, expertly folding the note into squares until Mr. Caws returned to grading papers. She passed it to me.

I bet Corbin sends you flowers for V-day. I need a Valentine so I'm not a total loser. Maybe we can go—

I balled up the note. What was she even talking about? Her note, this classroom, this desk, the Battle of Saratoga, seemed so unimportant. Vickie looked horrified. The bell rang, and I bolted up from my chair.

"What's your deal?" Vickie asked. "You'd think it was Corbin coming over for dinner, not some criminal."

"You don't understand," I said, slinging my bag over my shoulder. "You just don't. You're completely dense."

In the hallway, Vickie tucked her binder under her arm. "You're right, I don't. But I do understand I'm not driving you home. Find your own ride," she said, walking off.

"No, Vickie, wait." The hallway filled with students. I held my history book to my chest and did my best to push through. "I'm sorry," I said as I caught up, matching her long strides. "I didn't mean to—"

I nearly ran headlong into Val coming out of Physics. "Hey," she said.

I grabbed Vickie's elbow at the last second, and she whirled around. "Seriously, Lake. You've been such a bitch lately."

"*Whoa*," Val said. "Totally uncalled for."

Stopped in the middle of hall, our classmates were forced to scatter around us. "You're right, I have," I said. "I've been under so much pressure."

"So have I," Vickie said. "You think just because you're going to a top college that nobody else's life matters."

"What are you talking about?" I asked.

She took her arm back. "You haven't even asked how this has been for the rest of us."

"That's not true. You want to go UNLV and major in communications. What else is there to know?"

"Um, I don't know. Maybe that I'm not going to get in. That I've also applied to ten other schools as backups."

"*Ten*?" I shouted, causing people to look over at us.

"Yes, ten. That's totally normal, Lake. You're the only one who applied to *one*."

That was because I could only *go* to one. I wasn't going to jinx myself by even considering other schools. I looked at Val, surprised that I hadn't ever asked her how many schools she'd applied to. "What about you?"

She twisted her lips. "Five or six," she said. "I lost count."

"Which ones?" I asked them.

As we headed out to the parking lot, they listed off fifteen schools they'd applied to between the two of them. The thing was, while I'd been sick over applications, they actually sounded *excited*. They had options. Their futures were wide open. As of now, neither of them had any idea which city they'd be moving to at the end of summer. There was nothing mysterious about my plan. None of this process had made me giddy. It'd felt about the same as having an elephant sit on my chest, getting heavier and heavier the longer I didn't hear anything.

While they argued over the differences between University of San Diego, San Diego State University, and University of California San Diego, I thought back to the similar conversations I'd had with Corbin about NYU. All this time, I'd thought he'd just wanted me to be where he was. I hadn't seriously considered picking up and moving to a completely different place.

"Lake?" Val asked, lowering her sunglasses to squint at me.

"What?"

"We asked where else you *would* apply."

"Where else?" Could I see myself as anything other than a Trojan? USC football or basketball or baseball had been playing on our TV since I could remember. We had flags we hung outside the house during big games. My dad hated that Tiffany hadn't gone there, and I suspected he even resented my mom for not attending USC, which made no sense because they hadn't met until after she'd graduated college. My chest constricted at just the thought of asking about other schools.

Val's eyebrows gathered as she inspected my face. "Are you okay?"

"Her dad would never go for it," Vickie explained. "He puts her under a lot of pressure."

"Yes, I'm aware," Val said. "I have eyes and ears."

"USC is all he's talked about for months," I said, my voice sounding far off. "For my life." This had happened a few times lately, this rise of panic in my chest. I thought about USC a lot, but when I began to really think hard about the details, all the ways it could go wrong, my breathing became shallow. What if it wasn't enough? All the volunteering, studying, rigorous SAT prep and near-perfect score. What if my letter never came? What if it did, and the classes were so hard that I flunked out my first semester? Would Dad begin to look at me the way he did Tiffany, distantly, as if she'd wound up in his presence by mistake somehow?

"He doesn't have to know about it," Val said. "You could always apply without telling him."

"You can use my address," Vickie said excitedly.

"She'd use Tiffany's *obviously*," Val said. "She's her sister."

Oddly, their bickering calmed me a little. It wasn't like giving myself options, adding a little *unknown* to my life, was a crime. Surely, my dad would see that . . . but what if he didn't? If I asked to apply somewhere else and he said no, pursuing it would be defying him. But if I never gave him the *chance* to say no . . .?

There were other things he didn't know about the past few months—like how I'd stopped showing up to piano because I hated piano, and it was already on my application so who cared? Or that I'd spent the night at Val's a few times when her mom wasn't home so Val and I could stay out on the boardwalk until midnight or drink wine coolers on her couch and watch *Party of Five*.

I hadn't wanted to lie to my parents, but Val had made a valid argument. "You're going to be on your own soon anyway," she'd said. "If you don't start slowly, you'll go crazy when college starts and eventually have to drop out because you can't control yourself."

It'd made sense to me, but I knew it wouldn't to my dad, so I'd done it behind his back.

I supposed this was kind of the same thing. I'd gotten a job before the holidays serving yogurt and smoothies at a country club, so I had a little money saved I could use for applications.

"I think we lost her," Val said.

I blinked a few times. "Sorry."

"It's okay. You need a ride?"

Vickie blanched. "I already said I'd give her one."

"She's on my way home." Val pulled my elbow. "Come on."

"Are you sure?" Vickie asked. "I could always stay for dinner in case things get weird."

"Weird?" Val stopped pulling. "Why? What's for dinner?"

"Six-foot-five inches of delicious man meat," Vickie said.

I looked over at her. "You've never even seen him."

She shrugged. "I've heard rumors. Tiffany said he was that tall, *at least*, and that he looks like he should be riding a horse across a Tuscan landscape. Like an Italian model."

"Wait, Tiffany's boyfriend is coming over?" Val asked, bouncing on her toes.

I wrinkled my nose at Vickie, irritated. She was being rude and flippant about something that really mattered. Manning was so much more than a handsome face. "What Italian models do you even know?"

"*Please* let me come for dinner," Val said.

"No," I said. I hated them both in that moment for making light of something I'd been agonizing over for more than a year. "It's not that kind of dinner. It's for family."

"Yeah," Val said and resumed pushing me toward her 1979 convertible Beetle. "Family only, so run along, Vickie."

Vickie scowled, watching us go. "Fine. I have better things to do anyway."

Val had a noisy car you could hear coming from down the block. My dad hated it, said it left grease stains on the street outside our house. By all reasoning, he should've hated her, too. Her skateboarding in our driveway, her revealing outfits, and her single, airhead mom who wore red lipstick to match her Mustang. He'd met Val a few times, though, and called her "a smart girl," nothing more. That meant he liked her. He rarely volunteered much about any of my friends.

Val and I tumbled into the house. I threw my backpack onto the kitchen counter and opened the fridge.

"Lake?" Mom said from upstairs. "Is that you?"

"And me, Mrs. Kaplan," Val called.

"Oh, hi, Val." Mom came down with a mild grin, dressed in a gray skirt and blouse. "What are you girls up to?"

"When are you starting dinner?" I asked, handing Val a Yoo-hoo.

Mom checked her watched. "I have a house to show right now, and then I'll be back. Probably around five. Tiffany wants to eat early because she thinks Manning will be exhausted. Do they not get to sleep much in prison? I would think so. What else do they do?"

Val looked at my mom blankly, and I imagined my expression was the same. It was weird to hear her say it so casually. In the library, I'd tried looking up information about prison. There were things to do like jobs and exercise and even TV, but I wasn't naïve enough to think I understood anything about the experience.

"I'm going to go for a run," I said. "Is there anything else I need to get for tonight? I can pick it up on my way home."

Mom smiled and came over to fix my hair. "You've asked me that every day this week. We're all set. Don't be uncomfortable. I'm sure Manning is still the nice young man he was before all this. Try not to think of him as a criminal, but as a human being."

Of course he wouldn't be the same. *I* wasn't, and I hadn't been through a fraction of what he had.

"Enjoy your run. Don't overdo it, okay?" On her way out of the kitchen, Mom patted Val's shoulder. "Nice to see you, honey."

Val and I went upstairs to my bedroom. At my dresser, I opened up the drawer with my running clothes.

"What's she mean by overdo it?" Val asked.

"I don't know." I held up a pair of running shorts. "She's been saying that a lot lately. She was all worried because I ran on Thanksgiving Day. And Christmas Eve. And Christmas. Like a holiday is an excuse not to exercise?"

"Well," Val said in a tone that said, *It kind of is.*

I needed to run. It wasn't really a choice at this point. When I missed a day, the pressure caught up with me. Test scores and college apps, USC and extracurriculars. Not just the pressure, but my mistakes, too. I began to think of things I shouldn't, memories that'd gone from happy to sad, like talking to Manning on the bus to camp about his college classes and impending law enforcement career. Others haunted me—Manning being led away in handcuffs all because I'd gotten the wild idea he wanted one night alone with me. His orange jumpsuit. The judge ordering him away from us. The courtroom shrinking in the BMW's side mirror. I pushed the heels of my hands into my eye sockets to expunge the images.

Look what you've done, Lake.

"Hey," Val said. "What's wrong?"

I turned to her. She was lying on my bed, Birdy under her bare armpit as she absentmindedly picked at the blue fur. "You'll get deodorant on her," I said, frowning.

"She doesn't mind." She puckered her lips at the stuffed animal and crooned, "Do you, Booby?"

"It's *Birdy*."

She took the toy out from under her and walked it along the bedspread. "You should've named her Booby, though."

"Why?"

"Because that's what she is. A blue-footed booby."

"She's a pelican."

"This is not a pelican." Val gaped at me. "You should know that. You grew up by the beach."

My heart panged in my chest. That couldn't be right. She had always been a pelican, and that didn't just change. "Why would you say that?" I asked.

"Exhibit A." She tapped her head. "I'm a black hole of useless information." It was true. Val was always pulling random facts out of her ass. "But even if I weren't, see exhibit B. Blue feet." She showed me Birdy's webbed feet which were, in fact, blue like her beak. I'd just assumed she was colorful because she was meant for kids. "Plus, the tag says 'Blue-footed Booby.'"

My eyes dropped to the comforter. Had I been so blind that night at the fair that I hadn't even seen what was right in front of me? Maybe I was kidding myself thinking Manning was looking forward to tonight. What if he blamed me for what he'd lost? Tiffany certainly did. What if he wasn't happy to see me at all? Was there any other explanation for why he'd never responded to my letters, had never bothered to even call?

I couldn't think that way.

Tonight was *not* going to go wrong. Manning would see me, and just like that first day on the lot, we'd be drawn together. We'd know the truth without saying it—Manning was doing what he needed to until I was eighteen. Nothing else mattered until then.

Val was suddenly standing in front of me, my shoulders in her hands. "Hel-*lo*? What's wrong?"

I shook my head, clearing my thoughts away. "Nothing."

"Not nothing. You've been moping since the day I met you, and I'm not going to let you get away with it anymore. Why does this pelican-turned-booby bother you so much?"

My mouth wouldn't open. It was too weird to say out loud. *I'm in love with a man my sister calls her boyfriend.* If you hadn't lived the story like I had, it sounded awful. Val was as open-minded as anyone I knew, and even this was asking for a lot of understanding.

"Is it about a boy?" she asked.

"How'd you know?"

"It's always about a boy. Corbin?"

"No."

"So there's another boy." She tapped a light fingertip on my shoulder, studying me. "Why don't I know about him?"

I wriggled out of her grasp and went to my closet for running shoes. "Because he's not a boy."

She gasped. I could feel the delight coming off her in waves, even with my back turned. "He's older?"

"Yes."

"Older than Corbin?"

"Yes."

"I need to know *more.*"

"I can't tell you." I sat on the edge of my bed to lace up my sneakers. "If I could, I would."

"*Please*. This is too juicy. Is he in college? Is he a teacher? Is it Mr. Caws?"

I made a gagging noise, then giggled. "I'm not going to tell you."

"I'll tell you all my secrets." She leaned back against my dresser. "Hmm. In sixth grade, I peed my pants at my desk and didn't tell anyone so the next person sat in it."

"Oh my God, how disgusting."

"I know." She laughed. "All right, here's a good one. It's not funny, though. I wasn't completely honest with you about the first guy I slept with at my old high school. I told you it was no big deal, but I actually really liked him."

"You said it was with a stranger."

"I was embarrassed. He stopped talking to me after and rumors spread."

Once in a while, Val reminded me of Tiffany. Mostly tough, but their weak spots were arguably more sensitive than other people's. Val also had issues about her dad, who'd left her mom when Val was entering high school. "I'm sorry."

She shrugged. "It's fine. It taught me some things about men."

"Like what?"

"Mostly that they're immature . . . which is why I'm excited about this older guy."

"It's not . . . we're not, like, together or anything."

"You have a crush. Who doesn't? Is it the good kind of crush? Like one you want to act on or one you don't? There's a difference."

"Definitely the first one."

She went over to my closet. "Well, you never dress sexy at school—your closet is sad—but I guess that's because he already graduated, huh?"

"How can a closet be sad?"

"Do you have *anything* red?"

"I don't think so. Maybe a sports bra. How come?"

"Hmm. Red makes men horny. It's, like, biology. Plus, it looks great on blondes." She held out a knee-length, maroon corduroy skirt. "This is kind of red, but it's also . . . hideous."

"It's from middle school. I meant to take it to Goodwill, but—"

"Perfect." She held it up to her waist. "Cut it and wear it next time you see him."

"Really?"

"Yeah. With a pair of Mary Janes or clogs or something, you'll be all legs. He'll forget his own name."

I took the skirt, examining the button-down front and plummy color. It never would've occurred to me to do anything other than donate it. "Okay. Thanks. Anything else?"

"Nope. Just be yourself."

I rolled my eyes. "Yeah, okay."

"What? I'm serious. You're smart and beautiful. You hold all the power—haven't you ever watched your sister?"

My mood dimmed. Val had only been around Tiffany a few times, but I guessed that was all it took to see her charm. I wasn't really in the habit of emulating her—if anything, I was genetically predisposed to do the opposite of whatever she did—but in this case, I could see Val's reasoning. Tiffany had spent the last year getting to know Manning while I'd stayed here, getting further away from him.

Val picked up her backpack. "I have to go record *Wings* for my mom or she'll flip. When are you seeing this guy next?"

I turned away so I wouldn't have to lie to her face. "Not sure. I'll let you know."

"'K. Later."

As Val's Beetle rumbled down the street, I picked up Birdy and held her to my chest. I could *almost* convince myself I smelled campfire in the woods, sweat and sawdust on Manning's skin, lingering smoke on his clothes. As comforting as Birdy was, she would never be the real thing, and in just a few hours, that's what I'd have. Manning—big, strong, and real, right in front of me.

117

8
MANNING

Back against the wall, cigarette in hand, I watched the parking lot for Tiffany's car. I'd stood like this lots of times on the other side of these walls, but today I didn't see any orange jumpsuits, fried grass, or cracked concrete slabs. Just freedom.

I had a plastic bag with the contents of my life. Wallet, a check for what was left in my store account, and two-hundred dollars gate money. I'd filed Lake's unread letters away within my paperwork. Everything else I either left behind for Wills or trashed—except my dad's confession. The paper was worn from the number of times I'd read his letter. I wanted to memorize it. There was no worse thing in my life than what was in those pages—but also no better motivation for me to work toward becoming the opposite of my dad.

Tiffany was late. Maybe she wouldn't show at all. I closed my eyes, rested the back of my head on the brick, and tried to imagine what I'd do, where I'd go, but all I saw was Lake. Waiting for me at the curb. Opening her arms to make it all better. In the back of my mind, I knew there was a small chance she'd show up today. She'd always shown her youth in her persistence to get what she wanted, at least when it came to me.

I heard Tiffany's car before I saw it. I lifted my head as she came speeding around the corner, her BMW thumping as she flew right over a speedbump and then slammed on her brakes.

She parked in a loading zone and hopped out. "Babe, you're free!"

Before I could think, she was running at me, all blonde hair, her skirt flapping up. She jumped, and I caught her with an *ooph*, my arms locking around her. I moved her hair aside so it wouldn't catch on my cigarette. As soon as I got a whiff of her shampoo, I buried my nose in her neck and surprised myself with a long, fat sigh of relief.

Babe, you're free.

This nightmare was over.

She pulled back to look me in the face. "There must be so many things you want to do."

With her skirt up around her hips, and her pussy pressing warmly on my crotch, the first thing that came to mind was sex, but I couldn't let myself think too hard about it without getting us into trouble. For Christ's sake, she could probably wiggle a little harder and I'd come in my pants. "Yeah." I patted her ass. "Let's get the fuck out of here."

She slid down and led me over to the car.

I held open my hand. "Keys."

"You want to drive?" she asked nervously. "Do you remember how?"

The thought of getting into the passenger's seat made the collar of my starchy, puke-green release-shirt feel tight. I'd had enough of other people having power over me. There was no way in hell I wasn't driving us out of here. "Keys," I repeated, and she handed them over.

Despite the time of year, the car was already muggy just from sitting idle a few minutes. I had to push the seat all the way back before I got in, and my head still touched the roof. Immediately, I rolled down all the windows, turned on the A/C, and got to adjusting all the mirrors.

Before long, air blew ice cold on my face. I'd showered before leaving the facility, but I was already hot, horny, and sweating. I needed things—a cold beer, a monster burrito, and a good, solid, knock-me-out-cold fuck.

I shifted the rearview mirror again, envisioning Lake in the backseat, pretending she'd come to greet me at the gates. She hadn't, though. Knowing how persistent she could be, maybe that meant she'd accepted the way things were between us. I was glad. She was too fragile, like a little bird. My little bird. I didn't want her anywhere near here. Even so, I couldn't stop thinking it—she hadn't come.

"Manning," Tiffany said gently.

I snapped out of it, looking over at her. "Yeah?"

"Are you sure you're okay to drive? You've been sitting there staring out the windshield for five minutes."

"Yeah." *Don't think about Lake.* Not like this, when I was feeling a little strung out. I rubbed the bridge of my nose. "It's a long drive."

"I know. I've made it lots of times." She wrinkled her nose. "Are you sure you're okay? Should we stop for anything? Are you hungry? I'd want sushi first thing. Have you ever had sushi?" She paused. "Are you listening?"

"Yeah. I don't want sushi. I think—I'm feeling a little zoned out."

"You're probably, like, overwhelmed. Let's just go home. We shouldn't eat anyway. We're going to my parents' for dinner, and we might spoil our appetites."

It took a moment for her words to register. Sleep, food, sex. That was all I wanted. The necessities. I turned my head to Tiffany. "What?"

"My mom's making ribeye for you. She wanted to welcome you home."

If I knew Lake, she'd have a hand in that. My first meal as a free man, and Lake would be the one to make it. I wasn't sure how to feel about that. It was almost too much to take. "I don't know. I have to meet with my parole officer tomorrow, and I'm exhausted."

"I know. That's why we're eating early."

"What about your dad?"

"He'll be there," was all she said.

"I could eat right up until the steak was served and not spoil my appetite," I said.

"Then should we stop for food?" Tiffany asked, sounding confused.

"No. You have some of my stuff at your place?"

"Mostly what I could move in by myself, like clothing." She reached over to squeeze my bicep with a wink. "But I'm not sure it'll fit anymore."

———

After a three-hour drive, we hit a Target for the essentials, and then Tiffany directed me to her place. Palm trees lined the entrance to a complex of bi-level, standalone apartment buildings. Each cluster of beige stucco buildings had covered parking and access to a gated pool.

Tiffany's place was on the ground floor, underneath an outdoor staircase for the neighbor above her. Reddish-pink bougainvillea grew around the entrance and over the brick wall of her back patio.

She let us into the apartment. From the doorway, I looked around my new home. Or, at least, the place I'd be staying until I figured out my next move.

"It's nice, right?" she said, dropping her keys on the breakfast counter. "I mean, it's nothing special now, but we'll fix it up." I stepped inside with my plastic Target bags of boxers, undershirts, some new clothes, and toiletries. She brushed the arm of a couch in the center of the room, the same dark brown as the front door, then fluffed some blue throw pillows. Her TV sat on the ground. "I can make a few dollars go a long way. I wanted to wait for you anyway, to see what you like."

There was nothing too personal about the apartment, but it was bigger and nicer than mine had been before I'd gone away. For fuck's sake, it had a second room. Even growing up, there'd been no spare space.

In any case, I had more pressing things on my mind. I set the bags on a glass-top kitchen table and turned to Tiffany. The last thing I'd wanted to do was a Target run, but now that it was out of the way, the first and only thing I wanted to do was sink myself into a woman. "Show me the bedroom."

"Come." She motioned for me to follow her across the apartment to a door at the end of the hall. The bed was good, white and fluffy, twice as large as the twin I'd had at my place, and flanked by light-wood nightstands. Compared to a jail cell, it was the Taj Mahal. My limbs wouldn't hang off the edges of this one.

"I picked white for now," she said, "but I figured we could get some blue in here. Think beachy but masculine. Maybe even an ocean theme with turquoise—you know about Tiffany blue, right? The color of a Tiffany's box? That would be funny. Or if that's too girly, there's nautical with sailboats . . ."

Not blue. I couldn't do blue. It reminded me too much of endless skies, crystal-clear water, Lake's eyes . . . "Anything but blue."

She turned to me. "Sailboats are for like a kid's room, huh? I'm rambling. I'm a little nervous. This is weird."

"Yeah, it is." I came into the room, tilting her chin up for a kiss. "Don't worry. This part won't be."

She softened but took my hand. "I'm sure you're dying to, you know, which is why I told my mom we'd do an early dinner. I figured we could come home and spend all night catching up."

I arched an eyebrow. "Seventeen months inside, and you're asking me to wait? You think I'm superhuman?"

She pouted playfully. "Just a few hours. I guess I could call and tell them we'll be late, but they probably already started—"

They. Lake's cooking. If there was something worth postponing sex for, it was that. I imagined her moving around the kitchen like she had that first day we'd met, slicing avocado a little too carelessly because she couldn't keep her eyes off me. Telling *me*, an adult man seven years older than her, that I shouldn't drink beer and operate heavy machinery.

I planted a kiss on Tiffany's mouth. "No, don't call. I can wait."

"Okay. We're supposed to be over there soon, and we should probably shower."

By we, she meant me. I'd been sweating since I'd been released—no, since I'd been *taken in*. Since I'd left that courtroom at the dead of summer, I'd been perpetually hot, inside or outside, even in winter.

Tiffany left me alone to change and clean up, which was good, because I wasn't sure I'd be able to keep my hands to myself otherwise. Need burned through me, a heat I'd never felt, even as I turned the water stark cold. I had to be skin to skin with someone. I wanted to see how Tiffany and I got on after we'd been circling this for so long. Even if she wanted romance, I could do that, I just had to fuck before my head exploded.

I wouldn't be able to wait much longer.

9

LAKE

I'd misjudged my measurements.

In Tiffany's mirrored closet, I turned, inspecting the results of my afternoon. I'd taken a ruler and a pair of scissors to the corduroy skirt, but it had come out shorter than I was comfortable with. Tiffany wouldn't think twice about exposing so much leg, and Val probably wouldn't, either. They knew about boys, and tonight was too important to mess up.

Mom had bought me a pink bra from Nordstrom with Tiffany's discount she'd thought was "so cute." Well, cute wouldn't cut it, so I put it under a skin-tight, white baby tee I'd found in the back of Tiffany's dresser. The hem stopped where the skirt started, a sliver of skin between the two.

As the steaks marinated downstairs, I sat on the bathroom counter and slathered my tanned legs in lotion. I plucked any stray eyebrow hairs and inspected my pores. When two car doors slammed out front, I straightened. They were early. Given Tiffany's track record for tardiness, I hadn't expected that. But could I complain? I hopped down and quickly swiped on mascara. I heard voices in the foyer. *Damn it.* I didn't want to miss a second, especially not watching him come into the house, see the dining table set for him, smell the steak. The only heels I had were from the Homecoming dance and barely two inches. They didn't match my outfit, but there wasn't time to raid my mom's closet. I tried to buckle them on so quickly, I kept fumbling, convinced I heard Manning's sturdy footsteps moving to the kitchen.

I got the shoes on and flew down the stairs faster than I thought possible. The heels were low, but I must not've completely secured the left one, because it came loose, and I stumbled on the last step, blowing into the entryway, nearly falling on my face. I took a balancing step and stopped short.

Manning stared at me from the open doorway. His gaze slid down my top to my skirt, my legs, and shoes. He paused on the unbuckled clasp, then began to make his way back up.

He was ten times bigger than I remembered, ten times at least, and how was that possible when he was already the biggest man I'd ever met? He was taller, broader, more imposing. I'd expected him to look worn and weary, but his black hair, while longer than I remembered it, was cut, and his jaw shaved clean. He'd rolled up the sleeves of his crisp, white t-shirt and paired it with blue jeans and tennis shoes, also brand-new white. His muscles didn't overpower him, but they were real. Solid.

Manning was still looking at my body like it was a piece of chocolate cake, and I figured that was a good thing. People turned down chocolate cake all the time, but nobody ever *wanted* to.

Our eyes met. His expression remained smooth, but my face flushed with the undeniable heat in his stare, so intense that he almost looked angry. Maybe he was, because he curled one hand into a fist. Was he seeing me, finally, not as a kid, but as a woman? There was more to the moment that I didn't understand. A hardness in his eyes, frustration in his tensed arms. As I looked closer, I noticed the visible signs of his time away—a scar on his upper lip, the way his nose now crooked a little to the right.

Tiffany came through the door, holding up a bottle of wine. "Got it. It rolled under the seat." She looked at me at the mouth of the stairs and burst into laughter. "Why are you dressed like that?"

Her fingernails were the color of a firetruck.

"Red makes men horny."

She'd one-upped me. Again.

"You mean like *you*?" I asked. "You wear slutty stuff all the time."

Tiffany balked. "You look like you got dressed in the dark."

"Half of it is *yours*."

"Girls," Mom said.

I turned, startled. I hadn't heard my parents come in. Dad stood in the doorway of his study, staring at Manning, who hadn't noticed him, either. He followed Manning's line of sight to me. I saw the same anger in Dad's face I'd just seen in Manning's, but there was nothing exciting about it.

"Go put some clothes on," he said. "Now."

"I'm wearing clothes." I sounded more confident than I felt—but it wasn't fair! I did everything I was told, even if I didn't want to. I'd waited so long for tonight, seventeen months to be exact. This was my time.

"You are so obvious," Tiffany muttered, storming past Mom into the kitchen.

"It wasn't a request," Dad said. "Get upstairs, take off that ridiculous outfit, and put on some *goddamn* clothing."

The back of my neck tingled, heat creeping up to my cheeks. *Oh my God.* This couldn't be happening. There was nothing more childlike than being sent to your room by your father. It was so unfair and so typical of him to ruin anything important to me. "No. I'm not sixteen anymore," I said, glancing at Manning. "I—"

"*Please*," Manning said. "Just do it."

We all turned to him. He wanted me to change? With his tormented words, I felt suddenly selfish. I had no idea what Manning had been through, or what he needed from me. I wanted him to *see* me, but not if it hurt him, so I took off my left shoe and returned upstairs, changing quickly so I wouldn't miss anything. In a plain t-shirt and jeans, I went back down without shoes—but I still took the stairs two at a time.

Mom had set out a dish of black and green olives and was pouring two glasses of wine. "Charles," she called as I entered the kitchen. "Why don't you make Manning a drink?"

"I shouldn't," Manning said. "I'm meeting my PO tomorrow." Before I could wonder what that was, he added, "Parole officer."

"Oh, of course. Lake, go tell your father never mind. Could you drink in jail?"

Ugh. Seriously? I blew a sigh out of my nose and hurried out of the kitchen while trying to listen. "Prisoners can make alcohol if—"

"*Make* it?" Mom asked.

"It's called pruno . . . not like cigarettes, which you can get—"

I stuck my head in dad's study. "He doesn't want a drink," I said, then ran back through the house.

"What'd you miss most?" Mom asked as I entered. I moved out of the way so she could get in the fridge. "I should've had Tiffany call to find out so we could've had it here."

Seated at the breakfast bar with a glass of wine and a half-smile on her face, Tiffany tried to get Manning's attention. He leaned on the counter in one corner of the kitchen, keeping his eyes toward the doorway. I inched a little closer to him. I remembered him being stiff the last time he was here, but it was as if he weren't completely present. His guard was up. I couldn't fault him that. I needed to be alone with him to feel his presence like I had that night in the truck, and who knew when that would be?

"I missed a lot of stuff," Manning said without inflection. "Carpet. Towels that aren't falling apart. Privacy. But especially steak."

Mom blushed. At the kitchen's island, she checked on the tray of meat, turning the slabs over in the marinade. "You're just saying that because I have it for dinner."

"No, ma'am. The food inside was sh—excuse me. It was no good."

"Poor thing. I can't imagine how hungry you must be."

Manning dropped his eyes to mine. "Starved."

The word, only the second he'd said directly to me, pulled at my heart. No man of his size and importance should ever go hungry. I decided then and there—he'd never starve as long as I was around. It was worth the time and effort I'd put in to make sure every detail of tonight's dinner would be perfect for him.

Mom hummed. "It's a wonder you stayed so . . . healthy."

Healthy was one way of putting it. I couldn't remember Manning having any fat on him before, but somehow he looked more angular, hardened, his jawline sharper and his arms carved from stone.

"Wasn't much to do in there worthy of a mention, except hard labor and education," he said.

"Like school?" Mom asked.

"They had a guy come in for some classes, but I did a lot of reading myself." Manning swallowed, as if talking this much was hard for him. "I'd like to go back and finish my degree at some point."

Tiffany perked up. "Really?" she asked, smiling. "For criminal justice?"

The room got quiet—Tiffany didn't even realize her blunder.

Manning scratched above his eyebrow. "No."

"He's not able to be an officer anymore," Mom said quietly. "You knew that, honey."

"Of course I know." Tiffany sniffed. "I just meant, like, the other things he can do besides being a policeman . . ."

"Yes," Mom said, "but you have to be more aware of what you say . . ."

While they argued, Manning's gaze returned to me. His pain showed, the absolute depth of his hurt, right there in his eyes. It only surfaced when he looked at me. *I* did that. I caused him pain. His behavior began to make sense. His silence since the day he'd gone inside. My unanswered letters. His curled fists and quiet plea earlier.

Manning blamed me for this. The way he looked at me, like he couldn't bear it. The way he wouldn't speak to me. He'd probably done nothing for the last year-and-a-half but sit and wish I'd never forced my way into his truck or into his life.

"*Sorry,*" Tiffany said, exasperated with Mom.

Manning turned to her. "Don't be. That wasn't the path for me. I took a business course offered by the prison and did other stuff, like helping manage the construction of a new wing of the facility. Taught me a lot."

"But you already knew how to build a house," Tiffany said.

"I did, but I was self-taught or I learned on various jobs. Inside, I was forced to be involved in everything—planning, electrical, framing, roofing, welding, woodworking. When I got out of SHU, I spent a few months manufacturing furniture. It was a good education."

"You can do more now," I said. "You could be in charge on a site."

Manning cleared his throat but didn't look at me. "I could use some water if you don't mind," he said to nobody in particular.

I went and filled up a glass from the fridge while Mom took the steaks out to the grill. As soon as I gave him the water, he tilted back his head and drank. His throat worked, strong and veiny, his Adam's apple bobbing. When he'd downed half of it, he wiped his mouth with his sleeve.

"Was it bad in there?" I asked. I sought out his chocolate-brown eyes, but he stared into his drink. *Do you hate me for what I did to you?*

Tiffany set down her wineglass with a *clink* that echoed through the kitchen. "Don't be rude, Lake."

I wasn't sure how that was rude, it seemed worse not to ask.

We ate on the patio. January nights called for it. But even outdoors, tension thickened the air. Dad wasn't happy. Tiffany stole glances at him and then Manning. Manning barely let an emotion surface. Mom had chosen a safe topic—décor for Tiffany's apartment—that didn't include me because I'd never decorated anything other than a wall in my room. But to be fair, it was a good wall that I was pretty sure Manning would appreciate. I'd cut up the inside flaps off some of my favorite albums, and hopefully my favorites were Manning's, too. Pearl Jam, Jeff Buckley, Pink Floyd. I'd posted the album cover for *The Dark Side of the Moon* above the one of *The Wall*. The irony of that was lost on everyone in my family, or they just had no sense of humor was more like it.

"What are your plans, Manning?" Dad asked finally, cutting Tiffany off in the middle of a story about mispriced picture frames at Nordstrom. Sometimes I felt as if I worked there, too, I knew so much about that place.

"Maybe we can talk about that another time, Charles," Mom said. "Let Manning just enjoy his meal."

"It's okay." Manning swallowed his food, clearing his throat, the only sound except for crickets chirping on the other side of the pool. "I won't lie. I don't know yet."

"No?" Dad cut aggressively into his meat, and I jumped when his knife scraped the plate. "But you'll be living with Tiffany."

"Yes, sir. At least, as long as she wants me there."

Tiffany tried to throw an arm over Manning's broad shoulders, but could only clasp as far as his neck. "I want you there, babe."

She and Dad exchanged a look, but he quickly refocused on cutting his steak. "What about work?"

"He hasn't even been out twenty-four hours," Tiffany said.

"And he's had a lot of time with nothing to do but sit and think about it."

"I'm looking for something in construction," Manning said, his voice deeper than usual. "I've got word out that I'll take anything."

"That sounds wise," Dad said. "It's not as if you'll have a shot at law enforcement now."

I set down my fork. Dad wanted to embarrass Manning by pointing out his mistakes, but he didn't know those mistakes were mine. *I* was the one who was embarrassed. *I'd* ruined Manning's future, probably in ways I still didn't even know about.

Manning caught my eye. He stared hard at me as he intoned, "Like I said, I no longer want that. I don't. Not at all."

"Why not?" Dad asked. "A little disillusioned now, I imagine."

"You could say that."

"We'll find you something else, babe," Tiffany said.

I looked at Tiffany. She needed to stop using the word *babe* before I flipped out. It sounded worse than Dad's steak knife scraping the china.

"I have some money saved up from inside," Manning said.

Dad looked impressed. "How'd you manage that?"

Manning didn't answer. "I'm happy to help with the rent."

"Don't worry about that," Mom said. "You just focus on finding work. Use what you have to get yourself a nice suit for interviews."

Manning closed his mouth, his jaw ticking. This was too much for me. I couldn't imagine how hard it was for him. I wanted it all to go away. To go back in time and undo the mess I'd made. Opening my mouth to tell the truth would just make things worse. I was trapped.

Mom stood from the table. "I think we have some ice cream. How's that sound?"

Nobody answered.

"Tiffany, help me clean up?"

"Why can't Lake?" Tiffany whined, but took her plates into the kitchen. Since she'd left everyone else's, I got up as well.

"Sir," Manning said, "would it be all right if I went over to the wall and smoked?"

As much as I loved the smell of cigarettes for taking me back to Manning, hearing that he still smoked gave me a pang of disappointment. I'd hoped, even though the guards had taken the bracelet I'd made Manning, that he'd quit like he'd promised before he'd gone away.

Dad pushed his chair back and got up. "Just keep it away from the house."

I picked up my plate and glanced at Manning from under my lashes. I might've expected him to be distracted by the mental warfare happening at the table, but he looked right back at me. It was our first moment alone. I went around the table to him, and his head tilted back. He didn't look angry—just curious.

I piled his dish on top of mine. "Hi," I said.

"Was the steak your idea?" he asked.

It wasn't the question I'd expected. There was so much to say. I smiled. "Yes."

He nodded once. Before I could say anything else, and there was a lot on the tip of my tongue, he shifted to get cigarettes from his back pocket and stood. His presence was suddenly so huge and hovering that I fumbled the dishes, dropping a couple forks.

He stuck a cigarette in the corner of his mouth, picked up the silverware, and gestured for me to go. "After you."

We were closer than we'd been since the morning he'd been taken away—since that night in the truck. Remembering his hand inching up my shorts, my face warmed. I ducked my head and went around him, into the kitchen. Tiffany and Mom were arguing in hushed tones, but stopped when we walked in.

Manning stopped in the doorway and held up his cigarette. "I'm just going to . . ."

"Sure," Tiffany said. "I'll call you when dessert's ready."

He disappeared into the dark.

"But dad's being awful," Tiffany whined to Mom when they were alone again. "He's going to scare Manning away."

"It's just because he cares about you. He doesn't want you getting mixed up with trouble."

"Manning isn't trouble. I swear. *I'm* probably a worse influence on him than he is on me."

"Trust me, I believe that," Mom said.

I put the dishes in the sink, snuck by unnoticed, and slipped back outside. I spotted Manning's cigarette first, a pinprick of orange light near the bushes, and then him with his back to the wall.

Crossing my arms into myself, I went to him, the grass damp on my bare feet.

"Shouldn't be out here without shoes," he said when I was close. "You might cut your foot."

"On what?"

"Who knows."

In that way, he was still my Manning. Overprotective, always thinking the worst. I breathed a little easier knowing he hadn't changed too much. "You're smoking again."

"I never stopped."

"You said you'd try."

He didn't answer, but he didn't have to. I knew what he'd say. A lot had changed since that morning we'd stood outside of Reflection and I'd asked him to be better. "I still have your bracelet," I said. "If you want it."

It was mostly dark in our corner of the backyard except for the glare of the moon and the lights from the patio. Just enough to see him. Manning's beautiful, angular face was even better than I remembered but undoubtedly harder. When he narrowed his eyes toward the house, little wrinkles formed at the corners like he was thinking. Or maybe he was just looking. For Tiffany.

"Are you really going to live with her?" I asked when the silence became too much.

He took a long, long drag, then turned his head over his shoulder and blew smoke out. He coughed a little, then squatted to put out his cigarette in the dirt.

He was going to walk away. Almost a year and a half he'd been kept from me, and he was just going to walk away when we finally had a moment alone?

"Are you okay?" I asked.

He shook his head up at me. "I don't want you to worry about me."

"I can't help it."

"You have so much ahead of you. Focus on that."

"*You* don't. And it's my fault."

He stood quickly and flicked the butt over the side wall, into the yard of the house he'd helped build. He stepped a little closer, looking down at me. "You did what I asked. You did good."

"I want to do more. Tell me how to fix this. Can I go to the cops once I turn eighteen? Will they erase the charge if I give them your alibi?"

He hesitated, then raised my chin with his knuckle. "I don't want to hear another word about it, Lake. You're not going to the cops. You're not going to ruin your life by trying to help me."

"And what about you?" I asked. I wanted to be cool, to not care so much, but it was all I'd thought about since he'd left and the words wouldn't stop coming out. "Things are already ruined. You can't do what you love and you're with her—it's all ruined. *Everything.*"

He lowered his hand. "I chose this knowing what it would mean for me," he said. "I've accepted that. You need to also."

I shook my head hard as tears formed in my eyes. I didn't like to be told no. Maybe Dad was hard on me, but I normally got just about anything I wanted. Anything I could think to ask for. Manning belonged to me, even if I was still too young, even if Tiffany was still holding on to him. "You don't understand," I said.

"Yeah, I do. You have to trust me, Birdy."

Hearing his nickname for me again, my façade cracked a little. I closed my lids, my lashes wet on my cheeks. He tried to pretend he didn't care, but he did. He hadn't forgotten. "I can't live like this," I said. "Knowing what I did. That you're mad. That you blame me."

"I don't blame you."

I blinked away the threat of tears. "Then why didn't you answer my letters? Why couldn't I visit you?"

"Lake—"

"You could've called or written to tell me you were okay. I thought about you every day."

"Christ, Lake." He ran a hand through his inky hair, and it stuck up, slowly easing back into place. "Don't tell me that."

"Why not?"

"Because I don't want you thinking about what-if or why this, why that. It's just the way it is."

"It doesn't have to be."

"Doesn't it?" he asked.

It was all he needed to say. What were our options? I was still seventeen, and he'd always be seven years older. He lived with my sister. My father hated him and would never let me be with him while I lived at home.

I launched forward, throwing my arms around his middle. He didn't hug me back, but his smoky scent calmed me even more than the new t-shirt smell underneath it. This was exactly where I wanted to be. "I have to know what it was like in there. I can't stop thinking about it. I tried to get in to see you. I borrowed my friend's car and lied about where I was going. I checked out books from the library—"

"Lake, stop. Just stop." His torso expanded with an inhale, and his voice wavered. "Please stop. You don't know what it's like . . . and you're . . ." He pinched the bridge of his nose and breathed out what sounded like, "*killing* me."

"I missed you so much." I hugged him more tightly, hoping to wake him up, make him stop pretending this didn't affect him. "I still do."

He put a big hand on my forearm, a touch that put all my hairs on end, and turned it up a little. He ran a fingertip over my small scar. It was dark, but he looked almost longingly at it. "You miss the man I used to be."

"That's not true."

"This is too hard. You gotta understand."

I wanted him to slide his hand up, cup my face, and show me he'd missed me. Instead, he pried my arms from his middle. "Not yet," I begged.

"Lake, it's too dangerous."

I shoved him away, but he was so solid, I was the one who stumbled back. "It's *always* too dangerous with you. Everything." I curled my toes into the damp grass. "If it were up to you, I'd live in a padded room without access to anything."

"Maybe," he said. I thought I detected a small, almost imperceptible smile, but it was quickly replaced with a scowl. "And I don't want you dressing that way. Earlier."

The cut-off skirt and tiny top both thrilled and embarrassed me. Dad had made me feel like a prostitute, but the heated look in Manning's eyes was the only thing that made sense to me in all of this. He still wanted me, and not just a little. "It seemed like you liked it," I said lightly.

He wiped his temple with his sleeve despite the temperate night, then took a step back. "What would make you think that?"

For the first time in a while, I read his body language clearly. The outfit made him uncomfortable. In the house, he couldn't take his eyes off it. A minute ago, it'd made him angry. Now, he was looking toward the house, scratching under his collar. All that because of a short skirt and heels. I shrugged. "I guess it was the face you made."

"I didn't make any face." He backed away a little more but didn't try to leave.

"What didn't you like about it?" I asked. "Was it the skirt? Was it too short?"

"I . . . it . . ."

I leaned in a little. "What?"

"Never mind. Just don't dress like that."

"How am I supposed to know what you mean if you won't tell me what you didn't like?"

His demeanor shifted. With the set of his jaw came the same white-hot glare from earlier. It could've been passion as easily as it could've been hate. I was upsetting him, but I wasn't sure if that was good or bad. "I didn't say I didn't like it." He spoke slowly. "I said I didn't want it."

"Doesn't it matter what I want?"

"No."

And wasn't that the truth? It was a good thing I wanted to go to USC, because it wasn't like I had a choice. Dad would've made sure of it, just like Manning made sure I kept my mouth shut about his case, dressed like a pre-teen, and stayed away from him. I had no input about anything, and I was beginning to wonder if eighteen was just another number or if it'd actually mean a shift into adulthood. "I'm not sixteen anymore, Manning. I don't even feel sixteen. You got older in there, and so did I."

"Yeah? Did you?" he asked. I couldn't tell if he was joking, and for a blissful moment, we'd turned back time. The weeks before his arrest, I'd lived for

145

those moments when he'd teased me in his own subtle way. "Tell me, what'd you do while I was away? How'd you spend your days?"

"I told you everything in my letters."

He frowned a little. "I want to hear it from you."

"I ran a lot," I said.

"Why?" he asked.

There came a certain kind of peace once I pushed past the pain, the wheezing, the sweating. I had yet to find anything else that had gotten me there—except maybe the beer and joint I'd had with Corbin. "It helped."

Closing his eyes, he said, "Me too."

"You run?" I asked, straightening my back. We could run together, me and him, it could be our thing. He couldn't say no to it, because it was something innocent and good.

But then he blinked a few times. "Nah. I mean physical activity. Labor. It helped me, too."

"Oh. What else did you do? What else helped?"

He shook his head and trailed his eyes down my arm. "How'd you get the scar?"

"You know how."

"No, I don't, because I didn't read your letters."

My heart fell. "You never got them?"

"I got them. I just didn't read them."

Of all the scenarios I'd considered, that wasn't one of them, especially since I'd have done anything to read even one letter from Manning while he'd been away. I'd spent hours of my life writing them, one of the only things outside of running that'd kept me sane. "Not even one?"

"You wasted your time."

"Maybe I did," I said, "but time never feels wasted on you."

He swallowed, turning his face up to the sky. I loved when he did that, not just because the stars were ours, but because he exposed his strong, veiny throat to me. It made him, a man with callused palms and overpowering strength, seem vulnerable. "It was too hard." He spoke quietly. Maybe it was easier for him to say when he didn't have to look at me. "I wanted to, but I couldn't."

Though it hurt that he hadn't read them, I understood. If he'd ever written me back, a letter from him would've been salt in my open wounds. A sting I would've welcomed, but painful nonetheless.

I wanted to look at the stars with him, but not as much as I just wanted to soak him in. Still studying him like he might disappear at any moment, I asked, "What's up there?"

"Doesn't matter. I saw the night sky once the whole time I was in there." He inhaled through his nose. "It was only for a second, but you know what I saw?"

My heart skipped. *Summer Triangle.*

"Ursa Major," he said. He took a breath and looked back at me. "What gave you that scar?"

There was only one answer to that question. "A great bear." My great bear.

"Manning," Tiffany called from the house. "You out here, babe?"

He wet his lips. "Be right in."

He stepped back once then again. I put my fingers to my chin, attempting to hold on to the ghost of his touch. His eyes went to my mood ring. If he was shocked, he didn't show it, just looked at it for a long minute.

Then he turned and stalked back to the house. Back to Tiffany.

10
MANNING

Starved. Even after a full steak dinner, that's what I was. I hadn't eaten nearly as much as I'd planned. I'd have to work my appetite back to where it'd been.

I drove Tiffany back to the apartment, taking in everything through the windshield. The one time I'd been outside in the past year and a half, it'd been because of a fire in one of the dorms. They'd handcuffed all the inmates on my floor with one chain and walked us out to a van to transfer us to a secure spot until it was taken care of. In solitary, I'd had a nightmare or two about being locked in a cell while the building burned around me.

Just thinking about it now, I got hot. Tiffany's car was too fucking small. My knees were nearly at my chin. I'd rolled down the window before I'd even pulled away from the curb, but it wasn't enough, so I played with a few buttons to get the sunroof open.

"Want me to do it?" she asked.

"No." Eventually, it slid open. The night was cold, and Tiffany pulled her sweater closer, but I couldn't help it. I needed the air.

I'd made a mistake putting off sex with Tiffany. I'd known it as soon as I'd stepped into the Kaplan's home. Lake had come running down the stairs, her skirt practically up to her crotch. I'd taken one look at her long, tan legs and gotten hard on the spot. I'd had to refrain from chasing her back up the stairs, into her bedroom, and locking out the world for a few days.

If Charles hadn't sent her back to her room to change, I would've. The outfit was too much. She didn't know she was tempting a dangerous man, and if she did, she wasn't as smart as everyone gave her credit for. Did you put a juicy, bloody steak in front of a caged animal and expect him not to break through the bars?

As soon as I parked, I remembered what I'd forgotten at Target. "*Fuck.*"

Tiffany eyes sliced to mine. "What? What's wrong?"

"I meant to stop and get some things."

"What things?" she asked.

"Condoms."

"Oh. Don't worry. I've got it covered." She opened the car door, smiling at her pun.

I shut off the engine and followed her through the complex. The apartment keys were on the BMW's keychain, so I unlocked the front door. "Wait here," I said.

"Why?"

Walking into a dark apartment, I tensed. The quiet made my stomach hurt. I flipped on some lights, looking around.

Tiffany clomped in behind me, kicking off her shoes next to the couch. "It's a really safe neighborhood," she said.

I wiped my hands on my jeans. "I know."

She came over and stood in front of me, hands on hips. "You got taller."

"Or you got shorter."

She smirked and held out her hand for me. "Come on, big guy."

"Where we going?"

"Take a guess." She led me to the bedroom and left me standing at the foot of the bed. I'd never seen a sweeter sight than a bed that could be mistaken for a cloud.

Tiffany went to her nightstand and opened a drawer. "Condoms, lube, toys."

"No toys," I said.

I watched her light a candle on the side table. "This is for ambiance, so don't get any kinky ideas. I hope you like vanilla."

I was partial to anything that didn't smell like mold, shit, or piss. "Are you on the pill?"

"Yes," she said, then turned to me. "Manning, I've got this. I've been thinking about tonight for a long time."

I scrubbed my jaw. If that was the case, she probably wanted this to be special. I guessed that was the reason for the candle. I'd have to rein myself in, because right then, I could've fucked until my heart gave out. Or maybe it was like the steak, and slow was better at first.

"Toss me one of those."

She brought a condom over and put it in my open palm. "I got the extra-large. Wishful thinking, I guess."

I couldn't help my laugh. "Careful what you wish for."

Her eyes lit up. "Really?"

I kissed her. I wasn't sure how much longer I could wait. She pressed her body up to mine and I put a hand on her ass. When she had my pants down, she pulled back to look down. Her eyes widened. "Holy shit."

I was hard as a rock, but that wasn't the reason for her shock. My rock was more of a boulder. Thanks to communal showers, I'd seen more dicks than I ever wanted to, and I knew what I had. My hard-on was painful, and I was ashamed to admit I'd had it since dinner. Tiffany had run her fingernails over my thigh under the table like it was nothing.

Smoking that cigarette was supposed to help, but then Lake had shown up. Something about her bare feet was so sweet, it'd pissed me off. She made my emotions go haywire. One moment it was everything to keep my hands off her, the next I was reacting to her, helpless, and I hated that feeling. I never wanted to give up control again. If I'd never met her, I wouldn't be in this mess, but I cared too deeply for her to just walk away. It was confusing as hell.

And so was this, my girlfriend stripping down to her black lingerie while I thought about her seventeen-year-old sister. I needed to be more careful. Shouldn't be thinking about Lake that way at all, and definitely not while I was with Tiffany.

I pushed all thoughts of Lake out of my head and put my hands on Tiffany's shoulders. "Listen. I'm going to go as slow as a man in my position can," I said. "If I get a little too rough, stop me."

She blinked at me. "Why would I stop you?"

"To put it nicely, I'm eager, Tiff."

"Manning." She wrapped her hands on the outsides of my forearms. "I'm not breakable. I'm not like some innocent little virgin who has *no* experience whatsoever." I only just grasped the dig at her sister before she pressed on. "Did I expect classical music and roses and lovemaking tonight? No. We can do that later. Right now, I want to be what you need."

Her words worked their way down my chest, straight to my cock. What I needed was a girl who could take it as good as I gave it. That was Tiffany. Had it been Lake before me . . . the filthy things I wanted to do . . .

153

Overnight she started to change . . .

Was that any way to think about the wide-eyed girl who'd come onto a construction site to thank me for finding her bracelet? She'd been fucking timid and kind and sixteen, and I'd still looked at her and wanted to possess her. That was how I knew I was no good. A decent man would've looked at Lake and seen a girl, nothing more.

You don't know what it's like to watch a girl become a woman.

I stuck the condom between my teeth, ripped open the foil packet, and spit out the top scrap. I had to be inside Tiffany now. I needed her. I needed to lose myself, set fire to my thoughts. I rolled the condom on.

"How do you want me?" she asked.

My balls tightened as I turned Tiffany around and unhooked her bra, tossing it aside. I took a minute to appreciate what was in front of me, running my hands over her slender shoulders, over the tiny dark freckles that spotted her back, down her spine.

She shuddered.

I tested her with my finger, and when I found her wet, I nudged my cock between her legs.

She fell forward over the bed, spreading for me. My fucked-up brain saw long blonde hair and smooth back and Lake and I drove into her.

She hissed. "Mmm."

"Sorry." My heart pounded. She wasn't wet enough. Why would she be? I'd done nothing to warm her up. She writhed a little on the mattress, and I only grew harder for her squirming. All those sordid fantasies I'd had about her, now I was living them. I needed to calm down.

"Babe?" she said.

"Yeah."

"Get the lube, okay? It's in the drawer. Then you can go as hard as you want."

A sense of gratitude came over me. She could've told me to fuck off for going too fast, but she was trying to give me what I needed. I slid out of her and went to the nightstand. While I was there, I peeled off the condom in case I'd broken it. I put a new one on and turned back to her. I did the best I could in my animal state to make sure she came.

———

Uncomfortably hot, I woke with a start when I didn't recognize my surroundings. The sheets were soft and white, and sun came through the slatted blinds, warming up the bedroom. I had no idea when I'd fallen asleep or if Tiffany was by my side or what. In the kitchen, the faucet ran.

I sat up to grab my jeans off the floor and get my cigarettes from the pocket. I lit one and leaned back against the headboard. My head was clear for the first time in months. Maybe years. I shut my eyes and let the nicotine work through me. As soon as I did, I saw her. *Lake*. Lake, nearly falling at my feet in the foyer.

Physically, she'd changed. Her legs were still too long for her body, but now, she was lithe, not gangly. She had real breasts, ones that were just the right size for her frame. It made me equally uncomfortable and aroused. I liked them, but as they'd never be mine to memorize, to worship, I hated them. I hated the idea of other men looking at them, drooling over them, *touching* them. I breathed through my nose until the excruciating image passed.

She'd come to a hard stop when she'd noticed me, her lips parted, cheeks flushed. Why? Did I scare her? What would she have done if things'd been different? Leapt into my arms the way her sister had? In that short skirt, she would've pressed her heat right against me. *Fuck fuck fuck.* For what had to be the hundredth time in twenty-four hours, I was getting hard again.

Could I deny it? I wanted Lake. I wanted her bad. I always had, but I'd been able to control it before. She was still young, but she was seventeen now, and every inch the beauty I knew she'd become. She had lush blonde hair that was a little ratty and, like her legs, too long. Her breasts were high and round. For dinner, she'd worn tattered jeans and a t-shirt but why, why the *fuck* did she still look like the sexiest thing I'd ever seen?

I took a drag of my cigarette. All the times I'd fantasized about Lake inside, and when she was standing right in front of me, I couldn't even speak to her. What was there to say? I'd wanted to fall to my knees and pay homage. To overwhelm myself in her. Soak my senses with her. Touch her body, smell her neck, taste her mouth, hear her moan, feel her relief that I was home.

And still, she made me so fucking mad, demanding answers, pushing me places I didn't want to go, wearing an outfit that'd rouse a dead man. If just being in her presence was enough for me to feel the blood *rushing* through my veins, having anything more with her would be too explosive. I couldn't do explosive. Not with my history. I'd destroy everything good about her . . .

I looked up at a noise in the doorway. In a terrycloth robe, Tiffany held a glass of water and a Domino's box. "It's half pepperoni, half Meatlovers. I wasn't sure what you like."

I swallowed thickly. That small gesture brought me back to where I should be—to this bedroom, to Tiffany. It'd been so long since anyone had taken care of me. Had made me a monster sandwich or explained the constellations to me or put a roof over my head. Over the years, those I thought I'd taken care of had actually been taking care of me. "Thanks, babe," I said and meant it. "It's perfect."

She smiled a little and came into the room. "You look hot."

"A little."

She set the stuff down and flipped a switch for the overhead fan. On her way back to me, she pulled a bottle from her robe pocket. "I took this from the house for you. It's the bourbon my dad drinks, so it must be good."

I looked longingly at the liquor. I could count on one hand the sips of alcohol I'd gotten behind bars, and I missed it. "Wish I could, but I have that meeting with the parole officer at three. What time is it?"

"Noon."

"Damn. Normally by this time, I'd have already had breakfast, lunch, and worked half a day."

She played with the bedsheet. "You were so tired. I didn't want to wake you."

I kept my half-smoked cigarette in hand and chugged the water in one go.

"We're not supposed to smoke in here," she said.

I shook my head. "Have to be able to smoke if I'm gonna stay here, Tiff. I can't not do it."

She sighed. "All right. We might have to disable the fire alarm."

"Yeah." I sighed at my cigarette. I didn't want to set off the alarm and have to get up just yet. I dropped it in the remains of the water. "Didn't think of that."

She took a paper plate from the top of the pizza box and lifted the lid. "How's pepperoni sound?"

"After sex, a good night's sleep, and a cigarette, exactly what I need."

She gave me a slice. "Good," she said flatly.

"Was it too much last night?" I asked, worried I'd scared her. "You have to tell me if it's too much."

She smiled. "It was great. It's just that we, like, didn't kiss very much."

I set the paper plate on the nightstand. "C'mere."

She leaned in. I took her by the back of her neck and pecked her mouth a few times. It wasn't enough to thank her for what she'd already given me, but I had to ease into any kind of intimacy. Tiffany and Lake were worlds apart in my eyes, but I couldn't ignore their physical similarities, and I didn't want to imagine Lake during this part. Not even for a second. After I locked Lake into another part of my brain, I kissed Tiffany for real, as a boyfriend would his girlfriend.

When she pulled back, I focused on things that were unique to Tiffany, the way her nose turned up a little at the end, or the unusual, icy shade of her eyes. She had freckles, dark little ones around her chest and face, including a faint one that could've been a beauty mark.

"This is nice," she said softly. "I like to see you."

She didn't deserve to feel like I didn't care. I'd have to make more of an effort to show her that. "Thanks for all you did. Coming to the arraignment when you didn't have to. Dealing with my landlord, the truck, my furniture. I won't forget it." She'd gone above and beyond for me. I'd told Grimes to give her my things, but I'd pretty much expected her to turn them down. Instead, she'd stepped up to the plate. "And you can kiss me, you know. You don't have to wait for me to do it."

"I . . ." She looked into my eyes. "I love you."

"I know." Unfortunately for her, I wasn't really capable of returning it. I had lost Maddy, my entire family even, at an age when I was learning what love was. Maybe one day, with the right person, I would've figured out how to move past that, but not after what I'd seen inside. I was pretty sure I'd never let myself get too deep with anyone now. People were fucked. Life, too. If I loved someone, they could be taken away from me at any time.

It was a lesson I'd had to learn twice, and no way in hell would there be a third.

11
MANNING

Gary came out of my apartment with a beer in each hand just as I turned off the sander. I'd set aside a couple days to build an entertainment unit for the apartment, but with Gary's help, it'd only taken us the afternoon. The complex had a large, open lawn by the pool, so we'd set up near the closest outlet. I followed Gary to some chaise lounges from the pool he'd moved under a tree. I dragged mine a few feet over, my back to the trunk, so I could see the whole lawn.

"That didn't take very long," Gary said, adjusting his seat next to mine. "Maybe we should keep going. You guys need anything else?"

"Coffee table. Dresser. The kitchen cabinets are shit. You name it, we probably need it."

"Then we'll have a beer and do some more."

I shook my head. "I still have to put the stain on, and I only picked out enough wood for the TV stand."

Gary shrugged. "Next week then."

"Hope to have a job by next week."

"Yeah? What you got going on?"

I sipped beer and looked across the lawn at nothing. I'd been back in the real world two months with nothing to show for it. A part-time position at a garage and a few construction jobs here and there— barely enough to give Tiffany half of each month's rent, forget food or anything else. "I'm working with my PO, but his caseload is so heavy, he isn't much help. There might be an opening on a site in Santa Ana. One of the guys got hurt, so I'm just waiting to hear. Problem is transportation. I have to work out the car situation with Tiffany and I can tell it's getting on her nerves."

"Good luck, man. I know it's been tough. I wish I could help, I just—"

"I know." Gary brought it up all the time. He wanted to help, but his hands were tied. He ran the youth program at the local YMCA and had given me a chance two years ago as a camp counselor. It went without saying that after I'd been arrested at that same camp, I wasn't exactly a hero amongst parents or staff.

"It's screwed up," Gary said. "You were better with those kids than half the staff we've got now."

I gave him a look. "It's not screwed up. It's reality. I'm a felon."

"You're not, though. Wrong place, wrong time doesn't make you anything more than unlucky."

I picked at the label of my bottle. Gary had visited me in prison all the way up until my release. In the beginning, I hadn't been able to figure out his angle. He'd been good to me during our first visit, asking if I needed anything, when I would've expected him to be pissed that I'd drawn negative attention to the program. But I'd come to find out that for some reason, Gary thought I was all right. He believed I hadn't committed this crime. I hated lying to him, but if he knew where I'd really been that night, he wouldn't've been so understanding.

"What if I did do it?" I asked. Sometimes I pictured Lake gliding on her back in the dark water, waiting for me. "What if I'd do it again? I'm not the same man I was when I went in."

Gary drank some more. "I don't know, man. Not sure why you're always trying to convince me you're no good."

"Not trying to convince you about anything. Just stating facts. You get a chance to talk to Bucky?"

Gary inhaled a deep breath. "Yeah, and it's like I told you. He's an asshole but he's not a rat. He had nothing to do with your arrest. Why would he?"

"I don't know. Just to be a dick."

"Let it go, Manning. Nobody's out to get you. Well, nobody but Tiffany." He grinned. "Didn't I warn you she'd get her hooks in you?"

"You did." I got out my pack of cigarettes. I was trying to smoke less to save money, but I couldn't quit completely. It was still the best part of my day, most days. Not even the disappointment in Lake's voice that night I'd gotten out was enough to scratch the surface of my cravings. She said she still had the bracelet she'd made me, but what could it do for me now, other than make me feel worse?

"You guys get along all right?" he asked.

"Tiffany? She gets on my case sometimes." Truth be told, I didn't mind it so much. Nobody had given a rat's ass what I did with my life since I'd graduated high school. It was kind of nice, but I wasn't about to admit that to Gary. "I look for work every day. It's hard without a car, and my credit tanked while I was inside, so I can't get a decent lease. My last resort is trucking. I don't really want to go on the road if I don't have to."

"Doesn't her dad pay the rent?"

"I give him as much as I can each month, and I've been getting Tiffany to contribute more and more. I've suggested we move to a more sensible place, but neither Tiff nor her dad want that."

"How'd you two get hooked up again?"

"I was on the crew that built the house next her parents'."

"And she just came over and introduced herself?"

My chest tightened the way it always did when I thought of those first days with Lake. Everyone on site had noticed the girls. The other men had only seen Tiffany, but not me. Lake had stood quietly by her sister's side, absentmindedly playing with her bracelet, looking uncomfortable enough to make me notice, to make me wonder what was running through her head. I'd been ready to step in if there was trouble. I hated to be part of something that scared a young girl, but looking back, maybe she wasn't so scared. I'd found the bracelet in the dirt and returned it to her, but she was the one who came back to talk to me.

"You know how Tiff is," I said with a drag.

"Yeah, I do. She always been your type?"

"My type?"

Gary paused, seeming to choose his words carefully. "She's got a big personality."

Even after we'd moved in together, I'd sometimes wondered why she stayed. It was taking me time to trust that she meant it when she said she loved me. That I wasn't still a way to get her dad's attention. I had been, but somewhere along the way, her feelings had changed. Maybe she secretly craved the structure she'd always rebelled against.

"*But* I gotta say," Gary continued, "I've seen a change in her. That first week at camp, I thought I had her pegged. Boy-crazy troublemaker. But Lydia tells me she's not like that."

Tiffany had gotten to know Gary's girlfriend pretty well, mostly because Gary was the only friend I really hung around with. "She's still got a little of that going on," I said with a laugh.

"You've been a positive influence on her, though. Lydia thinks it's because of you, too."

"Yeah?" I raised my chin, nodding a little. Any positive changes Tiffany'd made, she got the credit for that, but if I'd helped motivate her like she'd told me I had, I felt good about that. Real good. I'd struggled so much in prison with all the ways I'd brought Lake down, and I hadn't even realized how my visits with Tiffany had had the opposite effect.

"You know I work with kids a lot," Gary said, "and not that she's a kid, but I can kind of see how one person can really make a difference in someone's life. Let me ask you something." He shifted in his seat to face me better. Gary always got worked up when he talked about his job. In a way, what he did was similar to what I'd wanted to accomplish as an officer. He helped kids, gave them a safe place to go after school, talked to them like adults, provided them with tools to succeed they might not find at home. It was a shame my record meant I couldn't really get involved in any way. "Does Tiffany have issues with her parents?" he asked.

I shrugged. "I mean . . . yeah. Her dad. He sort of favors her sister. A lot, actually."

"I thought so, the way she seeks out attention." He took a pull from his beer. "It's good she has you. Dads can really do a lot of damage when you're young, you know?"

Fuck, did I know it. My dad's actions had changed my life irreparably. I could go on to get everything I wanted in life, but losing Madison, knowing what my dad had done to her—I'd never get over it.

"And the shitty part is, that stuff gets passed down, so you have to break the cycle."

I looked into my beer. "What do you mean?"

"The parents treat the kids a certain way, and those kids grow up to recreate those behaviors with *their* children. It's really fascinating, that stuff. How much is ingrained and how much is learned, you know?"

Ingrained. What Gary was saying, I already knew. I had my dad's darkness in me. It could flip on like a switch, but how bad could it get? It wasn't the first time I'd wondered what kind of dad I'd be. My control had already slipped with Lake, even though I'd known the potential consequences. Not just for me, but for a young girl getting involved with someone older.

"You think that's always true?" I asked.

"Not always, but often enough from what I've seen at the Y. You find out a kid's being abused, and, man," he shook his head at me, "making that discovery's not something I'd wish on anyone, but I guarantee, the abuser . . . he came from the same kind of household. You think it'd be the opposite. It's pretty fucked."

Abuser. That was my father. That was my grandfather.

What about me?

I'd snuck off with one of Gary's sixteen-year-old campers. I'd come from a history of abuse.

Terrified he'd start prying into my childhood, I changed the subject. "Anyway, not sure what's down the line for me and Tiff, but we're in a good place for now." We'd gotten into a routine. She worked most days, and in the evenings, she was—slowly—learning to cook. Or we got takeout. She was catching me up on movies I'd missed while inside. "This cohabitating thing isn't so bad."

"Don't admit that to her. She'll think you're ready for the next step."

I grunted. "I think this is the last step for a while."

"Sure," Gary said. "I thought the same thing about Lydia. She said she wasn't looking for anything too serious. Six months later, she's been hinting about the fact that her lease is almost up."

"I already bit that bullet."

"Exactly. You're one step ahead of us. You know there's more coming, too."

I frowned. "I don't think so. Tiffany's not really the settling-down type."

"Denial will only get you so far, bro. You've been together almost two years."

"One of which I wasn't around."

"That's not how chicks do math. Just watch. Can I bum one?"

I passed Gary the pack. I wasn't so sure. As well as things had been going between us, Tiffany got frustrated with me, too. She wanted us to do more stuff together, like hitting the bars with her friends, shopping, couples yoga. I didn't have the money, and except for absolute necessities, I wouldn't take more from her dad.

Not that I'd been so well-off before going away, but at least then I hadn't had a record, and I'd been able to pay my student loans. Inside, I hadn't made enough to keep up my payments, which once had felt manageable and now seemed to balloon.

There were some days where life had felt easier behind bars. I hadn't had much time alone with Lake in the two months I'd been out. We'd had moments here and there. Some days, I read her like a book, and others, it terrified me how little I knew about her. She had a million things going on, from classes at community college to study groups to pep rallies and even a fucking job at some country club for rich people. She was due to hear from USC any day now. She seemed more and more anxious, unhappy even, but I wasn't sure if it was just being around me that made her that way. Sometimes, she'd get a certain kind of look and go somewhere in her head—somewhere I wanted to be.

A guy I recognized from the apartment above mine came down the outdoor stairs and toward us. "You selling this?" he asked, admiring the TV stand.

Gary shook his head. "Nah. We just made it."

"No shit." He cocked his head to see the front. Just to make Tiff happy, I'd crafted two glass portholes on the cabinets. She wasn't kidding about the nautical theme, and had been adding seashells and shit all around the apartment.

"Can I buy it off you?" he asked. "Our furniture's falling apart and my girlfriend's been bugging me to take her shopping. You'd be saving my ass."

I took the cigarette from my mouth, letting it burn between my fingers. *Fuck.* I needed the money, but I knew how much Tiffany wanted this done. Plus, I'd personalized it for her. "Gotta save my own ass first. I need it for my place," I said. "But I can make you one, no problem."

"Yeah?" he asked. "I'll pay a premium, just so I don't have to spend the day furniture shopping."

Gary and I exchanged a look. The reclaimed wood from a boatyard had cost hardly anything, and I certainly had the time. "Consider it done."

"Cool." He pointed above my apartment. "I'm there. 2B."

"My girlfriend and I are the place below you," I said as we shook hands.

Gary and I took the entertainment center into the apartment. Tiffany walked in with a shopping bag as we were hooking up the TV.

"Finally," she said. "Now I don't have to strain my neck to watch *Melrose Place*."

I got off the carpet, brushing off my hands on my jeans. She came over to kiss me, slipping me the tongue even though I'd told her lots of times how much I hated public displays of affection. "It looks nice," she said about the unit. "Those windows are cool. Did you boys have fun?"

"Sure did," Gary said. "Where've you been?"

"Work." She dropped the word like an anvil and set a Nordstrom bag on the breakfast bar. "I bought myself a present."

"Tiff," I said, not bothering to hide my irritation. "In case you haven't noticed, we don't have a lot of disposable income."

"*You* don't," she corrected.

"Neither of us do. Just because our rent is covered doesn't mean we're off the hook. If you have extra cash, you should be giving it to your dad."

She waved me off. "I know, but it's almost my one-year anniversary."

"A year of what?" I asked.

"Working at Nordstrom." She dug through the tissue and lifted a black, ruffled bra up to her chest. "What do you guys think?"

Gary's eyes nearly popped out of his head. "Wow."

"You like it?" she asked, smiling with one corner of her mouth. "Babe?"

"All right, you made your point." I'd pissed her off with the money comment. If I was picturing her in the bra, so was Gary, and she knew it. "Put it away."

She leaned over to Gary. "He gets jealous."

I did *not* get jealous, not really. I just didn't want to make Gary uncomfortable, and I sure as hell didn't invite anyone into my sex life.

Gary's pager beeped. "I'd better take off," he said after checking it. "Lydia's making me dinner tonight."

"How's it going with her?" Tiffany asked.

Gary shrugged. "Fine."

She rolled her eyes, dropping the lingerie back into the bag. "What do you two even talk about when you're together? Neither of you ever answer my questions with more than one word."

I shook his hand. "You up to help with a coffee table?" I asked. "We could make it look like a dinghy, then top it with glass."

"I'm in," Gary said.

"Next week, then. Unless I get that job."

"Job?" Tiffany asked once Gary had left.

"I might get on a crew," I said. "No guarantee."

"Well, that's good," she said. "That'll be at least a few months of work, right?"

I went to the fridge for another beer. "I'd be replacing someone and coming in at the end. A couple weeks, maybe three."

Tiffany followed me out of the kitchen to the couch. "Then what?"

She'd been bringing up the job thing more and more lately, and I didn't blame her, but that didn't mean I wanted to talk about it. "Keep looking."

"What if you don't find anything? You need something steady."

"You got an idea?" I asked, gesturing at her with the remote. "I'm all ears."

"Can't you go see a headhunter or whatever?" she asked. "A recruiter?"

"I might, if I were cut out for a desk job. Or even if I thought anyone was open to hiring ex-cons."

"You don't know until you try. Maybe you'd like working in an office. It'd be better than sitting on your ass all day."

"I don't do that, and you know it," I said. "I'm at the garage half the week. Word of mouth is everything in my industry. I have guys recommending me for jobs, but it takes time."

"We can't mooch off my dad forever," she said.

"You think I don't know that?" I sat up too quickly, spilling some beer on my shirt. There was nowhere to goddamn put it without a coffee table. "I'm the one who's been saying that since day one."

"Well, he's on my case. He wants to know what we're doing. I swear, he can be so fucking annoying.

173

He still makes me drive Lake sometimes. I don't understand why she doesn't get her stupid license. Between the two of you, I feel like a chauffeur."

I grabbed for my cigarettes. Lake had been taking driving lessons and had failed the test twice. Everyone had been surprised, considering she aced everything else. I was glad. I hated to think of her taking off whenever she wanted, driving to see boys, to parties, to college . . .

At the same time, it made me wonder what was going on with her.

"As long as he contributes to our rent, we don't have much choice, do we?" I pointed out.

"No, that's why you need a job. So I can get away from him." She sighed heavily. "For the millionth time, can you *please* not smoke in here? My dad will be so pissed if he doesn't get his deposit back."

I didn't even realize I'd lit a cigarette. "Sorry," I muttered. "Just a few drags while I watch the news, and then I have to get in the shower."

"Shower? Why? Are you going somewhere?"

I raised my eyebrows at her. "We have Lake's thing at the school."

She groaned, flopping onto the arm of the couch. "I forgot. Let's skip it."

I shook my head. "We said we'd be there."

"So? She won't care." She winked. "I can model my new purchases for you."

I got up, put my cigarette out under the faucet, and headed for our bedroom. "Maybe when we get home."

"Why is it," she started, "when I make us reservations or invite you to come out with my friends or ask you to meet me at the movies, you always forget, every single time. Yet *this* you remember? Lake's stupid honor roll ceremony?"

I turned around in the living room. Tonight wasn't some run-of-the-mill event. Lake had made Principal's Honor Roll with a GPA over 4.0, and on top of that, she was the school's Student of the Month for April. I wasn't going to miss it, even if I had to go alone. "It's a family obligation," I told her. "We can't afford to piss off your parents."

"Really?" she asked, watching me closely. She sounded more curious than angry. "Is that all it is?"

We stared each other down. I'd been careful these past couple months. Lake and I were never alone. I barely looked at her, let alone spoke to her. Maybe Tiffany had caught me staring. I did that, sometimes, without realizing it. "Of course that's all," I said and disappeared into the bedroom, a pit of guilt forming in my stomach, because it wasn't true.

That wasn't all it was. Not by a long shot.

12
MANNING

For Lake's honor roll ceremony, I wore the nicest things I owned—slacks, a dress shirt and tie, and a light cashmere pullover. They were all gifts from Cathy, who shopped often and slipped us things without Charles knowing. It bugged the hell out of me to take more charity from Tiffany's parents, except in cases like this, where I wanted to look nice. I'd even gotten a real haircut at a legit barber for the first time since before prison.

I drove us to the high school, parked, and put the keys in my pocket. While Tiffany led the way to the auditorium, I looked around the campus where Lake spent most of her days. If Maddy were still alive, she'd have been eighteen this year. I would've done things like this with her, helped with college applications, quizzed her for final exams, watched her receive honors. She would've. She was smart, driven, and creative. She'd wanted to do something artistic, but even if she'd tried to get out of going to college, I would've made her do it.

The Kaplans stood outside the auditorium. My eyes went straight to Lake's profile as she spoke to her father. She was changing before my eyes, subtle things I doubted anyone else even noticed. I did. There were more freckles on her nose than she'd had months ago. Her hair fell longer down her back. It made her look younger when we were all just hanging around the house, but sometimes, like tonight, she wore it up in a twisty thing and could pass for early twenties. It made my gut smart each time it hit me— she was getting older every day, living a life that didn't include me.

I'd learned through dinner conversation that she'd been in a school play while I was inside, and since I'd gotten out, she'd been taking drama and improv classes. I could see the difference in her personality. She still didn't seek the spotlight, but she was more self-assured than she'd been when we'd met. It was a quiet confidence I could sit and watch for minutes at a time without even realizing it, and that was dangerous.

"How long will this take?" Tiffany asked as we approached her family.

Everyone turned to us. "This is a big honor for your sister," Charles said. "She's Student of the

Month *and* number three in her entire graduating class."

I met Lake's eyes, trying to convey how proud I was with a look. She smiled back. Wrapped up in her, it took me a moment to feel Charles's eyes on me. Quickly, I looked at Tiffany, my go-to whenever I was caught staring at Lake.

Tiffany put an arm around Lake. "Congrats, little sis," she said and whispered something in her ear—a long, seemingly detailed message that made Lake's eyes go huge and her cheeks flush.

What was it about? Not me, I guessed, since both girls started to giggle. They didn't often have moments like this, but it always threw me when they did. I was used to them bickering.

Tiffany returned to my side, and everyone looked at me. "Congratulations." I cleared my throat. "You should be so—proud." My heart tightened into a ball as I said it. I knew how hard she'd worked. How smart she was. How much she wanted to impress her dad.

"We all are," Charles said, kissing her on top of the head. "It isn't number one, but it's certainly still impressive."

Lake glanced at me and then the ground. Why was she embarrassed? Because she wasn't number one? In that moment, I wanted nothing more than to be the man who announced in front of everyone that she was number one in my eyes.

"Cut her some slack," Tiffany said. "Senior year is supposed to be fun."

"You've had enough fun for the entire family," he retorted.

Tiffany flipped her hair over her shoulder. "Can we go in? It's hot out here."

Tiffany's dad hurt her when he spoke like that, but she didn't show it. At least, not the way most people would. Tiffany's emotions surfaced in other ways. As we walked into the auditorium, I put a hand on her upper back to comfort her.

Lake looked away. "We're in the front row," she said and waved to where other students had gathered. We took our seats right under the stage, me at one end, next to Tiffany, Charles and Cathy at the other, with Lake in the middle.

After a short speech, the vice principal called each honor roll student to the stage to shake hands and get a photograph taken.

"Lake Kaplan," he announced. She stood, her strappy, loose dress flowing around her legs as she walked by me. She had red marks on her knees and thighs where she'd crossed her legs. I was tempted to reach out and smooth away that redness until it was white again. To tuck the strands of her hair that'd come loose back where they were supposed to go. She climbed the steps at one side of the stage and uncurled her fists to accept a certificate. Behind the podium, a row of students had formed.

All at once, I felt Tiffany's glare. "Do you always look at seventeen-year-old girls that way?" she asked.

She'd said it softly, but not so softly that her parents might not hear. I leaned into her and whispered, "What the fuck are you talking about?"

"You're practically drooling."

"Don't be ridiculous. She's your sister."

Tiffany narrowed her eyes. "I wasn't talking about Lake."

I swallowed down my irritation. It wouldn't do an ounce of good to make a scene here. Fact was, Lake was the most conservatively dressed of all the girls, and if I hadn't been so distracted, I probably would've looked at them. Thin and beautiful, they stood in a row as the vice principal spoke about their accomplishments, California beach girls with tans, mile-long legs, and golden hair, even though we were still a couple months from summer.

Why had it been Lake who'd captured my attention that day on the site and hadn't let it go since? I was grateful I didn't see these other girls and feel stirred the way I did for Lake, but at that moment, I wished it was anyone but her. I wished I'd never fucking met her.

I just didn't wish it enough to walk away for good.

———

After the ceremony, in the parking lot, Charles announced, "We're going to dinner to celebrate."

Even Cathy looked surprised. "We are?"

"Manning and I have plans," Tiffany said, even though we didn't.

"Cancel them. This is important."

"Oh, let them go," Cathy said. "Lake makes honor roll and Student of the Month every year. It's not as if it's her first time."

"I made reservations at the Ritz-Carlton in Dana Point," Charles said.

The girls gasped. "Really?" Tiffany asked. "It's so fancy."

"I'm aware." He smiled a little. "Lake's worked hard this year. I just want us all to take a night to recognize that."

"We recognize it every day," Tiffany said, but when her mom eyed her, she added, "but I guess tonight's a big deal."

"How come I didn't know about this?" Cathy asked.

"It was last minute. The hotel manager is an old friend and squeezed us in." He put his arm around Lake and nodded at me. "You two'll meet us there? Tiffany knows the way."

As we got in the car, Tiffany sighed. "I don't want to go."

"We have to," I said as I pulled onto Highway One.

I expected a rebuttal but got silence instead, which meant she was genuinely upset. I kept my left hand on the wheel and massaged her neck with my right. Touching her was becoming normal, automatic. I wasn't all that affectionate by nature, but Tiffany loved when I was. When she wasn't feeling well, a small touch went a long way. "Why don't you want to go?"

"I'm tired. It was a long day at work. I just want to go home and be with you."

"All right." I slowed for a stoplight. "What's the real reason?"

She looked over at me a few moments, then curled into the seat to face me, nuzzling my hand. "It's just like a constant barrage."

"What is?"

"All of it. I never made the regular honor roll, forget the principal one. Never had the grades to even *apply* to USC. Every time my parents make a huge deal of Lake's success, it just feels like they're pointing out everything I didn't do."

"You know they're not," I said. "They're just proud of Lake and they aren't thinking about how it might make you feel."

"That's almost worse," she said. "It's like I'm not even there."

The light changed. I squeezed her shoulder and took my hand back to steer. "They're just caught up in the moment. Your dad's wanted this for so long."

"Another assistant manager position opened up this week," she admitted. "I wasn't going to say anything, but . . ."

"Why not?"

183

"I didn't want you to be disappointed if I didn't get it."

"I wouldn't be disappointed as long as you tried. I bet there are a lot of people at the store who don't even have the guts to do that."

"Well, I might be one of them." She sat up straighter. "I mean, why should I bother? They didn't give it to me before, even though I'm one of the top salespeople in my department. They want to promote people who're more qualified on paper so they can keep moving them up into corporate positions. It's bullshit."

I glanced over. "You're one of the top salespeople? How come you never mentioned that?"

She shrugged. "Doesn't sound like much compared to USC."

"Your department's got a lot of people in it," I said, switching lanes. "Not only that, but it's not a small thing to be good at sales. People pay a lot of money to master a skill like that."

"It *is* hard," she agreed, talking faster, "but I wouldn't call it a skill. You just ask people about themselves and learn enough about the product to make it sound like you know what you're talking about, and before you know it, the credit card is out."

"Tiffany, taking people's money is a skill, believe me." I flipped on the blinker. "Could you imagine me selling anyone anything like that?"

Her laugh lightened the mood in the car. "I mean, there's even more to it than that, I was just being sarcastic." She gestured out the windshield at nothing. "Like, when I find the right outfit for someone's weird body type, it feels like . . ."

"An accomplishment?" I asked.

"Yes! It feels good."

Hearing the excitement in her voice caught me off guard. She rarely got worked up about her job, and her bad mood began to make a little more sense. If she said any of this to her dad, he'd probably undermine her achievement. "I'm taking you out to celebrate," I said.

"Celebrate what?" she asked. "I don't even know if I'll get the job."

"The salesperson thing. I'm telling you, it's a big deal. Especially somewhere as big as Nordstrom."

I didn't have to look over to sense her smiling. "Listen to this. There're people in the corporate office who get paid to *shop*. They travel around to designers and pick out the clothes and accessories we carry."

"Sounds perfect for you."

"I know, but I'd need a degree."

I wanted to finish my twelve credits, but I couldn't afford it, not right now. Tiffany might be able to qualify for a loan, though. "Maybe you could enroll somewhere in the fall. Not to make your dad happy, but because you want the promotion. Because you one day want to be that person who . . . *shops* for a living, Lord help us all."

She grinned, tracing circles on the console. "I don't know. It seems kind of impossible, but . . ."

"But what? Find out the requirements of those positions and see if there are any classes that match."

"I just don't know if . . . if I want to do that forever. I feel like I need to sit down and really think about my future."

I wanted to point out to her that that was a luxury most people didn't have—people like me—but I didn't want to diminish the fact that she was finally tapping into something that might interest her. Tiffany had some flaws, but those flaws could easily work in her favor if she aimed her energy in the right direction.

Her dad had tried to get her to do just that, and her mom had let her off the hook for too long now. It was a funny, almost rewarding thing, to be the only one who'd been able to get through to her so far.

13
MANNING

The Ritz-Carlton sat on a cliff, overlooking a dark expanse of Pacific Ocean. The white-columned and marbled-floored lobby had bouquets of flowers as tall as me.

"I've always loved this place," Tiffany said. "So many childhood memories."

Well, fuck me. I'd never been in a hotel this nice, and certainly not as a kid. In that moment, I was grateful for the times Cathy had wounded my pride by forcing nice clothes on me.

Charles stood at the opposite end of the lobby while Lake and Cathy had gone to look at the view.

"What took so long?" Charles asked, motioning for us to hurry.

"Manning insisted on self-parking," Tiffany said.

As long as I lived, no matter where I ended up in life, I hoped I'd always opt to walk an extra two minutes to save a few bucks.

"He's frugal," Charles said to her. "You could learn a thing or two about that."

I was pretty sure it was a compliment, and the first he'd ever paid me. I just wished it hadn't been at Tiffany's expense.

We met Cathy and Lake to walk to the restaurant. "I used to bring the girls here for tea time during the holidays," Cathy said. "Remind me to show you pictures, Manning. The girls were so adorable in matching red dresses."

Lake and Tiffany, ahead of us, turned to each other and made matching "gag-me" faces as they laughed. I could just picture them—pint-sized, giggling towheads. "What were you like?" I asked.

Both girls glanced back at me. I imagined as kids, they looked a lot like they did in that moment, young and confused and being silly.

"Tiffany was the apple of everyone's eye," Cathy said. "At family events, she'd perform for us. When we were in public, people would stop me to tell me how beautiful she was. Then, when Lake was born, I could hardly walk ten minutes without somebody gushing over them. Lake hated the attention, though, always hiding behind her big sister."

"Lake was shy," Tiffany said. "Who would've guessed?"

"She wasn't shy." Cathy looked thoughtful. "She could go up to anyone and start a conversation. It's just that she endured people fawning over her, whereas you, honey, ate it up."

"Not much has changed." Charles patted Tiffany's upper back, leading her into the restaurant.

The hostess took us to a table in the middle. Charles set down a yellow and red gift bag with "Congratulations!" printed on the side.

"Should we have brought a present?" I asked Tiffany.

Cathy turned to me. "Don't worry. I didn't even know Charles had anything planned."

He sat at the head of the rectangular table and wanted Lake by his side, so I took the chair next to Cathy, across from the girls.

"Champagne for the table," he said as the hostess turned to leave.

"I'll let your server know," she said. "Does everyone have ID?"

"They're twenty-one," he said. "Just bring a bottle of your best."

The hostess hesitated before walking away. "Yes, sir."

Lake's eyes twinkled. "Dad?"

"You'll be an adult soon. One glass won't kill you." Charles leaned his elbows on the table, giving her his full attention. "You've earned it. I'm so . . ." He swallowed, as if holding back tears.

I glanced at Tiffany as she sank in her seat, fiddling with the corner of her cloth napkin.

Charles shook his head at the table. "I just need a moment to collect myself. I'll be more articulate when we toast."

Tiffany opened her menu with flourish. "Can we get anything, Daddy?" she asked.

"Anything you like, princess." He put on a pair of glasses and, reading over the specials, said, "You should order the porterhouse, Manning. It's unlike any you've ever had. I guarantee it."

It was the most expensive steak on the menu. I'd never seen the man in such a good mood. In fact, I wasn't sure he'd ever addressed me by my first name before. "That sounds great."

Tiffany noticed, too. She ran her foot up the inside of my leg, waggling her eyebrows at me. "You want to get oysters, babe? I hear they're an aphrodisiac."

"Tiffany," Cathy said under her breath. "Don't say things like that at the dinner table."

Lake focused on her menu, her cheeks reddening. Well, it'd been over two months since I'd gotten out. Lake had to suspect her sister and I were having sex. Maybe she was still the same wide-eyed girl I'd known, but she was definitely less naïve than she'd been when I'd left her. Hell, she'd been headed down that path the week we'd spent together at camp. She'd taken her top off in front of me. Lake knew about sex. Maybe she'd even come close with one of the boys at school.

I'd wring the motherfucker's neck.

The unbidden thought made my necktie feel tight and the words and prices on my menu blur. I tugged my collar, downed some water, and took a breath. I had no right to think that way. None.

A server appeared with champagne and five glasses. "What are we celebrating?" he asked, popping the cork.

Charles gestured at Lake. "Tell him, honey."

"It's dumb," she said. "I made honor roll. But so did, like, a hundred other students."

"You are not like a hundred other students," Charles said. He picked up his glass and stood, waiting until all our flutes were filled and raised. He turned to Lake. "I know I've pushed you. I know you've worked harder than your friends, read more books, gone the extra mile for the *plus* on the end of your 'A' when an 'A' alone would've sufficed."

Charles swallowed, inhaling through his nose. His hand shook, and his eyes watered. "I'm so . . . so . . ."

Tiffany pretended to read her menu but glanced up when her dad's voice broke.

"Oh, honey," Cathy said, reaching out to hold his hand.

He picked up the gift bag and passed it to Lake. "I'm so proud. And I knew you could do it."

Lake looked confused, but it was then I realized this wasn't about the Principal's Honor Roll or even Student of the Month. She peeked in the bag, then up at her dad. Instantly, her eyes also watered. "Are you serious?"

He nodded. "Congratulations, sweetheart."

Seeing Lake's expression change from confusion to shock, my heart swelled. This was what I wanted for her. Everything. This was why I'd done the time, had kept my hands to myself, had watched from afar. So she wouldn't lose sight of what was important. I had to clench my own jaw to keep from getting emotional.

Lake's mom put her hands over her mouth. "Charles."

"What is it?" Tiffany asked.

Lake's hands trembled as she pulled a thick, white packet out of the bag. She turned it over, then held it up for us all to see. Proud of her as I was, in that moment, my eyes went to Tiffany. When she registered the USC logo on the packet, her expression remained smooth. I couldn't read her. Tiffany might put on a show sometimes, but I knew she cared about Lake. That first and foremost, Lake was her sister. I didn't believe she'd feel anything but pride watching Lake get everything she wanted, but the way her complexion paled, I wasn't sure. Could Tiffany ever truly be happy for her sister, who'd now done everything their dad had ever expected of her? Or would Tiffany see this as something else?

Cathy stood and went around the table to pull a still-in-shock Lake into a tight hug. Her dad did the same. Tiffany slid the unopened packet over to her side of the table. "What if it's a rejection?" she asked so only I could hear.

"You know it's not."

She tore one corner of the envelope right before I took it away. "Don't spoil this."

Tiffany's eyes fixed on me as she sat back and crossed her arms. Maybe she thought I was the enemy, but I wasn't. If Charles saw Tiffany with the envelope, he'd make a scene. I put it back in its rightful spot, in front of Lake.

Once they were all seated again, Lake ran a hand over the envelope.

"Aren't you going to open it?" Charles asked.

She slid a finger under the flap and removed a sheet with a cardinal red-and-gold booklet. She read her acceptance letter as we all watched.

"So?" Charles asked after a few seconds of silence. "How does it feel to officially be a Trojan?"

"Good."

"That's it?" he pressed. "Good?"

Lake's nostrils flared. A few silent tears tracked down her cheeks. Cathy had her hands clasped in front of her, looking as on edge as I felt. Lake's body began to visibly shake as she covered her face and dissolved into sobs.

Cathy's eyebrows drew together as she and Charles exchanged a glance. "What?" she mouthed.

"Overwhelmed," he said softly.

I reacted physically, my throat thickening with a lump, my hands aching to hold Lake. Her crying sent my body mixed signals. I was the last person at the table who should comfort her, but maybe the only one who knew her well enough to understand her tears. Was she overwhelmed? Relieved? Yes. But the intensity with which she cried told me there was more to it than that. Maybe she didn't want this after all. I'd tried to warn her, years ago, that she'd have to fight to be heard if she had any doubts about USC. Maybe she hadn't really believed me, hadn't realized that was true, until this moment.

When the silence at the table grew uncomfortable, Tiffany broke it. "She's been under so much pressure, she can't even enjoy this moment."

Charles rubbed Lake's back. "You don't know what you're talking about, Tiffany."

"She's right," I said. I hadn't planned to speak up, because *goddamn it*, Charles and I had started an evening off on the right foot for once. But Tiffany puckered her lips, blowing me a grateful air-kiss.

Charles glared at me a second, but then turned back to Lake. "She's just overcome," he said. "Isn't that right, Lake?"

Lake nodded her head in her hands, inhaled a deep breath, and looked up. Her mascara painted her face like watercolor. "I'm sorry. I'm happy. I was just so worried it wouldn't come."

Tiffany got some tissue from her purse and passed it to her sister but didn't say anything.

"Nobody doubted you," Charles said.

Lake dabbed under her eyes. "I know."

Cathy took Lake's hand across the table. "How about we go shopping this weekend? Get you some college clothes?"

"I can think of something she'll need more than new clothes," Charles said. "If only she'd pass her driving test. No more screwing around, Lake."

Lake's eyes went wide at the same moment as Tiffany's, in a way that made them look twin-like. Lake had been inspecting her champagne, but she put it down. "Really?" she asked.

"You're buying her a car?" Tiffany asked. "Because I'm not giving her mine."

"She'll have to get around," Charles said. "Not to mention come home to visit."

Tiffany blinked a few times, looking shocked. I was about to point out that she'd gotten a car in high school, when I noticed her look at Lake and tear up. It was as if it'd only just occurred to Tiffany that Lake wouldn't be around next year.

Lake started to put the brochure away, but Charles took it from her. "I can't wait to see which dorm you're in," he said, flipping through it. "We probably won't find out until closer to mid-summer—"

"Oh, we'll get to shop for your room," Cathy said. "Start thinking about what colors you want to decorate with."

"It's a dorm," Charles said, looking at her over his glasses. "She'll have approximately two-hundred square feet to work with."

"Maybe we'll do a beachy theme so she doesn't get homesick."

Tiffany's mouth fell open. "*We* were going to do a beachy theme. You can't copy us."

Charles turned a page. "Don't be ridiculous."

Tiffany was already pouting, and we still had a long night of USC-talk ahead of us. As much as I soaked up all the details of Lake's life, I didn't blame Tiffany for her frustration. It was always what Lake was doing, what she was getting, where she was headed. "Tiffany has an announcement, too," I said.

She looked up at me. "What?"

"About work." I nodded her on.

Cathy put down her glass and turned to Tiffany. "Did you get a call-back to model for that sunglass company? The one that needed a pretty blonde?"

Tiffany's face reddened. *Shit.* Maybe I'd just embarrassed her, and not in the good way I'd intended. "Better," I said, trying to show Tiffany that her achievements at Nordstrom were worth more than getting a job based on looks. "She's one of the top salespeople in her store."

Charles placed an elbow on the table and continued paging through the brochure.

Cathy's face lit up. "Really? Was there some kind of announcement?"

"Wow," Lake said. "Your department or the whole store?"

"Not the store," Tiffany muttered. "Just my section."

"It's still a lot of people, right?" Lake asked.

I cleared my throat, raising my voice. "Charles."

He looked up. "Hmm?"

"Tiffany's got news."

"It's nothing," Tiffany said. "I'm doing well at work. The real news is that I'm thinking about going to school."

I did a double take. I wished she'd think before blurting out things like that to get her dad's attention. When she didn't follow through, it just made things worse.

"And?" he asked.

"*Charles*," Cathy said.

"What?" He gestured at Tiffany but spoke to his wife. "She's been saying that for years."

"I'm serious this time. I don't want to get passed up for my next promotion. I don't want to be a salesperson forever."

"Good, I should hope not," Charles said. "Look into it and I'll do what I can to help." He showed Lake the catalogue. "Look at Tommy Trojan."

"I know, Dad," Lake said. "I've seen the statue in person."

It wasn't as if I'd expected Charles to order a second bottle or anything, but that wasn't good enough. "You can help now," I told him, "by listening to what your daughter has to say."

He lifted his head finally. The table went quiet, and even Lake's sniffling stopped. I half expected Charles to stand up and throw me out by the scruff of my neck. This wasn't my family; I had no place speaking up. But he'd put enough negative pressure on both girls for too long, and clearly Cathy wasn't going to stop it.

The fact that I cared enough for both girls to attempt to stand up to Charles made me realize maybe I was wrong. Maybe this *was* my family, in a weird way—and maybe I even wanted it to be.

Charles' gaze slid from me to Tiffany. "All right. Do you have a school picked out?"

"I think so."

"Bring the course catalogue next time we have dinner." He sniffed. "We'll take a look at it together."

In the car on the way home, Tiffany looked out the window. "If I hear about USC one more time, I'm going to lose it."

"Things'll calm down now. This is what they've been working toward for years." I rolled down my window to let some fresh air in. I'd never get enough of that as long as I lived. "I thought you'd be happy after the way I put your dad in his place."

"It was kind of great." I heard the smile in her voice. She turned back to me. "I'm sorry. I guess I'm PMS'ing."

Already, the tension in the car lifted. She sounded lighter. Tiffany just wanted to be reminded that someone cared. Someone noticed. Sometimes I forgot to show it, went days without doing anything special for her. I needed to try harder.

I hit the brakes and swerved into a left turn lane.

"Where are you going?" she asked.

"Get you some ice cream."

"Really?" She beamed. "But we had dessert at the restaurant."

"That crème brûlée shit doesn't cut it." She liked mint chocolate chip when she was on her period, cookies 'n' cream when she had cramps. "I'm thinking cookies 'n' cream."

"You're such a good boyfriend," she said. "I love you."

Knowing what she needed so I could make sure she was happy and comfortable—that was a form of loving her. It shouldn't be overlooked or undermined.

"You want to know what I whispered to Lake earlier?"

She asked it the same way a parent might offer a kid a cookie for completing a chore, which made me cautious. "All right . . ."

"She got something in the mail at the apartment today. She didn't want Dad to know about it, so she used our address."

"What was it?"

"An acceptance packet."

I knew from dinner conversation that Lake had only applied to one school. The fact that I might be wrong, that there were important things I didn't know about Lake's life, made my throat constrict. "You mean like the USC one?"

"Yep. Only *not* USC. A different school."

The lights blurred through the windshield. So Lake was taking her future into her own hands. That was good. It was what I wanted for her. But at the same time, mentally, I'd already placed her in Los Angeles. She'd be a two-hour drive away, a Trojan, and she'd remain a California girl. I didn't have much in my life that felt pure and good, not like Lake. I didn't want her any farther from my reach than she already was, but I'd also promised myself I'd let her soar.

"Where else did she apply?" I asked.

"Somewhere far away," was all she said.

14

LAKE

I went to the living room window to look into the front yard for the third time in an hour.

"Don't worry," Mom said, appearing behind me. She drew my mass of curls off my neck, settling them on my back. "He'll be more nervous than you."

I stared forward, wringing my hands. I wasn't on edge about Corbin. Maybe I should've been. He'd taken a weekend off from studying for finals to fly home and take me to the prom. I hadn't asked him to, but when he'd found out I wasn't going to go, he'd insisted. I hadn't fought him as hard as I should've, because spending time with Corbin was always good, and truth be told, I missed him.

But it was Manning who had my nerves buzzing. I wanted him to think I looked pretty. To wish he was by my side the way I did. To break things off with Tiffany and take me in his arms, to hell with everyone else. I'd be eighteen in just over a month. It wasn't that I thought we'd be together right away. Tiffany would need time to forget about Manning, but she would. She always did.

"I want you to be careful tonight," Mom said. "Corbin's been in college almost a year now. He has more experience than the boys you know."

I made a face. "It's not like that, Mom."

She cocked her head. "It isn't?"

"He's just a friend."

"Does he know that?"

"Totally." We'd kissed that one time on the couch, but he'd never brought it up or tried again. I mean, I didn't see him a lot, just during his breaks from NYU, but we spoke on the phone all the time, and Corbin even told me about the girls he was dating. "He's just coming because he didn't want me to miss tonight."

Mom fixed my hair, plucking at some curls. "That's sweet of him. I still don't understand why you didn't have a date, but I'm glad Corbin is such a gentleman."

I'd been asked, but I'd turned everyone down. They were children compared to Manning, the only one I wanted. In size, he dwarfed them, but it was more than that. He carried himself differently. He looked at me like he owned part of my soul. The confidence that came through when he spoke, the ways he used his hands. I shivered as goosebumps traveled up my spine.

"*Mom*," Tiffany said on her way out of the kitchen. "You'll mess it up. You don't understand how easy it is to lose volume."

Mom stepped aside to give Tiffany access to my hair. "It looks beautiful, Tiffany."

Tiffany checked the bobby pins. She'd spent over an hour drying and curling my long hair, then pinning half of it up. She'd hairsprayed the rest of the curls, but somehow, they were soft and bouncy on my shoulders. I hadn't asked her to do all that, but I had to agree with Mom—it looked beautiful.

Tiffany turned me around by my shoulders. Eyebrows drawn, she scanned every inch of my face as if she'd be tested on it later. "You already smudged your liner. Don't touch your eyes. Don't cry. Your mascara's waterproof but your eyeliner isn't."

"Don't cry," I repeated. "Got it."

Tiffany rolled her eyes. "I meant *happy* tears."

"You're not wearing that."

All three of us turned to my dad in the hallway.

My black, floor-length dress had a plunging "V" in the front and one in back. It was sexier than anything I'd ever owned, but I was so close to eighteen, I could taste it. It was time for Manning to see me as an adult. "Yes, I am."

"Cathy," Dad said in his *are-you-serious* tone.

"I helped her pick it out," Mom said.

"It's too revealing."

"It's too *late*," Tiffany said. "Corbin will be here any minute."

None of us had heard Manning come in the front door, but he walked up behind Dad. His eyes started at my hair and scanned over my collarbone, following the plunging neckline to the point between my breasts. "I agree with Charles," he said.

What? He couldn't be serious. I'd done all of this for him, from picking out the dress to giving Tiffany free rein over my hair and makeup.

"Man*ning*," Tiffany scolded. "You're supposed to be on our side."

"Find something else in your closet," Dad said to me. "I already conceded about you getting a hotel room with your girlfriends for the night."

Manning arched an angry, thick eyebrow. "A hotel room?"

Dad turned to Manning. "Her argument was that it was better she stay and watch out for her drunk friends. Do you believe it?"

Manning looked pissed. "No."

"I don't see why it needs to be so sexy," Dad said. "At least find a sweater to put over it."

"*No*," I said, curling my hands into fists. Why did I need their permission to dress sexy when I was nearly eighteen? It seemed unfair. "I've done everything you've asked of me the last four years—*longer* even. I deserve this."

"You're being unreasonable, Charles," Mom agreed.

"Because I want my daughter to come home safe?" he shot back.

"Daddy, she's going with *Corbin*," Tiffany said, walking over to stand in front of them. "You know Corbin. You know his dad and his family. Honestly, is there anyone safer she could be out with?"

Manning looked at the ground, but after a moment, Dad sighed in defeat. "I suppose not."

A limo pulled up outside. My house had been designated the spot for our photoshoot, so next came the parents, who parked along the cul-de-sac.

"Looks like people are arriving," Mom said, looking out the window. "Outside, everyone. Come on. Let's not ruin Lake's night before it's begun."

I'd gotten what I wanted, and maybe I should've been happy about that, but when Manning reached for Tiffany's hand to lead her outside, all I felt was shock.

He reached for *her* hand.

Not the other way around.

It was a simple gesture, and maybe it didn't mean anything—but maybe it *did*.

Corbin arrived next, slotting his dad's Mercedes into the collection of foreign cars. He stepped out in one fluid movement, all six-foot-two of him, and buttoned his suit jacket. He'd gelled his hair off his face. I wasn't sure I'd ever seen him wear it that way. Smiling, he walked toward me. The red corsage he carried almost matched the sun-kissed tip of his nose, and I knew from that alone that he'd already taken his board out in the twelve hours since he'd flown in.

"Oh, my," Mom said. "He's grown up. Even more handsome since leaving for college. You're a lucky girl, Lake."

Corbin swooped in to kiss my cheek. "You've got it wrong, Mrs. Kaplan," he said. "I'll be the luckiest guy at the dance for sure."

I smiled up at him. "Thank you for coming. It means a lot."

He covered his heart. "It's my pleasure."

Mom snapped a picture. Tiffany came over to position us for photos, tickling me in the process until I broke into laughter. "Stay still," she complained, but snickered.

My smile faded when I locked eyes with Manning. He stood on the front patio, arms crossed, his expression pinched. The line of his jaw as taut as the veins in his neck.

From behind, Corbin put an arm around the front of my shoulders, kissed my cheek, and turned me away.

At dinner, Corbin told stories from college that made everyone at the table laugh. Between bruschetta and gnocchi, he laced his hand with mine and leaned in. "Having fun?"

"Yes," I said honestly. Mona, Vickie and the rest of my friends didn't hide their envy. Even Val, who'd turned down a few boys to come alone, asked if I wanted to trade dates. Corbin wasn't just handsome but funny. He drew everyone's attention at the table, but his attention was all mine, and my friends noticed.

His skills carried onto the dance floor. Corbin and his brothers had attended ballroom dancing classes to surprise his mom for his parents' twenty-fifth wedding anniversary a few years ago, so he effortlessly took the lead during slow and fast dances. Some of my friends cut in, and after Corbin, their dates felt clumsy, grabbing at me. Corbin always came back for me.

After, we took over an entire floor of the hotel. Val, Vickie, Mona and I had our own room, but everyone congregated in a suite someone had rented. The boys pushed all the furniture to the perimeter of the room. Corbin played bartender while we danced, Val and I karaoke-ing to Shania Twain.

"Doing all right?" Corbin asked when I stopped by the kitchenette-turned-bar for a breather. "Have you ever had three drinks in a row?"

I laughed, pushing his shoulder, but I was the one to take a step back. "I'm *fine*. Did you say three?"

I was definitely buzzed—and more relaxed than I'd been in months. I hadn't planned to drink tonight, maybe a few sips before the sleepover, but part of me just wanted to let loose for a night. I'd thought getting accepted to school would get my dad off my back, but it was still non-stop with college crap. He and I were going over dorms and playing phone tag with my new roommate's parents and Mom took me shopping at Target practically every week. Dad had created a *college* summer reading list and had even taken off work early one day to drive me to the campus bookstore. The last couple weeks, we'd been getting into the really important things, like my class schedule. He wanted me to choose a major, and business was at the top of the list. He didn't want to talk about electives like drama. Not until I'd decided on a major, even though everything I'd read said I didn't need to right away.

Tonight wasn't the time to stress. I took a long sip of orange juice and rum, watching Mona drunk-dance in the middle of the room. She didn't seem to notice the song skipping until her date opened the tray and took the CD out.

"Hey!" she said, swaying.

He blew on the disc, wiping it on his dress shirt. "Just keep dancing."

"But you stopped the music."

"I'm surprised you even noticed. You're more smashed than a pumpkin."

She giggled as he put the CD back in and hit *play* on "1979."

"I can't believe I almost didn't come tonight," I told Corbin. "This is the best night I've—" I was about to say *ever had*, but that would be a lie. No night would ever compare to the ones I'd spent with Manning, especially the one under the stars. "The best I've had in a long time," I finished.

He smiled widely, as happy as I'd ever seen him. "Yeah? I'm so glad. My prom was shit."

Corbin and his friends had gone solo. From what he'd told me, they'd arrived at the dance, swooped in on some other guys' dates, and spent the night drinking and gambling.

A girl reached between us for a handle of vodka, her cranberry juice making my nose wrinkle. "Why didn't you guys take dates?"

"I didn't want to. If I couldn't bring the girl I wanted, none of them got to have a date." He shifted as the girl grabbed a stack of Solo cups and took them into one of the bedrooms. "In case it isn't clear, that girl was you."

I laughed a little. Corbin had always been charming, but he'd had a lot more girls to practice on since leaving high school. "You didn't even ask me."

He hesitated. "I was going to. I told Tiffany. She said your dad would neuter me if I tried, and you know something? I believe her. I mean, you're almost in college and your dad was still looking at me tonight like he wanted to put me underground."

"He's protective."

"They both are."

I shook my head. "My mom? She was more excited about tonight than I was."

"I don't mean her. I'm talking about Tiffany's boyfriend. He was giving me the same look."

My throat dried. To anyone else, Manning had no reason to act that way over me. Had he watched Corbin and wished it was him?

Corbin topped off his drink. "But that's probably because of me, not you."

"What do you mean?" I asked.

"I don't think it was you her boyfriend was being protective of. See," he cleared his throat, "I used to have this little crush on Tiffany. When I was a sophomore and she was friends with my brother."

"I know. She told me."

He leaned a hand on the counter. "I'm sorry."

"Why?" I asked.

"For not telling you. I was afraid you'd, you know, blow me off if you found out."

I shook my head. "I'd never blow you off, Corbin. You're a good friend. You always have been."

"I don't mean blow me off as a friend," he said and got quiet.

I looked into my drink. We'd been friends so long now, I'd thought it was clear that was all we'd ever be. But as he said it, I knew I hadn't really believed it, and that I'd almost expected this. Did it make me a bad person that I'd let him go through all this anyway? "Corbin—I don't . . . I'm not . . ."

He stepped a little closer. "Lake, I like you. I've told you this before."

"I know, but that was a while ago. I mean, so much has happened since then. You're in college with tons of girls, in a whole new city. We don't even live in the same state."

"We could."

We'd had this discussion on the phone before. Corbin liked to tease me that some secret part of me didn't want to go to USC. That I was only doing it to please my dad. It wasn't true, but after my conversation with Val and Vickie about schools, and before my USC acceptance, I'd been thinking *what-if*. "I got into NYU," I told him.

"*What?*"

"Nobody knows except Tiffany. And I'm not going. I already have a roommate and everything at USC, which is where I want to be."

He shook his head. "Come visit me for a week after finals. I'll take you around the city. You'll change your mind, you'll see."

"No. I didn't tell you so you'd convince me to go there." I flicked my nail under the edge of my Solo cup. "I just wanted you to know, I *have* thought about other options, and USC is still what I want."

"What about drama?" he asked. "I heard you were great as Sandy in *Grease* last year."

As the understudy, I'd only gone on two nights when Ashley Hurley, the real actress in our class, had lost her voice. It'd been so far outside my comfort zone, but thrilling, too. "USC has a great film program," I said, even though I hadn't worked up the courage to point that out to my dad.

"And New York has fucking Broadway." He took my hand, pulling me a little closer. "And it has me."

"Corbin."

"What?" His lips quirked into a knowing grin. He took my drink out of my hand and slipped an arm around my waist. "Want to dance?"

"We already did," I said, but smiled as we swayed back and forth. "Like five times."

"Sixth time is a charm."

I gave him a look. "Like you need any more charm."

"Yeah? You think I'm charming?" He lowered his mouth to my ear. "How do you resist?"

Could he feel my cheek warming against his, the uptick of my heartbeat? I hoped not. If he thought I was giving in to his advances, he'd never let me off the hook.

"If you guys were both seniors, you so would've been voted cutest couple," Vickie said, passing through the room. She spent enough time around me to know Corbin and I weren't more than friends, but she refused to believe it anyway. While I was looking at her, Corbin leaned in and put his lips to mine. Automatically, I kissed him back before a wave of guilt hit me. I started to pull away like I had on the couch, then stopped. Maybe it was the alcohol, but I wondered what it would feel like to keep going. Kissing Corbin felt more natural than kissing anyone else, probably even Manning. I knew I'd feel a lot of things with Manning, but I wasn't sure *natural* would be one of them.

Corbin pulled away. "So you had a good time tonight?"

"Yes."

"There's a game of Kings going in the other room," he said. "You want to go play?"

I'd enjoyed the first round, but I didn't think I could keep up now without getting too drunk. The day was beginning to catch up with me, and nothing really sounded better than just hanging out with Corbin. "I think I'm good," I said. "But I can watch if you want to."

"I don't. This is your night. Is there anything you wanted to do that we haven't yet?"

"Not one thing."

Corbin looped our intertwined hands around over my shoulder. "Come on. I want to show you something." He handed me my drink and took his before leading me through the suite. Some of our friends began to whistle, even though I was pretty sure all the bedrooms were occupied.

"Where are you taking me?" I asked.

"Away from these goons," he said, opening the front door to lead us into the hotel hallway.

I didn't want to think too hard about it. I leaned my weight on him, snuggling into his side. His cologne smelled good, but underneath, he was pure Corbin—surfboard wax and sunscreen. He took a sip of his orange juice and rum, then leaned down to give me a wet, citrus-y kiss. Was just kissing Corbin so bad? We zig-zagged down the hall, leaning left before overcorrecting to the right. Our drinks sloshed, our teeth clinked. He tasted good, felt good, too, but it was still weird to be kissing my best friend.

He stopped all of a sudden, setting his drink on the carpet. He fished his wallet from his back pocket and held out a room key.

I released his hand, flipping the plastic over in mine. "What is this?" I asked dumbly.

He nodded at the door behind me, and what he was trying to tell me clicked. I looked from the door to the key and back. "You got us a room?"

"Yup. Before you say no, just come in and look around." He swiped the key, and the door opened with a *click*. He turned his blue eyes on me. "I know you weren't expecting this, so there's no pressure, Lake."

I peeked into the room, more out of curiosity than anything. It was smaller than the suite but just as nice. Nicer, even, because there wasn't music blasting or people everywhere. I spotted a bottle in a bucket of ice. "There's champagne," I said.

"I know. I put it there."

"When?" I asked. "You've been with me all night."

"Earlier." He opened the door wider to reveal a white bedspread dotted with red rose petals. "I know it looks romantic, and that's because it's supposed to be." He crooked a corner of his mouth. "But it doesn't have to be if you don't want."

"Oh."

"You all right?" he asked. "You're a little pale."

I touched the doorframe. "It might be the alcohol."

He laughed. "It might be the sex."

I smiled despite my apprehension. It was so easy with Corbin. Easy to talk to him—like Val, he actually listened when I spoke instead of trying to one-up me like my other friends. Easy to laugh with him, to be around him. Easy to love him. I *did* love Corbin, so why couldn't it be easy to fall head over heels for him? To get butterflies? Maybe it would be, if only I gave him a chance. After all, Manning seemed to be doing that for Tiffany. *He'd* taken *her* hand earlier tonight. I downed a courage-bolstering sip of my drink and entered the room.

The door closed behind me as Corbin dimmed the lights. He followed me in and lifted my drink from my hands to set it on the nightstand with his. Tucking some of my hair behind my ear, he said, "We can take it slow. Talk for a while, even." Then, he kissed me again. I forced myself to focus on his lips, his breath, *him*. I wasn't doing anything wrong. A lot of girls in my class had either had sex or were planning to tonight. None of them had someone as sweet and fine as Corbin, I was pretty sure.

Corbin deepened the kiss, and my body pressed into his of its own accord. Feeling how solid his chest was, my nipples hardened. Doing this didn't necessarily have to mean we were official or anything. I wasn't sure I could ever be official with anyone, not as long as my heart belonged to someone else. Was that fair to Corbin? Maybe. He'd had sex before and hadn't made anything official with anyone. He'd always been a gentleman to me, but I knew that wasn't the case with other girls.

Corbin circled my waist and walked me backward to the bed. The thought of lying down with him pulled at something deep in my belly—the *something* I was pretty sure I was supposed to feel about sex. He slid his hand down my lower back and over my backside, pulling me against him. As his hardness pressed against my belly, I couldn't help my small gasp.

He groaned. "I've wanted this for a long time, Lake. This is so perfect."

"I don't know if I want to do this," I blurted.

"Why not?" He kissed my temple. "Give me one good reason."

Manning.

"I've never . . . I don't think about you like that."

He lowered my hand to his pants, right over his zipper. "Like what? This?"

I was touching Corbin's penis. I might've laughed, except that it felt very serious. "This could change our friendship."

"I hope it does."

Corbin could have college girls, but he wanted me. My existence didn't anger him. He didn't keep things from me, not even his feelings. He didn't hate me or my clothing or my choices. He took my face in his hands and kissed me harder, sweeping my desire up to the next level. I slid my hand along him. I didn't know what to do, except that I knew I was doing it right, and not just by the pained moans coming from him. I was the one touching him, and yet *my* tummy was fluttering.

He grazed his fingers down my spine and I moved against him. Cupping my butt, he squeezed me from behind. My knees buckled, my body going limp as a rag doll. Holding me up, he laughed into my mouth. "I've barely touched you."

A deep, ache-y sensation throbbed between my legs. How was it possible someone I'd never even thought to fantasize about could make me so warm and squirmy? I had the confusing urge to pull him closer, to push his hand under my dress.

He undid his pants, opening them just enough to get his hand down his underwear. "You have no idea what you do to me," he said.

I didn't, but I could. My skin tingled as he kissed me. I no longer had any urge to laugh. I reached out tentatively, fingering the waistband of his underwear as I worked up the courage. He paused, then stretched the elastic of his briefs to make room for me.

I put my hand in, grateful we were still kissing so I didn't have to look at his face, and wrapped my fingers around him. The skin down there was surprisingly soft. I had nothing to compare him to, but his penis seemed to go on and on. I'd seen two in my life. The summer between third and fourth grade,

Alex Smith had come running out of the ocean and lost his trunks to the tide. The other time, I'd walked into my parents' bathroom as my dad was getting out of the shower. Where Alex's penis had been small and pink, like an eraser, my dad's had been larger than life, hairy and angry. I'd run away both times as if I'd been the one doing something wrong.

Corbin's was definitely *not* an eraser. I had no idea what to do with it, so I just held it. I couldn't ask him, because that would mean stopping our kiss and having to look him in the face. The longer I just stood there, the more uncomfortable I felt. The contents of my stomach sloshed as if they were swimming in alcohol. My palm began to sweat. Corbin was the one with experience, so why wasn't he doing anything? Was this how it was supposed to go?

The only other time I'd tried anything like this was with Manning, and he'd done nothing more than graze his hand up my thigh—but that was because he'd been fighting himself. I'd known, instinctively, I'd need to push Manning to get what I wanted. With Corbin, I was afraid to take the lead. What if I did, and I couldn't go through with this?

My stomach hurt. My chest. Everything in my body. Manning'd never liked me hanging around with Corbin, and from the look in his eyes earlier, that hadn't changed. I felt like I'd betrayed him somehow, even though I knew I hadn't. I hadn't even looked at another boy, and even if I had, who cared? Manning had held my sister's hand without her forcing him to.

I couldn't do this. I didn't want to, and it wasn't right. It wasn't us. It wasn't Manning. I took my hand out quickly, wiping it on my dress.

Corbin pulled back, looking offended by my reaction. "What's wrong?"

"I told you, I just . . . I'm not ready."

"But why?" He buckled up his pants, frowning. "We've been close for years. I've never even seen you *look* at anyone else. Why not me?"

My heart fell. I hadn't meant to lead Corbin on, but there was no doubt that was what I'd done. As long as people thought he was my boyfriend, they left me alone for the most part. And that was what I wanted. To be left alone by everyone but Manning. To save myself—not just my virginity but my heart, my soul, and everything in me . . . for Manning. How could I say that to Corbin? I couldn't. "I'm sorry."

"I flew all the way here from New York for you." He gestured behind himself. "I blew three hundred bucks on this room and spent an hour setting it up—I even went to Bath and Body Works and picked out that girly Juniper Breeze bubble bath you like."

"It's so sweet, and it means a lot that you did all this, but you didn't ask if—you knew I had plans to stay with my friends—"

"It was supposed to be a surprise," he said incredulously.

He sounded upset, even though I'd never even asked him to be my date, and that made *me* angry. "So I'm supposed to sleep with you just because you went

219

through the trouble?" I asked. "That's a stupid reason."

His mouth dropped open. "I didn't mean it like that. Like that you owe me or anything. I just wanted you to, you know, feel special."

Corbin would respect whatever decision I made, but still—he'd assumed too much. That I'd be okay with this. That I *wanted* this. That he could swoop in and take away everything I'd been saving for someone else.

The air conditioning kicked on, blasting on my bare skin. I crossed my arms over my nipples, embarrassed by how hard they were. "I know that's not how you meant it," I said, "but I think I should go."

"Come on, Lake. I'm not trying to make you uncomfortable." He picked up my wrist, running a finger under the strap of my corsage. I'd tried to take it off a few times tonight, but he wouldn't let me. The red petals matched those on the bed. "We're a good match. I've held back these past two years, waiting my turn. When other girls want more from me, I just see you."

I wished I could tell him the same was true for me, because I knew the agony of being in his position. Maybe it should've made me want to try with him, but instead it presented the horrific possibility that if I was feeling the same way about Manning as Corbin did about me, then maybe

Manning's feelings for me equaled mine for Corbin. At the end of the day, they were nothing.

"I don't like drinking," I said, touching my temple. What could I say to Corbin other than *sorry*? Apologizing didn't even seem right. "I don't trust myself to make decisions . . . and I don't feel right. I just want to leave."

"Fine." I heard the disappointment in his voice. "But I don't have my car, and everyone here is wasted."

I looked away. It was my first night out on my own, and I was drunk. I wasn't about to get my parents to come down here. Dad would be pissed, and I'd be the baby who'd gotten picked up by her parents from the prom. "I'll call my sister."

Corbin made an irritated gesture toward the phones on his way to the front door. "I'll be in the suite."

Once I heard the door latch, I sat on the edge of the bed and called Tiffany.

"Hello?" Manning answered on the first ring.

My heart clenched. "It's Lake."

"What's the matter?"

"Nothing. Is Tiffany there?"

"She's asleep." That made sense, it was after midnight, but it didn't sound as if Manning had been sleeping. "What is it? Are you okay?"

"I'm fine, I just . . . I don't think I want to stay at the hotel."

He was quiet a few seconds. I didn't know what else to say. I didn't want him to think I was childish for not wanting to have sex on prom night, but I hadn't thought up another excuse.

"I'll be right there," he said.

"What about Tiffany?"

"You want me to get her up?"

I picked up a velvety petal, rubbing it between my thumb and index finger. Part of me wanted my big sister. Even though Tiffany would undoubtedly tease me about this, she had real experience with boys. She'd know how to handle Corbin. But time alone with Manning was precious. More than precious. A bigger part of me wanted him. "No."

"Go down to the lobby and wait there," he said. "Not outside. Don't come out until you see my car. It's late."

"I'm at the—"

"I know where you are," he said. "Ten minutes."

I hung up. When I stood and turned, Corbin was in the entryway. He had my overnight bag slung on his shoulder. "I'm sorry, Lake. I really didn't expect anything. I'd be happy just to hang out all night."

Guilt crept up my chest. "I'm sorry you came all the way here."

"It's all right," he said. "I got to surf at least."

I smiled a little. "Sydney's date went home. Maybe you could take her back to the room."

"I don't want Sydney," he said simply. "I want you."

I wrung my hands in front of me. "I didn't realize . . ."

"That was my fault," he said, holding out my bag, "but now you do."

Corbin insisted on walking me downstairs. We stood silently in the lobby, watching through the windows until Tiffany's car pulled up with Manning behind the wheel.

He got out, stood against the driver's side door with a cigarette, and watched us through the floor-to-ceiling windows. His expression was so dark, it dimmed the harsh light of the lobby.

"What's his deal anyway?" Corbin asked. "Your dad has no problem with you hanging around an ex-con?"

I wanted to say he wasn't an ex-con. And that no, my dad was not okay with it. He still hated Manning and I wasn't allowed to be alone with him, but none of that meant anything to me. In my eyes, he was just Manning, my Manning.

"He's a good guy," I said.

"Then why is Tiffany with him?"

It was a joke, but I didn't laugh. Why *was* Tiffany still with him? I'd asked myself over and over. At times, I could read my sister easily, but on this, I wasn't sure. It had started as a way to piss off Dad, and Manning's presence still upset him, but not as much. I almost thought Dad was beginning to accept him in our lives. So what would happen if Dad no longer cared that they were dating?

I worried my sister actually thought she loved Manning. Sometimes I caught her watching him the same way I did . . . with stars in her eyes.

Corbin kissed me before I could stop him. "Call me, okay? This doesn't change anything between us."

I gave him a close-lipped smile. If Corbin wanted to stay friends, I definitely wanted that, too. "Thanks for a great night," I said.

I turned away, back to Manning, who watched me through the glass. I crossed the lobby toward him, suddenly aware of how low cut my dress was, of the silky way the fabric whispered around my smooth legs. Aware of Manning's eyes on me, and of the fact that in a moment, we'd be getting into a car alone for the first time since that night almost two years ago.

15

LAKE

Manning didn't look at me as I exited the hotel lobby and approached the BMW. Leaning against the passenger's side door, he flicked his cigarette away, but continued staring inside—at Corbin. "Get in the car," he said.

He didn't need to tell me twice. I was eager for time with him, something I hadn't had much of since the night at the lake. Manning didn't follow right away. It made sense if he had reservations about being alone in a car with me, but he'd picked me up anyway.

When he finally slid behind the wheel, I asked, "Can I come over? I don't want to go home."

He started the car and pulled away from the curb. "What happened?"

"Nothing. I just didn't want to stay."

"Did he pressure you?" He looked over with a fire I hadn't gotten from him in the months since I'd nearly fallen at his feet in the foyer. "Did he, Lake?"

"No."

"Because he's got it bad for you."

I gaped at him. "You knew?"

"Of course I know. I've got eyeballs."

The irritation in his voice irritated *me*. What right did he have to get upset about someone having a crush on me? I crossed my arms tightly over my chest. "He got us a room."

"And?" he pushed when I didn't continue.

I stared out the windshield. Everything I'd been holding in since the last time we were truly alone flooded over me. He'd given me close to nothing since he'd gotten out, while I hadn't thought about much other than him. I loved him, and it hurt. Because of that, I let him fill in the blanks. It would be just a *taste* of what'd been running through my head these last couple years.

"Lake, if he hurt you—"

"He didn't."

"If he tried to get you to do anything you didn't want—"

"Maybe I wanted it."

He white-knuckled the steering wheel, breathing audibly. Manning's frustration was better than nothing, but at the same time, our time together was limited. I didn't want to sit in silence, fire-breathing or otherwise.

"Nothing happened," I said. I was fairly certain in adult terms, nothing *had* happened. If I told Manning I'd held Corbin's penis the way I'd shake his hand, he probably would've laughed. "Corbin's a gentleman."

"Then why are you here?"

I shifted in my seat, the "V" of my dress gaping. I tucked the fabric back into place. "I'm sorry I woke you."

He sighed. "You didn't. I was up."

"Why?" I smiled a little. "Were you worried about me?"

After a few seconds, he blew out a breath. "So much can go wrong."

He *had* been worried. Manning always seemed to be running the worst-case scenario in his mind. Who could blame him? He'd lived it once already with his sister. Then again when he'd gotten picked up for a crime he hadn't committed. "I'm sorry if you worried," I said. "It's hard to tell if you even care."

He stayed focused on the road.

"You can tell me if you do, Manning."

"What happened that night in the truck was wrong. I'm not looking for a repeat."

"Neither am I," I said quickly, and it was the truth. I didn't need to make the same mistakes, to deepen my already profound guilt. "I learned my lesson, but . . . what happens next month?"

He set his lips in a line. He understood what I was asking. "Nothing," he said.

"I turn eighteen."

"I know."

"And then I'll go to college. I'll be away from all of them."

He wiped his upper lip with his sleeve and turned on the air conditioning. I tried not to shiver. "I'm sorry you think I don't care about you," he said, "but it couldn't be further from the truth. I care too much."

"What does that mean?"

"Just leave it, Lake. It is what it is."

"It doesn't have to be that way. If you care about me at all, you'd break up with her before—"

He slammed his palm against the steering wheel. "This isn't about her, it's not even about me. It's about you going off and accomplishing everything you're supposed to. Do you want to end up like your sister? No education, in a job she hates, living with a felon who can't even take care of her?"

I mashed my teeth together. Tiffany might not have much in everyone else's eyes, but she had Manning, so she had everything. I'd take that life in a heartbeat just to be with him.

"Forget about me. Go to 'SC. Do something meaningful with your life and I promise you, one day . . ."

I waited, hopeful, as he turned on his blinker and took a left into the apartment complex. "One day?"

"You'll find the man who's right for you. Who's good for you. Who brings out the best in you. Like I do for your sister. You deserve someone who can take care of you."

"I don't want to be taken care of. I want to be loved the way you love me."

He looked away, out the driver's side window. His throat rippled as he swallowed. "You don't want me to love you, Lake."

The words were too absurd to even hurt me. "I know why you're acting like you don't, and I know that you do."

He didn't argue. "If you believe that," he said, "then you know I only want what's best for you—and it isn't me."

He was already parking the car, our time together over before it had begun. A fiery rage burned up my chest. This went beyond being overprotective. Manning refused to see what was right in front of him. Everything he wanted. Everything I wanted. It made no sense to keep pretending it wasn't there. "Take me back to the hotel."

"What?"

"Take me back to Corbin. If you honestly feel nothing for me, nothing at all, then I want him."

He stayed where he was, the car idling.

"I mean it," I said. "I'm going to do it. I'm going to let him take my virginity since you don't want it."

Manning winced. "Stop."

"You don't want me, but nobody else can have me? Fine. If you feel nothing, turn on the car and drive me back—"

He tore his gaze from the windshield to look at me. "I feel it," he said through gritted teeth. "Of course I fucking feel it."

The night expanded around us, the world, the universe.

"That doesn't mean anything. You're a kid, and don't tell me you're not, because if you weren't, you'd understand—people don't just end up together for love."

That hurt. Him pretending he didn't love me was a lie, but this, he really believed. That it might not last. That it wasn't enough. That I wasn't enough. "Yes, they do—"

"They don't," he yelled, his voice too big for the small car. "Damn it, Lake. This is exactly what I'm talking about. You get under my skin like nobody else does. I have a temper. I get so fucking frustrated with you sometimes. You don't listen, you keep pushing me, you act like an adult when you're . . ."

"You're frustrated with me for acting like an adult?" I asked. "I'll be eighteen *next month*."

"It's not about your age." He shook his head. "It's not."

If that was true, then I didn't know how to fight him. I wasn't equipped for this. If there was some fundamental reason he didn't want to be with me, how could I change it without knowing what it was?

"Your sister loves me, Lake." He shut off the car. "I'm sorry if it hurts you, but it's the truth. The sooner you accept it, the better."

"But do you love *her*?"

We sat in silence for a few moments. When he didn't answer, I grabbed my bag, got out of the car, and slammed the door. My entire body shook. Rum and orange juice burned its way up my throat. I was going to puke. The door to Tiffany's apartment was unlocked, so I ran into the bathroom and dry-heaved until I was certain nothing was going to come up. I slid down against the bathroom wall to the floor and put my head between my knees.

Why? Why couldn't he just admit he loved me so we could start our life together? I'd waited long enough, spent almost two years keeping my distance. We were so close to the finish line, or so I'd thought. What did everything else matter once I turned eighteen? What was more important than this fiery, all-consuming love I felt for him?

The answer was nothing. Not even my sister, whom I loved, but whom I'd been willing to hurt to get what I wanted.

I tried to get up, but the room spun. It could've been the alcohol or just Manning's effect on me, but either way, I rested my head on my forearms and stayed put. I drifted to sleep, and by the time I opened my eyes, the dizziness had worn off.

I stripped out of my prom dress and changed into the cotton pajama set I'd bought for tonight's sleepover. It seemed childish and stupid now, a pink, gingham strappy cami and matching boy-shorts. When I came out of the bathroom, the night sky looked less like a sinkhole and more of a deep ocean blue. The faucet ran in the kitchen. I followed the noise, crossing the living room. The green glow of the oven's digital clock read 4:07 AM.

Manning stood at the sink in nothing but boxer-briefs, his back to me, an empty glass next to him. He splashed water on his face and leaned his hands on the lip of the counter. His torso expanded as if he was trying to catch his breath.

The moon was just bright enough to light some markings on his back. At first it looked like someone had drawn on him, but as I got closer, black ink made a triangle with three starred points. The muscles of his wide back worked as my eyes drifted over the simple tattoo, then his damp hairline, the sheen of sweat on the back of his neck.

Manning just stared at the running water until he finally flipped off the faucet. The drain gurgled and burped. Mesmerized, I reached up to touch the tattoo. He turned his head a fraction and spun. Within a second, my wrist was in a vice-like grip, my neck in his other hand as he pinned my back against the counter with his hips.

"What are you doing?" he whispered, voice hard, eyes black.

I forgot to breathe. His anger coursed through me like adrenaline, making my heart race and my nipples harden. "What's wrong?" I asked.

His grip remained strong, even as his fingers loosened. He pressed one thumb into my wrist and the other at the top of my throat. "You snuck up on me."

"Are you okay?"

The darkness hadn't left his eyes. He kept me caged against the counter like he'd caught me breaking in. He shifted his thumb up my neck, under my chin, as if checking for a heartbeat. "You know what I'd do to a man inside who tried to come at me while my back was turned?"

I swallowed against his hand. For all the times I'd tortured myself wondering what it was like in there, I said, "Tell me."

"It'd give you nightmares."

For some reason, that made my stomach tighten, my insides clench. It turned me on, even as realization dawned on me—Manning was the one with the nightmares.

When something twitched against my stomach, his eyes dropped. From this angle, he could see down my camisole, and he did. He looked right at my breasts. "Did you dress like this while I was away?" he asked, his whisper angry.

I sobered. "Like what?"

He put his hands at my waist, bunching up the cotton and exposing my midriff. "Why do you do this to me?" he asked. "Why can't you just . . . stop?"

My heart pounded. I knew what he meant without asking. Being around each other was as hard for him as it was for me. I hated that it took fear and nightmares to get anywhere with him, but at least he was here now. "I'm sorry," I said, because I didn't want to torture him, but I didn't know any other way.

He lifted me onto the counter and slid me back until my head touched a cabinet, like he was hiding a doll on the back of a shelf. He didn't let me go. His breathing labored, even though I knew lifting me was no effort for him. Something else made it hard to breathe. I put my hand on his bare chest, and it rose with his inhale. I ached to explore every inch of him. When he didn't pull me off, I traced the dip his collarbone created. He had the expansive torso of a man, unlike the boys I'd been around, and his stomach flexed into a six-pack. I was in awe. Breathless from the world opening up to me. As I went to touch, though, he stopped my hand and put it on his face. I scraped my palm along his stubble. I was touching him without asking. He'd touched me, too. I wanted to rejoice in that, but I couldn't ignore the anguish in his face. "What are your nightmares about?" I asked.

He kept his eyes down but pushed his thumbs into the soft space in the middle of my ribcage. As if he'd pressed a button, my insides melted like butter, warming my lower half.

"I'm fine," he said. "Don't worry."

"I do worry. I can't help it. I think the worst."

"What's the worst?"

"I worry that they hurt you. I worry they changed you. I worry you hate me."

"Hate you," he repeated, not a question. "There are some things I hate about you."

I was too wrapped up in him to be hurt. He could say anything to me when we were like this, and I'd take it. I shuddered. "Like what?"

"That you're not the girl you were when I went away. That you still are. That I could," he squeezed my middle, "ruin you in one stroke. That I could give you nightmares." He got closer, as if he were going to tell me a secret. "Cuts and bruises, broken bones, they heal, Lake. They're nothing."

"What doesn't heal?"

"Everything else."

My chest ached with the weight of my regret for what I couldn't change or take back. No matter how much time passed, no matter how life turned out, it would never be right what I'd done. "My mistakes hurt you. They did this. They're why you hate me."

He didn't say anything, but the way he avoided my eyes was answer enough. He put one large hand on my chest, spreading his fingers and wrinkling his brow as if trying to see if he could reach both my shoulders. "That's not what I'm talking about," he said finally. "There are things I can't share with you."

"You can," I whispered, locking my hands around the back of his neck. He was pushing me away by my chest, but I held on. "You can tell me. I'm stronger than you think."

"I was alone," he said. "For over two months. In a cell. That's what I dream about." He paused. "You're there sometimes."

"In the cell?"

Slowly, he raised his eyes to mine. "No. Just outside of it. Outside my reach. Everyone else can touch you, and I can't."

My limbs quivered, fatigued. This felt like a breakthrough and my entire body reacted to it. "Why does that scare you?"

I thought I knew the answer, and it could be summed up in one word—*helpless*. It described his role in Madison's death, his situation with the courts, and his relationship to me. It was maybe the only thing that could incapacitate a man as big and protective as Manning—knowing he could help, and being unable to.

"It scares me because things go wrong. Life isn't fair. Some people are bad. I don't want you to experience any of that."

"You don't have nightmares because you think I'll get hurt. You have them because you can't stop bad things from happening."

"I couldn't for Madison."

"You were helpless." I ducked my head to look him in the eye. "There was nothing you could've done for Madison, and you know you won't always be able to protect me."

"Helpless," he repeated.

"Why did you beat up that guard?" I asked. His gaze darkened. As close as his face was to mine, I couldn't deny feeling intimidated, but I held his stare. He didn't scare me. "What would make you that angry?"

He shook his head. "I can't explain it."

"Try. You're not protecting me by not telling me. When you don't, I fill in the blanks, Manning. I think these awful things, like that they took away your food or stole from you or—"

"I snapped, Lake. That's it. I snapped." His palm went clammy against my chest. "Just like him."

Snapped. It took me back to that night in the truck when he'd opened up about Maddy. Not only had Manning watched his dad's anger burst in an instant, but as a teenager, Manning had also been accused of, and nearly arrested for, snapping. "You're not like him," I said. I put my hand over his on my chest. "You are a better man. The best."

He looked toward the sink. "They wanted to get under my skin, and I let them. I went somewhere I shouldn't."

"Then what?" I asked. He wouldn't look at me. I grabbed his face and forced him to. "Then what?"

"I had to face the punishment. Solitary confinement for over two months, and I almost caught more charges, but for once, luck was on my side."

"How is that luck?" I asked, curling my fingers into his cheeks. "Two months alone, without anything or anyone. It's not right." Now, I was the one breathing hard, my frustration getting the better of me. I hated the idea of it, of them beating him and locking him up alone. Had he had enough to eat, been warm enough, had friends to confide in? "What did you think about in there?"

"Everything."

I moved my index finger down the crooked bridge of his nose, then touched the raised scar, the break in stubble on his upper lip. "Did they do this to you?"

It was no wonder he hated me.

His mouth parted, and as if by instinct, I dropped my finger to his bottom lip. Hardness nudged the soft inside of my thigh, but I was too afraid to look down. I used his solid body as leverage to slide forward on the tile and bring him between my knees. I couldn't believe I was just touching him. Just like that.

"Was I there? In your nightmare?" I asked. I ran my fingertip along his mouth. My other hand played with the soft ends of his hair.

He nodded.

"I'm still here."

He fisted my top and spanned his other big hand along the back of my head. The tips of his middle finger and thumb grazed each of my earlobes. He pulled me toward him, gripping my camisole so tightly that one of the thin straps snapped. My heart hammered in my chest. Manning and I were going to kiss. He had an erection, I was pretty sure. We'd have sex. On prom night. Just like I'd dreamed about. It was larger and more life-changing than anything I'd done up until then—and terrifying enough that I almost stopped him. I almost couldn't bear the weight of it.

"Manning?" I heard from a distance.

He stopped short.

It took me a moment to remember where I was, and that we weren't alone. That I had a sister who'd probably sat in this same spot. I looked over Manning's shoulder. Until then, I hadn't noticed the open bedroom door. Tiffany's bare legs were tangled in the sheets on the right side of the bed. For some reason, that shocked me. Like she should be in the middle the way she'd slept at home. It was the first evidence I'd seen of Manning and my sister sleeping in the same bed.

He let go of my top, and it uncrinkled like a piece of paper. He fixed it quickly, then stepped back over to the sink. "In the kitchen," he called. "Your sister's here." To me, he said, "Get down."

I slid off the counter just before Tiffany shuffled out in panties and nothing else, rubbing her eyes. "Lake?"

"Tiff." Manning jutted his chin behind her. "You're naked."

She rolled her eyes. "Lake's seen my boobs a hundred times."

It was true, I had, but never like this. Never in front of Manning. Not with the knowledge that Tiffany had come straight out here from bed, which meant she slept next to Manning every night like that. Naked. When I'd called earlier, he'd been in bed with her. When he left me now, that was where he'd go. To her bed.

"Why are you here?" Tiffany asked me.

I cupped my right shoulder, trying to hide that my strap had broken. "I . . ."

"Never mind," she said. "Tell me in the morning. Manning, come to bed. I need you for something."

Something? I looked between the two of them, my vision going fuzzy. Had it been this dark and hazy a minute ago? Had the clock glared this hard, green lasers cutting through my euphoria?

Tiffany plodded back into the bedroom. Manning picked up his glass, filling it under the faucet as he stared out the window over the sink.

"Manning?"

He shut off the water and turned away.

"Where are you going?" I asked, following him with my eyes.

"Bed."

"You can't." It came out softly, but I wanted to shout at him. Shake him. *You can't go in there. You can't!* He and Tiffany were going to have sex. They'd already *had* sex. Of course I knew it, but I'd never actually *known* it. Not until this moment.

He checked over his shoulder, then came back to stand in front of me. "You asked what I thought about in there," he said quietly. "A lot. Everything. You, and Tiffany, too. But mostly, I thought about my dad. All the awful things he did. The coward he was. And how I would never become him. Not even for you."

He returned to the bedroom. I had no idea what he'd meant, or why he thought I could possibly turn him, the man I loved, into his dad, the man he hated. *I* was the one who was helpless in all this. I got that same panicky feeling I had when I'd opened my college acceptance packet. My future had been set, but which, if any, of these choices had *I* made?

16
MANNING

I woke up next to my girlfriend, and there was nothing strange about that. Except that the night before, I'd just about lost my control to the urge to taste watermelon again, just once before I died.

Dried sweat made my hairline stiff. Last night I'd dreamed of Lake. She'd needed me and I'd been *helpless*. It'd shaken me even more than usual knowing Lake slept under my roof. She was close. Safe.

Except that she wasn't.

I'd turned into her instead of away. She'd radiated warmth and comfort, and having a nightmare about her had made me especially vulnerable. Maybe there was no more dangerous place for Lake than anywhere I was. I'd let myself get lost in her before, and one of those times, I'd paid a heavy price. Yet I'd still gone to pick her up, knowing we'd be alone in the car. She had a power over me that could hurt us both, and I had to be the strong one between us.

Like most mornings, I was up before Tiffany. By the time I'd showered, changed into a t-shirt and jeans, and downed half a pot of coffee, neither of the girls had gotten up. I was pulling eggs and bacon from the refrigerator when Lake shuffled out of the guest bedroom. Good thing for my sanity, she'd put a sweatshirt on. It didn't cover as much as it should, but at least I couldn't see her tits anymore. Those soft hills that peaked into hard little pebbles. They had to be close to a C cup, perky, perfect—and not mine to ogle or touch.

Lake rubbed her red eyes. I felt like a real piece of shit that there was even a chance she'd cried herself to sleep. "Sit," I said. "I'm making you breakfast."

She'd stopped in the middle of the living room, by the front door, as if she might make a break for it. "I'm not hungry."

I ignored her. "We don't have any fancy guest plates, but you can use my mug. It was a gift from Gary." I showed her my coffee cup, a man in black-and-white prison scrubs asking a zebra what it's in for. She didn't laugh. I filled it with orange juice and set it in front of a stool at the breakfast bar.

She blinked her puffy eyelids. Had she even gone to the bathroom yet? Or just stumbled out and into my orbit? I couldn't tell what she was thinking—

probably something about Tiffany and me. If she'd had sex with Corbin last night, that's damn well what I'd be thinking about.

"Take me back to the hotel."

"What?"

"Take me back to Corbin."

It made my stomach churn the same way it had when she'd said it last night. I knew in my gut she'd left because of him. He'd gotten her a hotel room for Christ's sake. How close had they come to sleeping together? Had he pushed her? Touched her? What if I hadn't been here, and Tiffany had refused to pick her up? That didn't matter, because I was here, and based on the sickness developing in my gut at the thought of her being stranded, I always would be.

"What kind of eggs do you like?" I asked to distract myself.

"How do you normally make them?" Tentatively, she took a seat. "What do you drink in the mornings?"

"Scrambled, but I'll eat them any way. Sometimes I'll make an omelet."

"With what?"

I continued about my routine, reminding myself when her gaze followed me around that I wasn't nearly as interesting as she seemed to think. "Whatever's around. Spinach, mushrooms, peppers. You sure you aren't hungry?"

"Yes. What do you drink?" she asked again.

"Coffee."

"I want some."

I gave her a look. "You don't drink coffee."

"How do you know?"

"I just do." No seventeen year olds I knew drank coffee. Not that I really knew any. I jutted my chin at the mug. "How about the orange juice?"

She took a long look at it, her expression contorting with disgust.

"What?" I asked.

"It's what I drank last night."

"Orange juice? At prom?"

"With rum."

She picked it up anyway and took a sip. I wasn't dumb enough to think there wasn't alcohol at prom, but it hadn't occurred to me she might've been drunk last night. I hadn't smelled it on her. The eggs sizzled on the pan behind me, but I couldn't get myself to move. "How much did you drink?"

She didn't look at me. "By the time you picked me up, I was fine."

"You have to be careful."

"I was." She raised her eyes to me. "You know I was."

I turned away. I hated the idea of it, her, drinking in a hotel room with men. No, I couldn't fucking *stand* the idea of it. Men were assholes to begin with, but they could be dangerous when they drank. Not that Corbin or any of those guys were men—they were boys, and that was worse. Drunk boys lost control. They made bad decisions. I ran a hand through my hair and pulled—I'd already been on this carousel all night before she'd called. I'd been in bed, staring at the ceiling long after Tiffany had gone to sleep, running through all the awful scenarios that could go down at prom.

I pulled the pan off the burner just as I heard a noise that sounded like her stomach grumbling. She twisted back and forth on the stool, looking not a day over her age. I scraped eggs onto a plate and set them in front of her. "Here."

"I said I'm not—"

"Bacon'll be done in a minute."

"But it's yours."

I smiled a little. "They're overcooked anyway."

"Oh." She watched me, wide-eyed, as she ate a forkful. Finally, she smiled, too.

The bedroom door opened, and Tiffany came out in just a t-shirt. My t-shirt.

Lake's eyes traveled over her sister, head to toe.

"What's so funny?" Tiff asked.

I realized I was still smiling, so I stopped. "Nothing."

She gave me a look as if I were in trouble, then went straight for the coffee. "How was last night?" she asked over her shoulder. "Did Corbin bring you?"

"Manning picked me up from the hotel," Lake said.

I stared at the back of Tiffany's head as she poured herself a mug, then moved by me to get her fat-free creamer from the fridge.

"She asked for you," I said, sensing her irritation. "But I didn't want to wake you. I was already up."

"What about Corbin?" Tiffany asked. "Still sleeping?"

"Corbin?" Lake asked.

"He's here, right?"

Like I'd let that little shit into my home so he could take advantage of Lake. "No," I answered.

Tiffany laughed, coming around the counter to hug a blushing Lake. "You didn't get laid on prom night? I thought that's why you came here. For privacy."

I couldn't do it. Couldn't let that image into my head. I pressed the heels of my hands into my eye sockets, forcing blackness. "Jesus Christ."

"What?" she asked, looking at me over Lake's shoulder. "She's seventeen, not ten. She can get laid on prom night if she wants. Lord knows I did, and if Corbin had been my date, I'd do it again. He's got that hot surfer bod. Better get to him before his freshman beer gut kicks in."

The room went silent except for the sizzle of bacon. Tiffany was angling to get under someone's skin, but I wasn't sure if it was mine or Lake's. Lake looked at her lap. "I wasn't—I'm not ready."

"Well, you're going to college soon. How much longer—"

"Lay off," I said. "She's a f—she's just a kid."

"I'm *not* a kid," Lake said.

I wanted to shake her every time she denied it. She needed to be young and carefree as long as possible. If not for herself, then for me.

Lake stood up, dropping her fork on the plate. "Just because I'm not a *slut* like some people doesn't mean I'm a child."

"No, you're not a slut at all, are you? You probably had the chance to lose your virginity to your crush and you couldn't even do that. You're a prude."

Lake's face went white, and maybe mine did, too. Did Lake have a crush on Corbin?

"Probably saving yourself for *the one*," Tiffany muttered. "Like a baby."

"What's with you?" I asked, my temper rising. "Why are you being so vicious?"

She shook her head at me. "What do you care? And why don't you ever make me breakfast?"

"I would, if you ate breakfast." I held up the pan. "Here. Want this?"

She made a face. "No."

"Then what's your problem?"

"Nothing." She came back to me and rose onto the balls of her feet. "I'm sorry. You know how I am in the mornings. Kiss?" When I just stared at her, she pouted. "Please?"

I leaned in and gave her what she wanted. I had no choice. When I pulled back, Lake had left the room. I didn't blame her. Just seeing Corbin peck her on the mouth last night had put me on edge. *Over* the edge. I'd wanted to wring his neck.

"Why do you say stuff like that to her?" I asked, scraping eggs onto a plate.

"You know why."

"No, I don't."

"She needs to hear it, Manning." She took a sip of her coffee. "She has a crush on you."

Fuck. I turned my back and opened the fridge, hiding my face. Why was she bringing this up? "She does not."

"No? What about that night?"

I froze, not even daring to take a breath, racking my brain for a night, any night, she could be talking about that wasn't *that* one. Dark highway, wind-in-her-hair, Summer Triangle on a black lake. "What are you talking about?"

"She forced her way into your truck the night you were supposedly committing robbery. What, you thought I didn't know?"

Her tone told me she *knew* I didn't. This was the first I'd heard of it. Lake had sworn to me she wouldn't tell anyone the truth about that night, but could I really blame her if she had? It'd all gone bad so fast, and she'd had no one to confide in. Slowly, I shut the door. "Nothing happened."

"Obviously—she doesn't have the guts. And yet you were stupid enough to get in a car alone with her again. Why? Do you have a crush on her, too?"

I turned quickly. *I* was the crush Tiffany'd been talking about just now. The one Lake *hadn't* lost her virginity to. Not Corbin. "Do I have a crush on

250

Lake?" I asked, trying to keep my voice level. "What's gotten into you? She's your sister."

Lake returned to the living room dressed in shorts with her bag slung over her shoulder. "I'm going."

"You didn't finish your breakfast," I said.

"I told you I wasn't hungry." She avoided our eyes as she walked to the front door. "Dad'll be here any minute."

"We could've taken you home," I said.

Lake didn't even glance back as she walked out, closing the door gently behind her.

I turned back to Tiffany, who was watching the door. "Did she have fun?" she asked.

I dumped the contents of Lake's dish onto mine. "Why don't you ask her yourself?"

Absentmindedly, she stirred more creamer into her coffee. "Did she?"

"She said she had a great time."

"Then why did she need to be picked up? Did something happen?"

I thought back to when I'd pulled up to the hotel, to Corbin and Lake standing in the lobby, smiling, kissing. I should've been grateful she hadn't slept with him, but I didn't like that Corbin had even tried. He probably hadn't been the first, and he definitely wouldn't be the last.

"I don't know," I said, forking some eggs into my mouth. It was partially true. Lake hadn't told me outright why she'd asked to be picked up. "She's a teenage girl."

"I'm sure it wasn't because of Corbin. He's too sweet."

Sweet. *Fuck sweet.* He was a teenage boy first. "How do you know?" I chewed. "Sometimes it's those guys you have to look out for."

"Because we've known his family a while. He and his brothers are perfect gentlemen."

I blinked a few times, unsure of where to start with that. Why did everyone keep calling him a gentleman?

"He used to like me," she continued.

"You mentioned."

She picked a piece of bacon off my plate. "Maybe he still does, and that's why he took Lake to prom."

There was no way Corbin flew all the way in from New York to make Tiffany jealous, but I wasn't about to argue. I was still wrapping my head around the fact that Tiffany knew about my night with Lake. How much had Lake told her?

"They're a good match, though, aren't they?" she asked, sliding onto Lake's stool. "Corbin and Lake. He's good-looking, smart, rich, and from a good family. Perfect guy for a perfect girl."

During prom photos, Corbin had put his arms around Lake and made her laugh like it was nothing. Like he deserved her. Even her dad approved of him. As if I'd needed the reminder that I was neither deserving, nor approved of. My stomach had churned watching his hands on her, his possessive grip on her shoulders.

"Nobody's perfect," I said.

"Except Lake."

I couldn't really argue that. Lake wasn't without her flaws, but I couldn't name a single one, and I doubted they'd be enough to keep any man away. I shifted gears. I could tell by Tiffany's sharp tone, agreeing with her would be the death of me. "Some people might say you're perfect," I pointed out.

She bit off a piece of bacon, narrowing her eyes at me. "Some people?"

"You're gorgeous. Clever. Funny. Hard-working." I handed her a paper towel when she spilled some coffee on her top. "You have everything going for you."

She patted the stain, glancing up at me. "Plus, I have you."

I nodded a little. "Perfect boyfriend, eh?" I was far from a perfect boyfriend. I wasn't even sure I was a good one, but sometimes, like now, she made me feel like I was, and it made me want to try harder.

Tiffany smiled. "Do you ever think about the future?"

I glanced out at the patio, at my pack of cigarettes. It made me anxious when I couldn't be sure if Tiffany was being genuine or angling for something. Instead, I picked up Lake's orange juice and took a sip. "What future?"

"Ours. We've been together a while now."

"Most of our relationship developed in a small room while guards watched." I wasn't joking, but Tiffany laughed.

"I'm just saying. We should start thinking about the next step. I mean, *I've* already thought about it—haven't you?"

I hadn't really until Gary had brought it up a couple months ago. I'd assumed Tiffany would want to talk about all this at some point, just not so soon. "Aren't you too young to start thinking about that?"

"You're not. And a few girls from my class got married last year."

"What about your dad?" All the times I'd been to his house, and Charles still gave me the cold shoulder. He didn't like me dating Tiffany; he might blow a gasket if he knew we were talking about getting serious. "He'd never go for that."

"He might. Maybe it'd get him to back off a little."

I piled the dishes and pans in the sink. "Or you and I getting married would just send him over the edge."

"Maybe," she said. She took her coffee into the bedroom and said, "Or maybe he'll finally relax a little knowing I'm taken care of."

Taken care of—by me? I barely made enough to put a roof over my own head. With my juice, I went into the living room and shifted the blinds aside to look out the window. Lake sat on the curb of the parking lot, her knees bent up to her chin. Still, at seventeen, her legs were too long for her body. And still, she was perfect. Tiffany was right—Lake had a crush on me, but that would pass. I couldn't take care of her. I brought nothing to the table for a girl who was on her way up.

Who was I to think I deserved perfection? That I even deserved perfection's older sister? If Tiffany was talking about the next step, then she was offering me everything a person could want out of life—to love and be loved. A home, a family, and a life I didn't think I deserved or would ever get.

She did better with me around. She'd gotten her shit semi-together. If I walked away now, she might get off track again and continue to put off school. I'd have to find a new place with no money, no credit, and no car. Living by the beach wasn't an option, it was too expensive, but I couldn't leave county lines, so what did that mean? Roommates?

I waited there until Charles pulled up to take Lake home. Once they were gone, I found Tiffany in the ensuite, taking a shower. Leaning my ass on the bathroom counter, I spoke over the sound of the showerhead. "I'm not even sure I want to get married. To anyone."

The only sound for a few seconds was water beating against the tub floor. "Well, if not, that's probably something I should know. It's something I want."

"Is it, or is it just what you think you *should* want?"

"This isn't the first time I've thought about this," she said. "Is it so hard to believe I want to find a good man? To take care of him, and let him take care of me? When it happens doesn't matter, does it?" She opened the shower curtain and stuck just her head out for a kiss. Automatically, I gave it to her. "Do you know what it'd mean to me to call you my husband? Can't you just picture it—everyone in our lives watching me marry the most handsome, wonderful man I've ever known?"

Stripped down and soaking wet, Tiffany looked up at me. It was the second time she'd said she felt taken care of, and not only that, but she thought I was a good man. A *wonderful* man. I hadn't realized how much it would affect me to hear her say that. A strange feeling rose in my chest. "You really feel taken care of?" I asked.

"Of course."

"By me?"

She laughed. "I know our little place isn't much, and my dad still helps with the rent, but it's the first thing that's ever felt like . . . mine. And I wouldn't have it without you."

When was the last time I'd done anything good or right for anyone? It had to have been Madison, those nights I'd taken her to the front lawn to distract her from our parents' blow-out fights. Even when my aunt took me in at fifteen, I couldn't be the support system she'd needed after losing her niece, and I'd always felt bad about that. But here I was, adding to Tiffany's life instead of detracting.

"Besides," Tiffany said before closing the curtain, "money isn't the only way to take care of a person."

I knew that, but I hadn't thought she would. The night of Madison's death, I'd learned valuable lessons about the importance of family. Not only had I lost my sister, the person I'd loved most in the world, but I'd been betrayed by my parents, too. I might've expected it from my dad, but when the officers had asked my mom if I was the one who'd hurt my sister and she'd nodded, I knew I'd never get over that. A good family shouldn't be taken for granted, and I knew that because I didn't have one.

Except maybe I did.

17
MANNING

Gary sat next to me on the bed of his truck, his legs swinging. He pointed to the ocean and shook his head. "Look at that. You don't take the first inside wave as a set approaches. You just don't."

The guy we were meeting hadn't shown yet, so we'd backed into a small alley by the pier between beachfront condos and shops. It was a three-minute loading zone, and we'd be unloading—just as soon as the guy got here. In the meantime, Sublime's *40oz To Freedom* played on the car stereo while we watched the ocean.

I followed a surfer down the line with my eyes until he jumped off his board. My gaze kept going and landed on the last person I expected to see— Lake. She and her friends spilled out of a surf shop onto the sidewalk, giggling. She wore a purple scrap of fabric around her torso like an oversized bandana. Two bathing suit straps tied around her neck. She took a pair of sunglasses out of a shopping bag and modeled them for her friends. As she removed them, her hair caught on the arms, but the strands were such fine, spun gold that they just fell back into place.

"Waves are shit, but I'd still get out there if I could," Gary said, oblivious to my wandering thoughts.

I couldn't remember all her friends' names, just Val, the one with the skateboard. The other two, Tiffany called *Dumb* and *Dumber*. To me they looked the same, except that one of them was always gawking at me. Tiffany said it was because she was scared.

Val dropped her skateboard on the sidewalk and pushed off, passing Gary and me in a slow, controlled ride down the sidewalk. Lake and the other two climbed on their bikes. Out of nowhere, a toddler ran up from the beach and crossed their paths. The two girls swerved, but the boy tripped and fell anyway. Lake slammed on her brakes and dropped her bike to go to him just as his parents swooped him up and took him away.

She got back on and started to pedal, but her chain had popped off and her foot slipped. I went to get up as she stumbled forward, then looked up, right at me, her blue eyes hitting me hard.

As seconds passed, something loosened in my chest. Four weeks had passed since I'd picked her up from the prom. I'd seen her at family dinners, but even then she was rushing in from studying or volunteering or whatever else, or she was hurrying off somewhere.

"Hey, Lake," Gary said when he noticed her. "What're you doing here?"

She wheeled her bike over to us, the chain clinking.

I nodded at the plastic bag hanging from her handlebar. "Shopping for a birthday present."

Lake's eyes lit up. "You remembered," she said before cinching her eyebrows. "Or I guess Tiffany told you."

June ninth. Lake's eighteenth birthday. Couldn't forget today if I tried. "She didn't tell me."

Either she blushed or she'd gotten too much sun. The pink tip of her nose and the bridge had a light smattering of freckles. I had the urge to run my thumb over them, to spend my afternoon covering her head to toe in sunscreen. "What're you guys doing here?" she asked.

Gary thumbed the coffee table in the bed of the truck. "Delivering some furniture."

"For who?"

He nodded at one of the houses. "This lady bought it from us. We're meeting her husband."

Lake looked around me. "You guys *made* that?"

"Well, Manning did."

"We did it together," I said.

"But you designed it." He grinned. "I'm just an extra pair of hands. And I'm making sure you don't scare off your customers."

It was just a table, not much to it except that I'd oxidized and stained the wood and added some metal detailing on the legs and corners. I'd built one for our upstairs neighbor, and his girlfriend's mom wanted one, too. The money wasn't much but every little bit helped and I had the time. I glanced over my shoulder and wished it was more. Something worth looking at.

"It's so good," she said. "I can't believe you can do all that. I knew you could make things but not that you were . . . creative."

As I went to speak, I realized I'd been holding my breath. "I'm good with my hands, that's all."

Her cheeks went pinker as she tucked some hair behind her ear. "Oh. Y-yes. I . . ."

I had to look away. She was way too cute when she was flustered. "Your friends left you," I pointed out.

"They'll be back."

A car pulled up behind ours, and Gary craned his neck over the top of the truck. "I think this is them. I'll go see."

Lake set her bike on the sidewalk and came to stand right by me. The threads of her cut-off shorts drifted against my jeans. She lifted her hair off her neck and fanned herself, showing me the delicate

curves of her shoulders. She was eighteen. *Fuck.*
Never had there been a greater test of my will.

"You're always saying at dinner how you're
looking for work. Why don't you just make things?"
she asked.

I blinked slowly, trying to pull myself from the
trance her nearness always put me in. "What kinds of
things?" I asked, hearing the rasp in my voice.

She reached behind me. I could've stared at her
all day, except that she got too close, her cheek right
by my face, smelling like lemon and Coppertone. I
could almost convince myself I detected watermelon
on her lips. I turned to watch her small hand glide
along the table's edge.

"These things," she said. "The wood is so cool.
Smooth."

Her short, bare nails were pale on her tan fingers.
I'd never seen her bite them except her thumb
sometimes when she was nervous. She had hangnails
and golden hair on her knuckles and more freckles.

"Don't you normally work today?" I asked,
changing the subject for my own sanity.

She chewed her bottom lip, bringing her hand
back to her side. "I ditched. Val says you don't work
on your birthday."

If it were anyone else, I would've laughed and
told them to suck it up. Lake not working on her
birthday made me happy, though. Part of me didn't
even like the idea of her working at all. She should
just have fun, shop with her friends, ride bikes along

the beach, at least until college started. "So you're getting into trouble instead."

She smiled a little. "What trouble? I'm just talking to you."

"Exactly."

"Maybe you're the one getting into trouble," she said.

I tried to enjoy the way she blushed as she flirted with me. The way the color of her eyes deepened. But a thought nagged the back of mind. Fun as it sounded, I could never get into trouble with her. Not even little things, like sneaking in somewhere we shouldn't be or getting caught drinking on the beach or taking off for a weekend in Vegas. All things she should be able to do. Being on parole meant playing by the rules and staying within state lines. I couldn't go far away with her. I couldn't soar.

Which would mean she couldn't, either.

"Tiffany mentioned that you applied somewhere other than USC," I said.

"Oh. Yeah. It's supposed to be a secret so my dad doesn't find out."

Pissed me off how she wouldn't even entertain other options because of her dad. He should've been encouraging her to look at lots of school for a decision as big as this, but instead he'd just packed on more and more pressure. "So where is it, this mysterious school?"

"Doesn't matter," she said. "I'm a Trojan now, that's that."

"Yeah? You never even considered this other place?"

"Why should I?" Her blue eyes shimmered like the ocean's surface on a sunny day. "Everything I want is here."

The look on her face said everything her words couldn't. I was what she wanted. I was here. It should've made me happy, but instead, it sobered me. The last thing I wanted was for her to make such huge decisions based on me. That made me no better than her dad. If I had anything to do with her choice to stay, especially after the way she'd broken down at the restaurant, it told me all I needed to know—she might've been eighteen, but she still wasn't making decisions as a grownup.

Lake reached around me to touch my hip, and my back went rigid. "What're you doing?" I asked.

"Trying to see what you're reading." She stuck her tongue between her teeth, patting around my back pocket.

"Other side," I said.

She couldn't reach that far, so she had to go around my knees. She slipped a paperback from my back pocket and read the title. "*Tropic of Cancer*.'"

"Not going to find that on your reading list," I said.

"Why not?"

"It's, uh . . . not suitable for high schoolers."

She bent back the flimsy cover with her thumb and flipped through the pages. After a few seconds, she looked up, scanning my face. "You're still having nightmares."

I tensed instinctively. Images I fought during the daytime flashed across my mind. Me, locked in a six-by-nine cell for eternity. Lake being pulled into the black water. Madison alone in a room with my father. Lake alone with my father. Sometimes I was in the room, too, stuck in a chair I couldn't get up from.

I could never give Lake those images. "No, not really," I said.

"Well, then something's keeping you up at night. You have these . . ." She reached up to touch my face. "Dark circles . . ."

When I noticed Lake's friends wheeling back toward us, I pulled my head away, and Lake dropped her hand. Val skated in the middle, eating a frozen banana and flanked by the other two. She stuck a foot on the sidewalk and gracefully flipped up her board. Like little green magnets, her eyes went directly to the cigarette behind my ear. "Can I bum one?" she asked me.

"No."

"I'll pay you for it. For a pack, even." With hardly a look, she tossed her banana into a trashcan a few feet away. "I'm not old enough to buy them yet."

"Don't bother," Lake said, her lips curling into a mischievous smile. "He'll never give in."

I narrowed my eyes at her ribbing. "Excuse me for trying to keep you girls pure."

"What's that?" Val asked, taking the book from Lake.

"It's Manning's."

Val flipped it over, reading the back cover. "Holy contributing to the delinquency of minors!"

My chest rumbled with an unexpected laugh. "Did you just quote Robin from the *Batman* series?"

"Yes, and you get points for noticing. It says this book was originally banned in the U.S. for being obscene. Is it like a sex book?"

The other girls went wide eyed. "No," I said, "but it's pretty graphic."

"How?" Lake asked.

To hell with it. She was eighteen now. "Lots of drinking, women, prostitution, and, ah, misogynistic language. Miller supposedly took a lot of it from real life."

"Ew." That was the gawker. She leaned over Val's shoulder. "Henry Miller. Remind me not to read any of his books."

"How come?" I asked.

She looked stunned I'd spoken to her. In her stupor, she fumbled her words. "Because he—well, prostitution? That's gross. His life was so obscene that the book was banned?" she asked. "Why would I, you know, support that kind of man?"

That kind of man. Being around Lake always made me feel like *that kind of man*, like I might lose control and corrupt her at any turn.

"You have a point, Mona," Val said, "but what do you think, Lake?" Val suddenly looked interested in my reaction. I didn't quite understand their dynamic, Lake and Val. It felt a little too familiar, or, familial.

"I . . . I think I disagree," Lake said.

"Why?" Val asked.

I watched the two of them like a tennis game. Lake furrowed her brows at the gawker. "What does his personal life have to do with his work? A good book is a good book."

"But are you then condoning his bad behavior by supporting his work?" Val asked. "If he's demeaning to women, like Manning said, how does that make you feel as a woman?"

"It doesn't bother me," Lake said. "I don't think it lessens his contribution to the literary world."

Val seemed to have come to that conclusion on her own, but she was pushing Lake to have an opinion. Maybe she wasn't so bad.

Lake looked to me, as if for approval. "I feel the same," I said. "An author's morals, or the morality of the characters for that matter, isn't a reason not to appreciate a well-told story."

Lake's shoulders pulled back. "Yeah. That's what I was trying to say."

"You said it," Val told her with a smile. "Anyway, we should get going."

"Already?" Lake asked, a little breathlessly, turning to me as if I were the one breaking up the party. "Can't you . . . we . . ."

"Go on," I said. "Have fun."

Val kicked up her skateboard, and the other girls got their bikes. "We still have lots of birthday festivities to partake in," Val called, rolling away.

I stepped down from the truck, took Lake's bike in my hand by the frame, and carried it back to the sidewalk. I flipped out the kickstand and squatted to reset the chain.

Lake came and stood on the opposite side, putting me face to face with the frayed ends of her denim shorts, her bony knees.

I lowered my eyes back to the chain. It was a quick fix, but it took me longer than it should, her proximity distracting me. "Try that," I said when it was secure.

She put one leg over the seat and rolled the pedals as far as they'd go with the kickstand up. "I think it's good."

I stared at some dried blood on the inside of her ankle. She must've scraped it when her foot slipped. I wet my thumb and rubbed it away, leaving a faint grease smudge on her skin in the likeness of a bruise. Goosebumps rose on her calves. It was all I could do not to slide my hand up and pull the soft-looking inside of her knee to my mouth.

I kept her ankle in my hand but didn't look at her. If half the ache I felt in my chest showed on my face, I couldn't trust that she wouldn't notice. And she couldn't notice. She needed to go on with her day, with her life, and not worry about leaving me behind.

My eyes caught on an anklet on her other leg—a brown, orange, and green wax band. The bracelet she'd made at camp, then given me to help me quit smoking. The one the guards had taken away with all my other personal effects. *My* bracelet.

"I'm keeping it for you," she said. "For when you're ready to quit again."

She didn't know I was in too deep to quit. Maybe there'd been a time when I could have, but smoking was a part of me now, an organ that growled when it wasn't fed on schedule. As I stood, she followed me with her eyes, tilting back her head when I hit my full height. Her lips were dry and parted as if she'd forgotten to do anything but watch me. I forgot everything, too, except what was right in front of me. The elegant slope of her freckled nose that ended in a cute but sharp button. The hidden dimple that would appear with even a hint of a smile. That cobalt blue that ate her pupils in the direct sun. She bit her lip, and I imagined reaching up and taking that pout for myself. Between my fingers, in my mouth, my tongue tracing the lines of her lips to each corner and back. My cock throbbing as I opened her up with my fingers until she was gaping and gasping and waiting for the one thing I'd always wanted to give her.

One minute she was my innocent little girl, and overnight she started to change. You don't know what it's like to watch a girl become a woman.

Bile rose up my throat with my dad's disgusting words, his self-righteous justification for the pain he'd inflicted.

I looked from Lake's mouth to her eyes. Hope radiated from her, some kind of sweet, gentle plea for me to see her while my mind had gone straight to the gutter. She'd been eighteen less than a day. I was no better than my dad. I knew it like I knew my own hands—if I gave in, I would ruin her and everything I loved and cherished about her.

I took the cigarette from behind my ear. Knowing it was my way of telling her to go, Lake's eyes darkened with hurt. My entire self responded, the need to take her pain away primal and strong.

Footsteps shuffled up behind us. "Wasn't them," Gary said. "How much longer you want to wait?"

The spell between Lake and me broke. "Happy birthday," I told her.

She swallowed, looking like she wanted to speak, but she just got on her bike. With a final glance at me from under her lashes, she left.

I returned to the bed of the truck to wait with Gary.

"Did I tell you Lydia thinks she's moving in with me?" he asked.

I raised my eyebrows at him. "Why's she think that?"

"Because I didn't say no."

"Huh. Congrats." I leaned my elbows on my thighs and watched the water. "Tiffany and I just had a similar conversation."

"How'd that go?"

"She brought up marriage already, man. You were right."

"I'm not surprised." He raised his sunglasses, appreciating a barreling surfer with a low-whistle. "What'd you say?"

"I . . . I didn't say anything." I opened my hands. "My parents had this bad marriage, and I never really thought I'd want that."

"What was bad about it?"

"They fought all the time. He was a piece of shit, but she'd forgive him, and then it would start all over."

"From what I've seen, it's the opposite for you and Tiffany. Maybe this is your chance to break the cycle."

I looked back at him. "What cycle?"

"Remember what I said about parents passing on their bad habits?" He pulled his feet up onto the tailgate to sit cross-legged. "Let me ask you something. Are you a piece of shit?"

I laughed a little, but he didn't. Was I? At times, I'd thought so. Like now, for instance—I wasn't sure if I loved Tiffany, but here I was, talking about marrying her. Maybe I owed it to her to walk away, knowing I could never love her completely, but I'd be good to her. I'd step up to the plate and eventually, I'd be able to take care of her. I'd find a way to love her as much as I was capable. Did that make me a piece of shit? "Sometimes I'm not sure."

"The answer to that was supposed to be no. And do you think Tiffany would let you get away with treating her like shit? You think she'd turn around and forgive you just like that?"

I had to smile. Based on the attitude I'd seen Tiffany give her dad, she wouldn't put up with that from a partner. "More like she'd remind me how many other men were lined up to treat her well."

He chuckled. "Exactly. You know how I felt in the beginning. I didn't understand your interest in her. But I think you saw something the rest of us didn't, and what's more . . . now I see it. You brought that out in her."

Just like my conversation with Tiffany last month, I got a sense of pride thinking I'd helped her. I'd improved her life. I'd done good.

There were things I wanted from the depths of my soul, but I understood how loving something too much could do irreparable damage. Because whether I wanted to or not, I did love Lake. Like my cigarette craving, it lived in me. I couldn't cut that cancer out, couldn't quit this addiction. It would've been easier to swim across the ocean.

Since the age of fifteen, I'd wanted to put on a uniform and stand up for those who couldn't for themselves the way Henry had for me. I'd lost my family, so instead, I'd decided to lead a fulfilling life protecting other people. I thought that opportunity had been taken away with my felony charge, but perhaps it hadn't. Maybe I could still make a difference, and maybe there was a way I could have both things.

I could help the ones I loved, and I could have a family of my own.

18
MANNING

Tiffany stood in Gary's doorway with her purse at her side. It must've looked to her as though I was living the life. At four in the afternoon, Gary and I were spread out in the living room, my arms and legs hanging off the couch, Gary slumped in a neon yellow beanbag while he strummed a guitar. On the coffee table sat a bong, an open pizza box, and a dozen empty beer bottles. Gary had muted the TV on *The Ren & Stimpy Show*, and Beastie Boys' *Licensed to Ill* had been on repeat for two hours.

Tiffany crossed her arms and surveyed the scene. "So this is what you've been doing all day?" she asked. "Getting high and eating pizza?"

"I'm not high," I said. "But I *am* eating pizza."

Gary giggled. "I don't know why I'm laughing," he said. "He really didn't smoke."

"We made another sale today," I told her. After moving our coffee table into its new owner's house this afternoon, a neighbor of his had asked for an armoire. I hadn't been sure what the fuck that was, but I'd said yes right away. I needed the money. "We've been working on it all afternoon."

"Oh."

"Can I get you something to drink, Tiff?" Gary asked.

"You've been smoking for an hour straight," I told him. "I don't think you could move if you tried."

It was clear Gary wasn't planning on doing even that. I got up from the couch. "Thanks for coming to get me."

She shifted feet. "Sure. Can I see the new piece?"

"Not much to see, but sure." I took Tiffany to Gary's small backyard. The tarp he and I had laid out covered the whole patch of grass. "Don't step on this," I said, bending over to fold back the corners. "There are nails and shit."

She looked over the large box we'd moved against the fence. "You already did all that?"

"It wasn't too hard. The devil's in the details." I winked at her, piling wood off to one side of the lawn. When she didn't smile, I asked, "How was work?"

"Fine."

"You in a mood or what?"

276

"I don't know."

I topped a can of stain. "What's wrong, babe?"

"They filled that assistant manager job I told you about."

"Ah. Damn." I pulled Gary's work bench up and sat, my elbows on my knees. "Come here. Sit."

"It's dirty."

Tiffany hadn't been born in makeup and heels. She'd built those things up around herself for a reason. She was, surprisingly, more fragile than Lake. When we went out to eat, she'd flirt with male waiters and bartenders. Not to upset me, but because it was the only way she knew how to communicate with men. This kind of stuff, this no-bullshit face to face, was harder for her.

I patted my lap. "Then sit on me."

I was dirty, too, but she perched on my knee. I took her little black purse out of her hands to stop her from fidgeting with it and set it on the ground.

"That's Prada," she said.

"Don't know what Prada is and don't care. It's a fucking purse."

She rolled her eyes but smiled, put an arm around my neck, and kissed my cheek. She wasn't ever afraid to just touch me. Sometimes it annoyed me, sometimes it was welcome, but if she felt it, she did it, and I liked that. She smelled like a field of flowers after I'd spent too much time around paint cans, pot, and freshly sawed wood.

"There'll be other opportunities," I said.

"I know, but . . . it just sucks to keep getting passed up."

"So how about that community college application that's been sitting on the counter for a month?"

"It might be too late for fall semester," she said. "I think I missed the deadline."

"I'll help you," I said. "We'll get the application in somehow if that's what you want. Is it?"

"I don't know. Maybe I should focus more on the modeling. I know it's been a while since I got anything, but it's because I've let Nordstrom get in the way." She played with the collar of my t-shirt. "I mean, if I start school on top of work, I'll barely have any free time. What if my agent wants me to run to a go-see and I miss the call because I'm in class?"

I rubbed my forehead. Sometimes, I was certain, she was sabotaging herself. She wanted to be the victim so her dad would come in and save her. No matter what success she found, it'd probably never be enough for him, so why not do the opposite? "If you want it, Tiff, you have to be the one to make it work."

"I don't know if I do."

"That's fine, but that goes for modeling, too. You can't just sit back and hope. You have to do the work, or you have to be okay knowing it's going to take you longer to work your way up at the store, or modeling, or whatever. There might be some positions you can't get without a degree."

She kept her eyes down. "Maybe I'm not cut out for school, though."

"College isn't like high school. You get to learn about stuff you actually care about. Hell, you could go to fashion school and make your own damn Prado bag if you want."

That got me a smile. "It's Prad*a*."

"Whatever."

She made a face. "Crap. To top it all off, we have Lake's birthday dinner tonight. I wanted to have good news to share, but I don't."

"Doesn't mean we can't have a good time," I said, and I meant it. Oddly, I'd come to look forward to dinner with her parents, and not just because it meant I got to see Lake. I always loved Cathy's cooking. I enjoyed Tiffany and Lake's bickering-turned-giggling. I didn't even mind Charles treating me like a stranger in his home. I was part of a family, and after years of feeling as if I'd go through this life alone, it surprised me that I actually wanted that.

"My dad will want to talk to you, by the way," she said.

"How come?"

"His company has a big construction project in Irvine, and he knows some guy in charge. He thinks he can get you on the job. It's all above board, and it pays well, so it's competitive, but my dad has pull."

I sat back a little. "Why would he do that?"

"Because I asked him to."

I shook my head. "He's given us enough. I don't need him to find my work for me."

"Yes, you do, Manning. After what happened . . ." She took a breath. "The odds are stacked against you, and it wasn't even your fault. You deserve a chance."

I rubbed my temples with one hand. I hated this. I wanted to work, and I was a good employee. It shouldn't be this hard for me. What kind of man did it make me to keep taking help from my girlfriend's dad? What kind of man couldn't provide for just the two of us? Then again, would a good man turn down an opportunity that could benefit both me and Tiffany out of pride?

"How long is the job?" I asked.

"All summer. Then maybe you can use that to get other jobs."

In the career department, my parole officer helped where he could, but he was overloaded. He'd tell me to take the job. I looked up at the sky, exhaling through my nose. "I don't need your dad to get it for me. I'll go myself and talk to the foreman."

"They've already hired everyone. You can't just go and ask." She ran her fingers along my hairline, behind my ear. "Just talk to him tonight. You don't have to commit to anything." She pulled fuzz or something from my stubble. "I mean, it kind of depends on what we're doing. Obviously, I don't think you should work for my dad if . . ."

"If?"

"If you and I decide to break up."

"Break up?" I asked. "Why would we?"

"I love you, Manning, I'm just not sure . . . I mean, if you're not interested in having more with me, then what are we doing?"

"More," I repeated.

"Have you given it anymore thought since we talked last month? The whole marriage thing?"

I swallowed. "Yeah, I have."

"And?"

And the more I thought about it, the more the idea grew on me. Tiffany and I were on a good path. The more comfortable she got around me, the more she opened up. The more she laughed and made me laugh. In the bedroom, I didn't have to hold back with her. She and I didn't have the explosive chemistry people wrote novels about, but I didn't want that. Not even a little. I wasn't ready to say goodbye to Tiffany or to her family. "I think we should do it," I said. "I don't mean right now or anything, but I want to be with you. I don't want to break up."

She pecked me on the lips, then wiped away the lip gloss she'd left behind. "Me neither, but if we're talking marriage, there is one thing I think you should know." Her shoulders curled forward a little. "The morning after Lake's prom, you know how I brought up the night at camp when she got in your truck . . ."

I tensed instinctively but forced myself to relax, hoping she hadn't noticed the pull of my muscles. "Yeah. What about it?"

"I never apologized for lashing out at you. It's not your fault Lake has a crush on you. It bothered me that you even let her in, but it's not because of her or even you."

My mind worked to keep up. The way she said I'd let Lake get in the truck made me wonder how detailed Lake had gotten about that night. "I told you, it was innocent," I said. "A drive, that's all."

"I know. It doesn't—it's not what I want to talk about. It's more about my dad."

I furrowed my brows. "Your *dad*?"

She took a slow, deep breath, as if working up her courage. "He had an affair."

I blinked once at her. Charles had cheated on Cathy . . . it took a moment to sink in, but it didn't shock me. I was more surprised Tiffany hadn't mentioned it before. "Are you sure?"

"When I was in middle school. I missed the bus one afternoon, so I walked to my dad's work. Sometimes he'd let me sit and do homework until he was finished and we'd drive home for dinner." She picked at nothing on the hem of her dress. "Anyway, this time I walked in on him having sex with his secretary."

I ducked my head to catch her gaze. "Why didn't you ever tell me?"

She shook her head. "I hate thinking about it. I hate *knowing* it. I wish I'd never seen it."

"What did he say?"

"He didn't see me. I just left and found another way home."

It explained so many of their issues. "You've kept it to yourself all this time?"

She looked away. "No. I was really confused. After a few days, I couldn't hold it in anymore. I broke down in tears and told my mom."

"And?"

"I thought she'd be shocked. She was, a little, but she covered it up quickly. She said men did that sometimes. That it took a lot to make a marriage work and that she and my dad had built a life over many years. Dad wouldn't let some secretary destroy that."

It didn't take much for me to put the pieces together. I pretty much knew all Tiffany's insecurities linked back to her dad, but I'd figured it was because he'd ignored her so long, pinning all his hopes and dreams on her sister. I hadn't suspected there was more to it. "Not all men 'do that sometimes,'" I told her.

"My mom just let him get away with it. All she did was start dressing in more expensive clothes, ask for a new car, and get her real estate license. He'd never let her get a job until then. She started taking me shopping a lot after that, like it was some kind of consolation. For me or for her, I don't know."

It sounded to me as if Cathy hadn't let Charles get away with it at all. Instead of putting a stop to it, she'd used it as leverage against him. No wonder Tiffany had issues with her dad and with money. As a pre-teen, Tiffany had learned that material things meant more than a healthy marriage. More than love. It hit me suddenly that Lake would've been just as young, just as impressionable when this had happened. "What about Lake?"

"She doesn't know. I thought about telling her so many times, just to have someone to talk to, but . . . I didn't want her to feel as bad as I did."

I put my arms around Tiffany's waist and hugged her closer for her selflessness. She'd saved her sister in many ways, even though it hurt her to keep it inside. It reaffirmed the many things I'd known to be true about Tiffany—she cared about her sister, about her family, and wanted to be good to them. She didn't always show it in the right ways, but maybe that was something I could help with. "Well, I'm not your dad . . . I think we've established that."

She smiled a little. "I know. I've just been wanting to tell someone for a long time, and my friends would just treat it like gossip. I wanted you to know, because, well, if we're getting married, it's kind of important. Cheating, and stuff."

"It's very important," I said, readjusting her on my thigh. "And it's wrong. I know that, Tiffany." There were enough ways to hurt people in the world, physically and emotionally. Some of it was intentional, like abuse. Some of it wasn't, like how Charles pressured Lake or ignored Tiffany. "That's not the man I am, and it's not the man I want to be."

I didn't know exactly the kind of man I wanted to be, but I did know it was the opposite of my dad. And apparently, Tiffany's, too.

19

LAKE

June had been a month to celebrate. My birthday had barely passed before senior class events and graduation parties began.

At the house, streamers hung everywhere, tied off with balloons. Red and gold for my new school, blue and gray for my old. Mom had transformed the backyard into a *fiesta* with cloth-covered tables and a catered buffet of Mexican food fit for royals. Members of her family and Dad's had driven in for my graduation ceremony, and I was being passed around like a hot potato, forced to answer the same questions over and over:

Was I excited for USC?

What would I major in?

Had I met my roommate?

A table by the door had been filled with presents, including stacks of envelopes I was pretty sure contained money. The sun lowered over our house as everyone under the age of twelve splashed in the pool. Vickie and Mona nibbled on taquitos. Val had been trying to sneak a margarita for twenty minutes while her mom flirted with dads.

I ducked into the kitchen and found Manning opening and closing cupboards. He'd attended my graduation ceremony with Tiffany in the morning, but we hadn't been alone together since my birthday on the beach a couple weeks earlier. "Hey."

He glanced over his shoulder. "I've been sent by your mom to find Tupperware so Clancy Stevens can take *frijoles* to go."

It was likely the most domesticated thing to have ever left Manning's mouth. I grinned ear to ear and held up the empty bowl I'd grabbed on my way in. "I'm refilling chips."

"Doesn't the caterer do that?"

"I needed a few minutes of refuge."

He opened another cupboard. "Keeping you busy, huh?"

I leaned my stomach on the island and set my chin in my hand, watching him. "You won't find them in there."

He paused, picked a gold-rimmed, leaf-patterned plate out of the cupboard and turned to show it to me. "Guest dishes."

Those two words were enough to send my imagination spinning into the future. Once, before he'd gone away, we'd talked about guest plates and the kind of wife he pictured for himself. Even with Tiffany yards away, I saw myself in Manning's kitchen, experimenting with new meals every day, made with love for him. That had to mean something. Tiffany would understand eventually, once she saw how right we were together. She would be mad, but she couldn't deny the unshakeable truth about Manning and me—this story was ours.

Maybe reading my mind, Manning put the dish away and turned to me. "Did you say hi to your sister?"

"I think we're in opposite rotations. I haven't talked to her, but she keeps scowling at me."

A caterer passed through the kitchen, fixing her cuff. She did a double take at Manning and stopped. I didn't blame her. In a short-sleeved black t-shirt, the way he'd crossed his arms over his chest, his biceps were front and center. "Anything I can help you find, sir?"

"Tup—"

I stood up straight. "We're fine."

She looked startled by my presence, then nodded and continued outside.

"Take it easy on her, all right?" Manning said. "This isn't easy for her."

"The caterer?" I asked.

"Tiffany."

"Oh. You mean because one day of the year isn't about her?"

He jutted his chin at me. "The past year has been about *this*, Lake. This party, your future. Your sister feels invisible."

"Tiffany, invisible?" I laughed. "Do you hear how ridiculous that sounds?"

He didn't even smile. He was seriously defending Tiffany to me.

"Whatever," I said, turning to hide my disappointment. This must've been how Tiffany had felt when Manning had scolded her at the Fun Zone. I didn't like it. I went to the pantry, grabbed a bag of chips, tore it open, and paused. My ears heated with my frustration. I whirled back to him. "It's not like I asked for all this," I said. "She hasn't even congratulated me once."

He glanced out the sliding glass door. "I'll talk to her, but it'd be good if you made more of an effort."

I went over to a cupboard. "Here." On my tiptoes, I tried to grab for plastic on the top shelf, but I couldn't reach. "You don't want to keep Clancy waiting."

Manning came up behind me, gently pressing his hips against me as he easily nabbed a container.

He was close. So close. His heat at my back melted my anger. I knew at any moment, he could take it away, so I asked, "How many?"

"How many what?" he asked, his voice low.

"Containers?" My throat sounded as dry as it felt. "Clancy looks like he eats a lot . . ."

"Not sure, but I can't reach any more. You'll have to move."

Move? I couldn't. I didn't even blink. I'd barely been in his presence ten seconds. I couldn't take it, catching a moment alone with him here and there, once every few weeks, *months* even. I wanted to soak this in. Manning stayed there, too. There was so much I wanted to know, so much to ask, but before I could, he put his hands on my hips. "Sorry, Birdy," he murmured, squeezing me gently before moving me out of the way himself.

He took down a stack of tubs and lids, and we turned at the same moment to find my dad across the island, looking at us.

"Lake, we need you outside," Dad said.

"I'll be right there."

"Now." His tone startled me. He'd been on cloud nine since the night of my honor roll ceremony, buying me USC gear and embarrassingly expensive electronics for my dorm, telling me how proud he was at every turn. After graduation, we'd all driven home for the party and found a black Range Rover in the driveway with a bow on top.

"Manning," Dad said as I slinked away, "let's you and me have a word when the party dies down. About the job."

"Yes, sir."

Job? What job? While trying to keep my eyes and ears on the kitchen, I walked right into a conversation between my aunt, uncle, and Tiffany.

"Fashion design, maybe," Tiffany said, beaming. "Or business. You can never go wrong with a business degree—"

"There you are, Lake." My dad's brother, Darryl, was more relaxed than my dad. He and my Aunt Roberta had driven down from Northern California just to watch me graduate.

My aunt wore silver bangles that chimed when she put her arm around my shoulder to pull me into the circle. "Look how tall you are. You girls have grown so much in the past couple years. How tall are you now, Lake?"

"Five-eight, I think."

"My word," Uncle Darryl said. "You might have to do some modeling on the side to help with that private tuition."

Tiffany's neck flushed. She was the model in the family, not me—God forbid there were two of us, even though we'd been mistaken last year for Niki and Krissy Taylor. Tiffany had taken it as a sign that *she* was supposed to be a model. Not me, though. "*I'm* almost five-eight, too," Tiffany snipped.

"Is that so?" my aunt asked. "Maybe Lake's legs are a bit longer. She gets that from your grandma."

I could've sworn Tiffany's head ballooned, and not with ego. Just as I braced myself for an explosion, Manning appeared at her side. He whispered something in her ear, and she took a breath. It was the first time in recent history, maybe ever, that Tiffany hadn't let her anger get the better of her and spat out a nasty comment.

My dad walked up and patted his brother's back. "I'm assuming that enormous present you brought Lake is a personal computer. More and more students have them these days."

I blushed at his teasing. "*Dad.*"

"I wish it was, kiddo," my uncle said to me. "If only I didn't have two college tuitions coming my way."

"Any progress with Craig?" Dad asked.

My cousin Craig was sixteen and, to the family's dismay, had his heart set on the military. My peace-loving, Berkeley-alum aunt and uncle couldn't wrap their heads around it, and my dad just all around disapproved of not going to college. "No," Roberta said, "but we've still got a couple years to change his mind."

Dad nodded. "It's a good thing Lake's around to carry on the Trojan line," he said. "I have no idea what I would've done if she hadn't gotten in. None."

Manning put an arm around Tiffany and tried to pull her away. Remembering what he'd said in the kitchen, I began to hear the conversation as she might, more reminders of what she *hadn't* done. But for some reason she glared at *me*, as if I'd orchestrated this whole thing just to embarrass her.

293

My uncle side-eyed my dad. "Give Craig five minutes alone with Charles and he'll bleed Cardinal-red and gold. I swear, Charles could get a Bruin into 'SC."

Manning, seeming to give in to the fact that Tiffany wouldn't budge, said, "Tiffany's headed to college this year, too."

Dad looked over her head and amended, "Community college. Which is fine. It's how I started out as well."

"She was just telling us about it," Roberta said. "And you must be the boyfriend. Madding, was it?"

Manning shook her hand. "It's Man—"

"Actually," Tiffany said, her voice an octave too high. She laced her fingers with his almost aggressively. "Not for much longer, right, babe?"

"Uh." Manning paused, his eyes darting over the ground as if processing her comment. "You mean . . . no, Tiff." He shook his head. "This isn't the time."

"But all of my family's here," she whisper-hissed.

"So, Lake," my uncle started, "where's the first place you plan to drive your new car?"

Manning and Tiffany were locked in a stare down, seeming to have a silent conversation. Something felt off. "Not for much longer what?" I asked.

Manning looked at me. The concern in his expression made my heart sink before Tiffany even spoke. "Manning won't be my *boyfriend* much longer," she said. "He'll be my fiancé!"

I stared at her. We all did. As the word *fiancé* began to take on meaning, I covered my stomach, my gut smarting.

That had to be some inside joke between them I didn't understand, some mistake. But why say it like that? Why say it at all? To be funny? Or get the attention back on her? Did she just want to ruin my party?

It didn't matter. It wasn't true—it couldn't be.

"Your . . . what?" Dad asked. "What's she talking about, Manning?"

Manning looked around the circle, pausing when his eyes met mine. He turned his head as if to look away but couldn't seem to. He swallowed. "Nothing's official, but yes. It's what we've decided."

Decided. It was such a cold, un-Tiffany-like word to describe a marriage. It also left no room for doubt. My throat closed. I was pretty sure I hadn't taken a breath since the conversation had veered into this territory. I tried to inhale, nearly choking, feeling as if hands pressed around my throat.

But I was eighteen now.

Manning and I hadn't even had a chance to talk since my birthday, and there was no end to the things I wanted to say. The things I wanted to hear.

Tiffany held up her left hand, wiggling a bare ring finger. "There are still some *minor* details to work out," she said, her tone light and airy for the first time all night, "but we really feel it's the right next step for us."

My mom walked over to us, her party dress flouncing around her. "What's going on over here?" she asked cheerily. "Why do you all look so glum?"

"Tiffany's just made an . . . announcement," Dad said.

A fly buzzed around the opening of my dad's beer can. It landed on his knuckle. He shooed it, so it tried the aluminum tab, then his shirt cuff, then my uncle's beer before disappearing for a few seconds and starting all over.

Mom took Dad's elbow, and he shifted his beer to his other hand. "What's your news, honey?" she asked.

"Mr. Kaplan," Manning said. "I'd planned to talk to you first—"

I flinched. *I'd planned to talk to you first.* He wasn't denying it. The idiot fly wouldn't quit. It just kept trying to get in the can.

The nightmarish haze of the moment began to lift. He wasn't denying it, because it was true. Manning actually planned to marry my sister, to become a permanent part of my family, and not in the way I'd often dreamed about.

"What's the matter?" Mom asked, her party-smile wavering.

Tiffany looked delighted to have the attention back on her. "Manning and I are engaged to be engaged."

My mom covered her mouth with both hands. "No. Are you serious? You know, I had a feeling. I can't describe it, but the other day, I was reorganizing some photos and I came across the trip to Napa Valley where your father proposed . . ."

My insides flipped as my mom's words began to run together. I was going to spew Mexican food right here, all over the lawn. I looked at my stupid new heels, which I'd bought to make my legs look good, because I'd wanted Manning to notice. The blades of grass under my feet seemed to come alive, squirming like worms, and the fly was back, doing a figure eight around my ankles.

I closed my eyes. One of the things I loved about our backyard was that if you listened hard enough, you could faintly hear the ocean. Waves crashed *that* hard, their impact echoing as far as this. I could almost feel the ground vibrate with the collision of water and sand, but I couldn't hear anything except the *wah-wah* of voices, the squeal and splash of my cousins in the pool, my mother's happiness. Not being able to hear the water made the world feel small, narrowed down to this moment and my inability to breathe. All the while, Manning's eyes were on me—that much I knew, without even looking. It was just the two of us.

How could you do this to me?

I didn't even know what *this* was.

How could you let me find out like this?

How could you have spent the past ten minutes in the kitchen without telling me?

How could you marry her?

How could you marry her?

I couldn't get a breath, my throat now swollen shut. I was an idiot. Either my heels were sinking into the grass, or the ground was giving out. I had to open my eyes to center myself as my balance wavered. My eyes connected with Manning's. They were the cruelest color of brown, even when filled with what looked like regret.

Val, Vickie, Mona and I had gotten our hair and makeup done for today, yet I'd never felt more like a child in an adult's world. Tiffany was saying things like *sweetheart neckline* and *cushion cut* and *something blue* and Manning wasn't stopping her. He just shook my uncle's hand and looked at me. Touched Tiffany's back and looked at me.

A gnat zoomed around my face and I slapped my hands together, smashing its guts on my palms. Somebody had to stop this.

My dad.

With that realization, the ton of bricks on my chest lifted. My dad would *never* let this happen. I turned to see why he'd barely spoken.

His eyes were narrowed on Manning, watching his every move. Each time Manning looked at me, my dad saw. His gaze followed Manning's to me and then went right back. Their back-and-forth made me dizzy. The circle around us had somehow grown and also tightened, *congratulations* flowing. I listed to the side as the dirt gave under my feet.

Manning crossed the circle in one step and caught my arm. "You need air."

"Manning."

With that one terse word from my dad, everyone went quiet. Dad's neck had reddened under his collar as he stared at us. I suddenly felt as if *I* was the one who'd made the announcement. As if *I* was about to endure his wrath, the weight of his disappointment. Manning's hand on my elbow warmed me, bracing me for the explosion about to hit.

When my father's silence had stretched a little too long, the air growing tense, Mom spoke to him softly. "Charles, come inside for a few minutes. I'll make you a drink."

"I have a drink."

He'd make a scene, and Mom knew it. It didn't matter that this party was his idea, or that he was as happy as I could ever remember him being. His temper couldn't be reasoned with. It was just a matter of how badly he'd ream Tiffany out for this. Or me. Or Manning, the way Dad was looking at him.

"What's wrong?" Dad asked me, glancing at Manning's hand.

"She was going to faint," Manning answered.

"I—"

"Come here." Dad opened an arm to me. I didn't want to leave Manning, but it wasn't a request. I went to my dad, and he hugged me to his side a little too hard, almost possessively.

Tiffany broke the silence, her voice timid. "Daddy—"

He held up a hand to her. I waited with bated breath until he inhaled through his nose and announced . . . "I think it's wonderful news.

Tiffany and I exchanged a glance, sisters first, shocked by his response. My dad was the one person I could rely on in this situation. For once, it elated me that he hated Manning. He couldn't stand there and say it was *wonderful*!

"You . . ." Tiffany hesitated. "Wonderful?"

Mom smiled politely at my aunt and uncle. "I'm sorry. I think we just need a moment—"

"That's right," Dad said a little too loudly, raising his beer in the air. "It's wonderful. A graduation and a wedding. What a night. Isn't it, Cathy?"

None of us knew what to do. Manning stepped forward, as if to diffuse the situation. "Sir—"

Dad transferred his beer can to shake Manning's hand. "Congratulations."

"You're happy?" Tiffany asked. The hopefulness in her voice both hurt me and made me hurt for her. She so wanted his attention—good or bad, it didn't matter.

"I am," he said, and then brightened up. "In fact, let me make a call. You remember that friend of mine over at the Ritz? He's the manager there, and he owes me a favor."

Tiffany gasped. "As in the Ritz-*Carlton*?" She squealed so loudly, even the kids yelling in the pool looked over. "On the cliff? Overlooking the *beach*? Are you serious?"

Words and hands flew by me. I couldn't keep up. Dad laughed at Tiffany as she bounced up and down, and a hesitant smile broke through my mom's skepticism.

"Tiffany, hang on." Manning wiped his upper lip with his sleeve and turned to my dad. "Thank you, sir, but the Ritz is—it's the Ritz."

Dad waved his beer but his other arm tightened on my shoulders. "Don't worry about that. It's customary for the bride's parents to pay." He nodded at my mom. "Cathy's father footed the bill for our wedding."

"He did," she agreed. "And don't let Charles try to convince you he protested. He was happy to accept the help."

"Bullshit. I did some protesting, but in the end, I realized it's a father's honor." Dad kissed the side of my head, then held open his other arm to Tiffany. She slipped into his side, looking up at him. "Besides, this is why I work as hard as I do." He locked eyes with Manning. "To see my girls happy."

If he wasn't going to put a stop to this, I had to. But how? I had no claim over Manning, not even a real kiss or a whispered promise. He'd never told me he loved me. I'd based an entire future with him on the things we hadn't said, on looks exchanged and almost-touches. I knew I hadn't imagined it, but I had no evidence of it whatsoever, not even a complete, unwavering certainty that Manning felt the same way I did.

Tiffany glowed. Mom saw it, too, how she and my dad wore matching smiles. My eyes watered. I wanted this for Tiffany, her happiness, my dad's approval. I never tried to steal her attention, because I didn't want it as badly as she did. But I couldn't find the graciousness to celebrate with her tonight. Instead, I wished all of this away—so I could get what I wanted. Did it make me selfish that given the chance right then, I would've taken Manning for myself?

"Hello?" came a familiar voice.

We all turned as Corbin came through the back gate into the yard. "It was unlocked, so I just—"

"Please," Mom said, beckoning him. "Come in. How are you, sweetheart? How's your father?"

Corbin crossed the lawn to us and I'd never been happier to see anyone in my life. I ducked out from under my dad's arm and vaulted myself into the comfort of my best friend with a hanging-on-for-dear-life hug that he answered with a deep laugh. "I appreciate your enthusiasm, Kaplan."

I buried my face in his sunscreen-scented neck. Corbin understood me. He wanted me to be happy. He'd never do anything as awful as fall in love with my sister and announce his engagement to her this way.

"Watch this one," Dad said to Corbin. "You thought she was a handful before? She's really on the loose now."

"You mean the Range Rover out front?" Corbin asked. "It'll be a shame to see such a beautiful car just sit in the driveway."

I turned, keeping Corbin's arm around my shoulders. "I'll get my license, geez," I said, my bad mood clearing a little. "I've just been too stressed the last few months to—" Manning's glare stopped me cold, and it wasn't even aimed at me—just behind me. "—to concentrate."

Corbin squeezed me to him. "Congratulations on today," he said. "You want to grab your friends and we'll head out?"

"Where are you going?" Tiffany asked.

"Bonfire," Corbin answered. "Bunch of people down on the peninsula celebrating graduation."

"Is that legal?" Manning asked.

"All the kids do it," Mom explained before telling us, "Go ahead, you two. No need to hang around with us old folks."

"*I'm* not old," Tiffany said. "And we're celebrating, too, so we should—"

"Will there be drinking?" Manning asked.

Tiffany hooked her elbow in his. "Why don't we go and find out?"

"Yes," Manning said. "Let's."

Tiffany slow-blinked, over exaggerating her surprise. "Really? *You* want to go *out*?"

303

"After we talk," Dad said to Manning, then looked at Corbin and me. "It's nice to see you again, Corbin. You never said how your family is."

"Doing well." His voice, always strong and confident, reverberated against my back. "Looking forward to our annual Hawaii trip."

"And how's NYU?"

"Great. I'm starting an internship on Wall Street next year, actually."

"Wall Street," Dad said enthusiastically. "How about that? Even at my age, that sounds daunting."

"I'm not worried, sir," Corbin said. "Just excited."

"Such ambition, just like Lake." Dad raised his beer can to us. "I can see why she's so smitten with you."

"*Dad*," I said, horrified. I had never once spoken to him about Corbin in a romantic way. My mom, yes, but only to explain there was nothing more than friendship between us. Corbin didn't need any encouragement.

"Sorry, sorry," Dad said, laughing. "I forget what it's like to have a teenage crush." He glanced at Manning. "It can feel like the whole damn world, can't it?"

20
MANNING

Mr. Kaplan's study was even more intimidating than I expected, and Tiffany had warned me about the guns. They sat displayed behind glass, which was too bad. If a man had a real reason to own a Colt .45, he shouldn't keep it pristine and locked up. I figured maybe it was so the girls wouldn't be able to get to them.

Charles came in with a bottle of Booker's and two glasses. "You like guns?" he asked as he went to his desk. "I guess you would since you wanted to be a cop."

I turned to him. "I'm not really supposed to be around them."

"Don't worry, I doubt your parole officer's going to come knocking tonight. Have a seat."

"I'll stand." Since becoming a free man, I didn't move for anyone.

"All right, then." Charles poured our drinks with surprising calm. I took that to be a bad thing. Like maybe he was about to stab me in the back, or in the front, or make me disappear. All because fucking Tiffany couldn't keep her mouth shut. I'd wanted to talk to both Lake and Charles before the topic of marriage ever even came up.

"I'm sorry I didn't come to you," I said. "Truth is, I haven't really wrapped my head around the marriage thing yet. Tiffany and I just started talking about all this a couple weeks ago. I would've asked for your blessing—"

"It's okay." Charles passed me a drink. "I meant what I said. I'm happy about it."

I took a bolstering sip. "With all due respect . . . why?"

He sat at his desk and smiled into his glass as if it were a movie screen playing back the good old days. "You've been good for Tiffany. I wouldn't've believed it if I hadn't seen it with my own eyes."

"I haven't exactly been your favorite person."

"No, and I'm not saying things are automatically erased between us. Do I like the idea of my daughter marrying a felon?" He shook his head. "But Tiffany and Cathy are both pretty convinced that you didn't commit that crime."

I crossed an arm over my chest, swirling my drink. "I didn't. I got screwed, but I did my time like a man, and I'd like if you could find a way to accept that."

He nodded slowly, assessing me. "I can do better than accept it. Do you still want to go to the police academy?"

It wasn't the response I expected. I narrowed my eyes. "Why?"

"I'm sure I can do some digging, see if I have any mutual friends who can help us out."

"I think it's going to take more than a good word to get a felon on the force."

"I'm talking about getting your record expunged."

I leaned in, as if I'd misheard. I'd thought, leaving the gates of prison, the hard part was over. I'd been wrong. I hadn't accounted for the stress of having a felony record. It gave landlords and banks and the general public the right to discriminate against me. It meant three years of checking in with a PO, living in Orange County, and staying within state lines. Charles might as well have placed the most decadent dessert ever made in front of me and handed me a fork. "You can do that? You *would* do that?"

"I appreciate how you've been with Tiffany."

It didn't take much for me to put it together. If you can't beat 'em, join 'em. He knew Tiffany would get what she wanted in the end, and if she wanted me, better she was married to a cop than a construction worker. Compared to Corbin's Wall Street internship, even law enforcement was pitiful. "I appreciate it," I said honestly. "But the truth is, no part of me wants to be involved with the system. I want my record expunged, but not bad enough to be a cop. Not anymore."

He chuckled. "I tried to tell you years ago. They're all rotten."

"I know that isn't true, but more rotten than not. I'm sorry if that changes how you feel about the wedding."

"It doesn't. How do you like construction?"

"It's what I know, and since prison threw me into some unfamiliar areas, I gained skills it would've taken me much longer to master outside."

He slid his heavy glass back and forth over his desk, the sound like a saw on wood. "So you plan to work your way up."

"Given the opportunity, yes. I know I can manage a crew, it's just a matter of getting there."

"Good." He nodded slowly. "I like to hear that."

It made no sense that he considered construction a suitable job choice. If this wasn't about making me into a more presentable son-in-law, then what? "So you're still on board with a wedding?"

"On board?" he asked. "I'm manning the ship. I'm going to put in the phone call tonight and book my baby the first available date."

"I think maybe we're getting ahead of ourselves," I said. "I'd like to be a little more stable before making a commitment like this. The timing just isn't right."

"It's the Ritz, Manning. The timing will be right, whatever they say. You don't want to disappoint Tiffany, do you?"

"No, but I don't see the reason for the rush."

"I never said there was a rush, but you know Tiffany. She's impatient." He finished off his drink and set the glass on the sturdy wood surface of his desk. "How would you feel about a summer wedding?"

"I feel summer is soon. Summer is *now*."

"When you know, you know, right? Like I said, I just want Tiffany to be happy."

The way he said *Tiffany* snagged my attention. As if he were clarifying something. "So do I, but like *I* said, it's not the right time." I couldn't help but think of Lake right then. Once she was off to college, she'd have so much going on, I wouldn't occupy a thought in her head. Then, maybe, it'd be the right time to go through with this. Once she'd moved on. "I haven't even proposed."

"Tiffany, like her mother, has expensive taste," he said. "It's probably my fault, and I'm sorry for that."

"She knows who she's marrying."

"I can help with that, too." He adjusted his watch. "The ring. She doesn't need to know."

309

"The wedding will be enough," I said. "Tiffany will have to make do with the ring I can afford."

"Very well. You can always add to it over the years like I have for Cathy. No need to let that get in the way of the wedding."

For some reason, he wasn't hearing me. "I'm not ready," I said.

"Why not?" He stood, coming around the desk to his bar cart. "Are you having second thoughts?" he asked, refilling his drink.

"No." As difficult as it'd been to watch Lake process the news of the engagement, a part of me couldn't help noticing how proud, how happy Tiffany was to make the announcement. Over the last couple weeks, she'd slowly been slipping in comments and details about weddings. Apparently, she'd been dreaming up ideas since childhood. I supposed that was normal for young girls, though I couldn't remember any of that with Maddy.

"Good. Once everything's settled, we'll get the details of your record sorted." He came back to the desk but didn't sit. "Maybe I can even find you a position at my company with a salary you'd be hard-pressed to get without a degree."

Finally, I sat, setting my glass on the edge of the desk and almost missing the lip completely. I steadied the drink, my mind spinning. It was no small thing, what Charles was offering—a fresh start. "Thank you," I said carefully, because I didn't know if I should be grateful or wary. "I'm happy with what I have, though."

"Well, if you change your mind, the job will be there," he said and winked. "Of course, I can't promise *I* won't change *mine*."

Now, he was speaking a language I understood. An unsubtle threat to take it all away. At times, all of this felt unreal, as if I'd ended up here by accident. I didn't belong in this world, and maybe Tiffany would realize it. Lake, too, if she didn't already. Tiffany had a tendency to self-destruct, and I didn't want that. I wanted to give her not just the wedding she'd dreamed about, but a good life, too. Maybe Charles could take that away from us. He certainly held power over Tiffany. I wasn't sure, but if I'd already decided to marry Tiffany, then I guessed there wasn't any reason to put it off if he was offering us things we both wanted to go through with it now. A wedding for her, and a fresh start for me.

"So what do you say, Manning?" He held up his glass to cheers.

Maybe if I hadn't had my pride stripped down every day since those officers had walked onto campgrounds and pointed a finger at me, I could've done better for myself. Maybe if Charles weren't making it so damn easy to get my life back on track, I could walk out on principle. Maybe if this was his other daughter, I'd have the will to fight him harder, to build her a life with my bare hands instead of taking the easy way out.

I stood. Clinking my glass with his felt like making a deal with the devil, and with his next comment, I understood why.

"Lake and that Swenson boy make a nice couple, don't they?" he asked.

I turned the comment over in my mind. It came out of nowhere, and yet, his timing was studied. That was what all this had been about. As long as I was married to Tiffany, I was off limits to everyone else—especially her sister. Whatever he'd seen when he'd walked into the kitchen tonight, I had a feeling it wasn't the first time he'd noticed it. I wasn't very good at paying attention to anything else when Lake was in the room, and she was hopeless at it. Maybe all the time Lake and I had been watching each other, Charles'd been watching us. And if he had, he'd no doubt know Lake thought she was in love with me.

It was shady, and I might've called him on it if I didn't accept why he was doing it. He didn't know he had no reason to worry. Nobody understood better than me that the Prince of England wasn't good enough for Lake, let alone me.

To make it clear that I got it, I said, "I care about Tiffany a great deal." I did care for her. I'd have to reach deep to find a love for Tiffany that I knew would be good for both of us. She didn't make my heart pound the way it did around Lake, but I was thankful for that. I didn't want that kind of all-consuming passion. I needed constant. Steady. Sturdy. Tiffany wouldn't get under my skin or bring out the worst in me, and when she tried, I would hold strong and show her the best in *herself*.

"She loves you, too," Charles mused. "I've never seen her blossom this way with anyone, not even under my guidance. I couldn't have predicted it, but there it is." He sipped his drink. "My girls really are growing up. It's not exactly how I imagined, but to tell you the truth . . . everything feels just as it should."

21
LAKE

A cool breeze came off the ocean, but the fire warmed my shins. Bundled into my sweater, I watched Corbin, his brother, and Val knock a Hacky sack around with their sneakers. It was about dark now and hard to keep track of the sack. Val had smoked half a blunt and kept missing it altogether. Anytime they got too close to the fire, I tensed.

Val had hijacked the boom box someone'd brought with one of her infamous mixed CDs. "Fade Into You" set a dreamy, romantic scene, stoking the embers of my heartache. It was as if I'd been walking through mud and fog since Tiffany's announcement. I held my heels by their straps, my bare feet heavy in the sand. I couldn't quite remember the words she'd used or her expression as she'd said them. If there'd been a tremor of uncertainty in her voice, if she'd checked Dad's expression at any point. Did it matter? There was the Ritz, and Dad's approval, and Manning's consent, and I knew without a doubt, Tiffany would never let those things go.

So I had to.

A future I'd known so surely to be true began to slip away.

I startled when the Hacky sack hit my calf. I set down my shoes to pick it up, catching sight of the friendship bracelet around my ankle. I'd made it for Manning with love, and he didn't even want it. What was I holding on to it for? I loosened it to work it off my foot.

"You're supposed to send it back," Corbin called.

I glanced up. The three of them waited. I abandoned the anklet and kicked the Hacky sack in their direction, but it landed in the fire.

"*Lake*," the three of them cried.

"Sorry. I'm sorry."

Corbin shook his head like I was the most adorable thing. He trudged over to where I stood, creaked open the lid of the blue cooler, and held out a beer. "You might as well since I can't," he said.

"Why can't you?" I asked.

"Jesus, Lake. I'm driving you home. When have I ever taken a sip of anything with you in my car?"

Corbin. Why did he have to be such a gentleman, even when my mind was so wrapped up in someone else? I owed him more than I gave him. "Go ahead," I told him. "I'll drive us."

"Then you should definitely drink. It'll be an improvement."

Val laughed, but I wasn't in the mood to even force a polite smile. I didn't feel like being here. I wanted to return to Manning, even if being around him was like sticking a finger in an open wound.

Corbin kissed my temple. "I'm sorry. I was only kidding. I'm sure it's totally normal to sideswipe stationary objects two out of two lessons."

That was only because Corbin had me laugh with impressions of Screech from *Saved by the Bell.* "You were distracting me."

"Was I?" He slid his hand over my backside and squeezed. Just like prom night, my knees buckled, my breath caught. "It's like pressing a button," he whispered in my ear.

I hated how my body reacted to him, but at least I knew my pleasure wouldn't always be bound to a man I couldn't have.

"Why don't you two just get married already?" Vickie asked.

Corbin dropped to one knee, looking up at me. "Marry me, Kaplan. Would you? I promise to make you real happy. At least twice a night."

Everyone laughed. I even smiled. God, if anyone could pull me out of a funk, it was Corbin. If only love was as easy as that.

But it wasn't. I looked over Corbin's head at some movement in the distance, squinting into the dark at the big, shadowy figure headed our way from the parking lot. *Manning.* The man who, hours earlier, had joked with me about guest plates and then stood silently by while my heart broke. Everything that'd happened the last couple hours sat dangerously close to the surface. I didn't know how I'd say all the things I needed to, but I'd never be able to stand here with him and pretend everything was normal.

I went around Corbin to meet Manning, to stop him from coming over here and making me look even more stupid. My nose tingled, words like *betrayal* and *how could you* and *stop this* bubbling up my throat as I pushed a few steps through the sand . . . and stopped where I was. Tiffany was on his back, waving at us. He touched her, carried her, kissed her, committed to a *life* with her and left nothing for me. It should've been me. I wanted it to be me so badly. Their playfulness shattered something in me, and I hiccupped, jolting some tears onto my cheeks.

A hand on my elbow pulled at me. "Lake," Val said, tugging me back. "Come on, Lake."

"No."

"Come on. Come here."

My body shook, my chest rattling. Val pulled me hard, away from the fire, away from everyone. "What

. . . is it?" I couldn't speak. It took everything I had not to burst into tears. "What do you want?"

"It's him, isn't it?" Val asked. "He's the one. Your sister's boyfriend."

I shook my head hard. "No. He's not."

She wrapped me in a hug and squeezed me so hard, some of my tears splashed onto her shoulder. "I see it so clearly now. You should've told me."

"You would've thought I was awful."

"No way." She swayed us back and forth. "You're my best friend. My right to judge you was automatically revoked when you earned that title."

Relief filtered through me. Finally, somebody knew, and not just somebody—a real friend. "I saw him first. I knew him first." My silent tears became quiet, snotty sobs. "I loved him first."

"Does he know?"

I nodded into her neck.

She pulled me away by my shoulders. Her eyes were bloodshot but deadly serious. "He does? And how does he feel about you?"

I shrugged pathetically. "I thought I knew . . . I thought we . . . but he's going to marry *her*."

"You thought what—that he loved you back?"

"He does, I know he does," I said. "But he won't admit it. He pretends he doesn't."

"Oh my God. Are you sure?"

"Yes, but she's my *sister*," I said. "What choice do I have?"

"Do you really love him, Lake? Really, *really* love him, the kind of love that makes Rhett pine for Scarlett or Miss Piggy terrorize Kermit?"

I hiccupped again, this time with a laugh. "Only him. Only ever him."

She sucked in a breath. "You have to tell him how you feel."

Val was a closet romantic. She wanted there to be some resolution I couldn't give her. It wasn't that simple. "I can't. I've tried, but he won't hear it."

"How long have you loved him?"

I couldn't raise my answer above a whisper. "Two years."

"If you live to be eighty, that's over sixty more years you have to live wondering what might've happened if you'd spoken up. It'll hurt when you rip off the Band-Aid, but only for a short time. Compared to sixty years, it'll be nothing."

Sixty years of this hell. I didn't expect the pain of losing him to ever go away, but surely it would dull. Surely it would get easier. But she was right. I didn't want to live that long wondering *what-if?* "If I tell him, I'm betraying my own sister, Val. How can I do that?"

She heaved a sigh. "I don't have a sister but if *you* ever tried to steal my fiancé, even if you truly didn't believe I loved him, I'd scratch your eyes out. Your sister is flighty. She'll turn it into drama and then she'll forget all about it." She tapped a fingertip on my shoulder, twisting her lips. "Or . . . it's possible she'd never forgive you."

It was more than possible. Like that night in the truck, she'd have something to hold over me for life. Something far worse than anything she'd ever done to me.

"I guess the question is whether he's worth it," she added.

The truth hurt. It hurt in my chest, and it hurt coming out, because I didn't want to feel this way, but I did. "He is."

"If he's your soul mate, then he's yours. He can't have two soul mates—it's a fact. You deserve a happy ending, even if it means you have to be selfish and greedy."

"You're stoned, and you're a film buff obsessed with happily-ever-after. Can I really take your advice?"

"Then don't," she said. She sounded serious.

I shouldn't tell Manning how I felt. I knew I shouldn't. But if I didn't speak up before the wedding, I definitely couldn't tell him after. "What if this is my only chance?" I asked.

"Then do."

The acoustic guitar song on the stereo strummed the painfully taut strings keeping my heart from bursting. "What song is this?" I asked.

She closed her eyes, listening. "'Into Dust,'" she said softly. "Also Mazzy Star."

A commotion by the fire made us both turn. Manning and Corbin stood a foot apart, arguing.

"Don't worry about me, and I won't worry about you," Corbin said to Manning as Val and I approached.

"Not worried about you, but you're driving Lake, and that *does* concern me." Manning waited as Corbin took a long, pointed gulp of his Budweiser. "But go ahead and finish your beer," Manning said smugly. "Tiffany and I will take Lake home."

"Not that it's any of your business, but I'm not driving her. She's driving me. So you can shove—"

"She doesn't even have her license."

Corbin raised his voice, taking a step forward. "Shove your self-righteous, judgmental bullshit—"

"*Whoa*," Tiffany said. "No need to get worked up, Corbin. He's just looking out for her."

"You'd think *I* was the criminal between us," Corbin spat.

Manning met Corbin's stride, getting in his face. Despite Corbin's height, next to Manning, he looked like the teenage boy he was. "I don't care if I'm FBI's Most fucking Wanted," Manning said. "I'm not going to stand by and let you put her in danger. You bet your ass I'll always call you out on that."

"Yeah?" Corbin asked, leaning in dangerously close. "*Why?*"

Heavy with meaning, the word sat fat and unsubtle between the four of us—*why?* A question I was pretty sure Corbin had been wanting to ask since the night he'd walked me back to my cabin and

322

Manning had gotten upset about it. Why should Manning care what I do?

"Because she's my girlfriend's little sister," Manning said.

"Is that all?" Corbin asked.

"Shut up, Corbin," Tiffany said, pushing between them. "You're being a drunk idiot."

Corbin picked up my heels. "Am I drunk, Lake? Am I an idiot?"

They waited for me to answer, Corbin and Manning's eyes intently on me. I didn't know where my loyalty should lie, but at that moment, it wasn't with Manning or Tiffany. I went to Corbin and slipped one arm around his waist as I placed a possessive hand on his chest. "No to both."

Corbin's heart beat strongly against my palm. Manning pushed up his sleeves, his forearms tense and veiny.

"Don't," Corbin said under his breath so only I could hear.

I looked up at him. "What?"

"You know what. Don't use me to get what you want." He peeled my arms off him and walked away as I stood there. *Perfect.* Just what I needed to end this night, being humiliated in front of Manning and Tiffany by the one person who rarely let me down.

"Let's go for a walk," Tiffany said to me, glancing back at Manning. "Is that okay? I need to talk to her about something."

He took a pack of cigarettes from his hoodie pocket, looking between both of us. "Fine by me. Don't go far."

Tiffany looped her elbow with mine to walk down to the water. It felt like cozying up with the enemy, except that Tiffany's shampoo and scent and hair and body were as familiar to me as my own. I needed the kind of comfort only a sister could give me, but I also didn't want to go anywhere with her right then.

"Everything okay with you and Corbin?" she asked.

"There is no me and Corbin." I sniffed. "You know that."

"But he's so perfect for you, Lake. You need to try harder."

"He's not . . ." *Manning.* "He doesn't . . ."

"So who *does*?" she asked. "Aren't there any guys at school?"

"They're boys."

"If you don't practice with boys, how will you handle men?" We stopped walking and she glanced back at the fire, presumably at Manning. I didn't want to look, but I couldn't help it. I wanted to know where he was. How he was. Always. Even while he was shredding my heart. Manning looked back at us as he talked to one of Corbin's brothers.

"I mean, I don't know why you don't just go for it," she said. "He obviously loves you."

My breath caught in my throat before I realized she was looking beyond Manning, at Corbin. "This is what you wanted to talk to me about?" I asked, annoyed.

"No. Yes. I don't know." She snuggled closer to me against a gusty breeze. "We haven't talked much since I moved out."

"We have dinner together every Sunday."

"You know what I mean."

It wasn't the distance causing our rift. Did she know that? Did she know what she was doing to me, how much it hurt to even look at her right now? I could barely swallow their kissing and cuddling in front of me, the knowledge they were having sex, and now . . . she was taking forever from me. It didn't belong to her, and she had to know that, even if I hadn't said it aloud. I might've kept my love for Manning in the dark, but it was as impossible to ignore as the sun. "Do you love him?" I whispered.

Either she didn't hear or pretended not to. She smiled. This time, she was looking at Manning. "You know what he told me in the car? Dad's so happy about the wedding that he might try to make it happen this summer."

My mind reeled. My thoughts had been spinning since the party, and I wasn't sure I could take much more. A wedding, this summer? My dad, happy? I wanted to take my arm back from her, but I was afraid I'd sink to my knees. "But it's already summer."

"If Dad's offering up the Ritz, I'm taking it before he changes his mind. We have a lot of work to do. I haven't been this excited to do anything in a while, probably not since high school. First, you and I should take a trip to Barnes and Noble to clean out their bridal magazines. We'll need to stock up on Post-its to color-code the dresses by length, neckline, fabric . . ."

I billowed my cardigan with my free hand to get some air against my skin. "Why can't Sarah help?" I asked. "You always say how bad my fashion sense is."

"I mean, she can." Tiffany looked at her pink-polished toes as she dug them into the sand. "I just thought you might want to."

The disappointment in her voice was evident even to me. Any other time, any other man, yes—I would've been happy to see Tiffany this way. More than happy. Normally everything was dumb or bogus or uncool or pathetic to her, yet on the biggest day of her life, she wanted to include me. But this was *Manning*. My Manning.

"I'm sorry, but I can't," I said. "Maybe there's some other way I can help."

Tiffany laughed so loudly, Manning, Corbin, and everyone else looked over at us. "Don't worry. I think we can find a *few* things for the M.O.H. to do."

"M.O.H.?" I asked.

"Duh. Maid—of—*honor*."

The maid of honor . . . Tiffany's maid of honor? *Me?*

326

22
MANNING

From where I stood, I couldn't see much more in the dark than the white foam of ocean waves and two heads of blonde hair, their figures shadowy in the distance. The girls who'd turned my life upside down. It hadn't been much of a life. No doubt, it was better now. After watching my parents' knock-down, drag-out fights followed by make-up sessions that'd keep them in the bedroom for days, I couldn't have predicted I'd ever actually *want* to get married. Tiffany and I wouldn't end up like my parents, though. When she baited me, I kept my cool. When she got upset, I'd do my best to help her manage her emotions. She was a catch, too, and I was the only one who'd caught her in any meaningful way. We'd build a good, sturdy life together. I'd find work that fulfilled me and made sure she did the same.

And I wouldn't be saddled with the constant worry that I wasn't enough for her.

I returned my attention to Corbin's brother, who was talking about restoring a T-bird. He took out a pack of cigarettes and held it up to me. "Smoke?"

I took one and stuck it in my mouth while I dug my lighter from my jeans pocket. "You're in college, right?"

"Santa Barbara."

"You live in a house or something? Where do you keep the car?"

"Here, in my parents' garage. I just work on it when I'm home for weekends or holidays. Corbin helped out before he left." He cupped his hand to light his cigarette. "He's not so bad, you know."

So everyone insisted on telling me. Knowing Corbin had driven Lake and her friends here tonight, I'd seen the beer in his hand and my mind went to the worst. Maybe some of my overprotectiveness was unfounded, but I'd actually known people who'd died as a result of drunk driving, and I'd bet Corbin did, too. My gaze went directly to the girls, as it had been every couple minutes. They stood right at the shore, the water creeping up to their bare feet, reaching for them after the smash and fizz of each wave. I shuddered.

"You go out with Tiffany?" Corey asked.

I nodded. "Are you the one who dated her?"

He laughed a little. "No, that's my older brother, Cane. I mean, I wouldn't say they dated. I think they probably hooked up a couple times in high school. Sorry."

I shrugged. "I didn't know her then. She says your brother had a crush on her. Not Cane."

"Corbin? Maybe. She was a senior when he was a sophomore. They all had crushes on her." He blew smoke out the side of his mouth. "But that was before he met her sister. Corbin's fucking whipped on that girl. He's so in love with Lake, it's stupid. And she treats him like crap."

"Yeah?" I asked. That didn't sound like Lake. "How?"

"She just strings him along. Says they're best friends or some shit, won't sleep with him. But he keeps hoping she'll change her mind." He shook his head. "He's a pussy. He gets lots of girls. Just not the one he wants."

Lake was a heartbreaker, that wasn't news to me. I'd seen how Corbin looked at her. I'd probably worn the same expression. She'd break more hearts than ours. I couldn't muster any sympathy for any other motherfucker. Maybe Corbin was the gentleman everyone claimed. Maybe he was in love with Lake and wasn't out to hurt her. Maybe he'd even be good for her. But he was still the one who could get everything I wanted with one word from Lake.

"It's not that she doesn't want Corbin." At some point, Val had inserted herself between us. She slurped from her beer can. "She just can't see him. Someone else is in the way."

"Who?" Corey asked.

"I'm not sure." Val glanced at me and then the girls. Tiffany had her arms around Lake. "I'd bet a hundred bucks that right now, Tiffany is asking Lake to be in her wedding."

Fuck. Tiffany wouldn't waste any time. From now until she walked down the aisle, all eyes would be on her. I couldn't do anything about it without making things worse for all of us. There were some things I couldn't protect Lake from. She'd have to handle herself. I looked into the fire, swallowing down my guilt.

"You guys getting married?" Corey asked.

"Maybe it'll be a beach wedding," Val said. "Right here. Picture it. The sun setting, all your friends and family in the crowd, Tiffany complaining that she can't wear heels, that her dress is dragging in the sand. Lake walking down the aisle, catching the bouquet."

I pinched the bridge of my nose. Val knew. Her attempts to get me to open my eyes were cute, but they wouldn't do much good. As long as I believed this was best for everyone involved—not just Lake, but for me and Tiff, too—it was the right choice.

"Sounds epic," Corey said, but neither of us looked at him. He flicked his cigarette into the fire. "I'm gonna go see if Cane's back with more alcohol yet. He'll need a hand."

I still had half a cigarette left, and I didn't like giving up something I'd once fought a man over, but I felt like I should offer. "Need help?"

"Nah, we're good," he said and took off, leaving Val and me.

"You think I'm an asshole, don't you?" Val asked.

I hadn't been sure what to make of Val when I'd met her. In some ways, Lake's relationship with her reminded me of hers with Tiffany's—one loud and attention-seeking, the other composed, reserved. Except Val seemed to recognize that Lake's quiet confidence wasn't to be mistaken for meekness. She challenged Lake in a way her friends and family didn't. Not even her dad, because Charles didn't really want Lake to think for herself. "I think you're a good friend."

"Because I don't have a dick?"

I pulled back, frowning. "*What?*"

"When Corbin tries to look out for Lake, you go caveman. Is it because you want her for yourself?"

I set my jaw. She had no right telling me my business, but my anger was diluted by the fire her words lit in me. *Want her for myself. Want. Lake. For. My. Self.* Lake did bring out the caveman in me.

"You can't have it both ways," Val said as Tiffany headed back in our direction. "But you can have her. Of that, I'm pretty sure."

Tiffany pulled her hands into her sweater sleeves, trekking through the sand toward us. "I haven't stopped smiling since the party," she called out to me. "My cheeks hurt."

"Why?" Val asked.

Tiffany's smile fell. "Because I'm getting *married*."

"Oh yeah." Val snorted. "I already forgot."

Val knew how to get to Tiffany. Unlike Lake's other friends, I hadn't seen Tiffany try to engage her. That could've been because she wasn't sure she'd win. "Maybe you've had enough beer," I told her.

"Maybe." Val tossed her empty beer can into a trash bag slumped by some lawn chairs. "I'll see if the guys need any help."

"So," Tiffany started, "how do you feel about hydrangeas?"

I looked over her head. Lake was walking away from the bonfire, along the water. "What's she doing?" I asked.

"Hydrangeas," she said. "What do you think?"

"Huh? What is that?"

"A type of flower. For the wedding."

"Tiff," I said, squinting to see into the dark, "you know I don't give a fuck about the flowers."

"All right, geez. I thought you might want to *try* to care."

I cared enough that I'd possibly made a deal with the devil, but I didn't have time to get into that now. "Where's Lake going?"

"I don't know. Probably to drown herself because I stole her spotlight."

My face heated as I dropped my eyes to her. I'd never gone into much detail about my sister's death with Tiffany, but she knew Maddy had drowned. "Why would you say that?" I asked. "You have any idea how insensitive that is?"

She rubbed under her nose, looking away as she muttered, "About as insensitive as ignoring me?"

Tiffany wasn't mean-spirited, but sometimes she did mean things out of hurt. I knew her comment about drowning hadn't been meant as a barb at me—it was too low of a blow. But she needed to think before she spoke. "I'm going to go get Lake."

"No."

I glanced down at her. "No?"

She put her hand in my free one. "She'll be fine. I need you here."

"For what?" I squeezed her hand but let it go. "I'll just be a minute. It's not safe for her to walk alone in the dark."

Tiffany folded her arms. "Manning." She thinned her lips into a bloodless line. "I said no."

She was telling me no. It was cute she thought she could. Before anything, I was a man, and I answered only to myself. Especially after the life I'd led. I'd bent over backward to make Tiffany comfortable, but I wasn't indulging this kind of behavior. I took a drag of my cigarette and watched Lake get farther away. "I have to."

"Like you *had* to let her in your truck that night? You couldn't have just said no and closed the door?"

I sucked nicotine into my lungs, hoping it'd morph into some kind of explanation for that night. I understood why she was paranoid after what she'd witnessed with her dad, but I didn't need Tiffany throwing that in my face the rest of our lives. "I tried."

"Try *harder*."

I didn't want to. Tiffany didn't know that trying harder meant me walking away from the whole situation. I'd given her as much as I was able these past couple years. This moment wasn't about her, though. Lake was hurting, and it was my fault, and I had to attempt to fix it. I kissed Tiffany on the forehead and started for the shore.

"She did this to herself," she called after me. "It's not your job to make it better."

Sand filtered into my sneakers until I made it to damp ground. The shore chased me up and down as I closed the space between Lake and me.

When I was at her back, she stopped and turned around. She didn't look surprised to see me, probably because she knew I'd come. "How could you do this to me?" she asked. "Why? I'm eighteen now."

I inhaled through my nose, then took one final drag of my cigarette. Maybe it was my fault Lake got so hung up on age. Had she thought she'd turn legal and we'd ride off into the sunset on a fucking bicycle? "It's not as simple as that."

"Summer?" she asked, sounding strangled.

"I know it's soon." Admittedly, the urgency of it made my collar tight. "But does it really matter when?" I asked. "Would it be easier if we waited a year or five?"

By the way her face fell, I had my answer. It was the same for me. Putting an end to this for good would never be easy. Maybe having the wedding now would give Lake the closure she needed to go off to school and live the life she was meant to. In that respect, summer wasn't soon at all. In fact, sooner was better than later.

"You're really going to do it?" she asked. "You want this?"

I squatted to put out my cigarette. "Yes."

"You won't even smoke in front of me," she accused. "I'm old enough to buy cigarettes, but I'm still a child in your eyes."

I looked up. The night sky spread out behind her. The stars weren't as clear as they'd been up in Big Bear, but it didn't matter. She was the only star I saw. No, she wasn't a child in my eyes, because if she was, that'd make me the same monster as my dad. I saw her naked underneath me. I saw her as a woman opening up for a man. I saw her soft parts giving way to my hard ones. And it sent my heart racing. "One day—"

"Don't tell me 'one day,'" she said.

Her beauty fucking radiated when she hurt like this. She couldn't control her pain, so it just seeped out of her. I wanted to tell her it'd go away soon.

She'd meet someone at school who'd do far better for her than I could. Some rich, California asshole who'd go on to run a Fortune 500 company or produce movies or something. Some finance guy like Corbin, maybe. She'd be his star, not mine. She'd forget about me in no time. If I had the smallest doubt about it being the right thing, I would've taken her somewhere right now. I'd have made her mine for real, even knowing there was a large chance she'd figure me out one day, and *I'd* end up the one with a broken heart.

"There's only now," she said. "There's no more time. You have to be selfish, even if people get hurt."

"*Selfish?*" I stood abruptly, training my eyes on her so she'd understand I wasn't fucking around. I gestured toward the parking lot. "This *is* me being selfish. I stayed when I should've gone. For you. Now, I have a life here. A family. Now, I'm not sure I could leave if I wanted to. And I don't want to."

She turned away from me, toward the ocean, her chin wobbling. "Whatever you say, whatever *she* says, I know the truth. I saw it."

I had to crane my neck to hear her over the waves. "What are you talking about?"

"Your tattoo," she said. "That night at your apartment in the kitchen. I know what it is."

Hands on my hips, I hung my head. What could I say? I'd been desperate. Locked up, unable to talk or even think too hard about the things that mattered most to me. Trying to forget the memories I'd made just months earlier. A lifer had been trading tattoos for cigarettes and I'd asked for the stars. It'd cost me three packs and a little bit of my bad-boy image, but having those three stars on my body had bought me some peace.

"It's for Madison," I said, which was partly true, and easier to swallow than the whole truth.

"No, it's not." Her long hair blew into her face with a breeze, and I had to cross my hands under my pits to keep from brushing it away. She took a breath, the words floating out on her exhale. "It's for me. It's Summer Triangle."

She fucking knew I'd put her star on my body, even though it didn't belong to me and never would. Wasn't that enough? I couldn't tell her I loved her. I couldn't tell her I didn't. It killed me, but that was how it was. It wasn't going to be any other way, no matter how many times she put me in this goddamn position.

"I love you," she said.

Hearing it aloud, from her mouth, made my throat thick. I allowed a second for the pleasure to sink in, for that euphoric warmth to spread from my chest to my face, to the lower half of my body. She loved me, and those words alone were doing things to me. She was going to get me hard with one sentence? God*damn* it. I was a grown man who thought with his head, not his dick. I had to get ahold of myself. "Don't do this, Lake."

"I can't just sit back and watch. I have to say something." Her face, open and sweet, pleaded with me. "You know it's true, Manning, you *have* to. You've always known that my heart doesn't function right without you, that food doesn't taste the same and air is too thick, and my mind is always wandering back to that night on the lake, because I'm all wrong *without* you, because I'm in love *with* you."

23
LAKE

Manning hardly moved an inch, arms at his sides. His gray hoodie hugged his biceps but opened as a breeze came off the water. My confession hung in the air. Slowly, pieces of it caught on the wind, scattering away from us.

I'm all . . . wrong . . . without you.

Meeting Manning had taken me apart, and he hadn't been around to put me back together properly. My limbs had been stitched on, my heart cut out of red construction paper, my cloth outside wearing thin. I wanted to be a real girl, but without him, I was just a bundle of body parts.

I'm in love with you.

I needed to hear it back.

Instead, Manning closed his eyes and asked, "Why are you telling me this?"

My paper heart tore a little. "Because I've never said it, and you need to know before you—"

"I *do* know, Lake," he said loudly enough to make me jump. "You've told me. Maybe not outright, but some way or another, you've told me, and it hasn't always been subtle. You told me that night in the truck. In the lake. On the horse." The waves had nothing on him, the way he grew bigger, his voice booming. "You told me in the car when I picked you up from the prom. You told me on your eighteenth birthday. You seriously think I don't fucking know?"

His anger vibrated between us, as loud as the ocean, as acute as the sharp pains in my heart. "You *don't* know," I argued. "You *can't* know, or you wouldn't go through with this."

"I do know and I *am* going through with it." His words, cold and hard, came down as if the sky stormed bricks. "You think I don't know how you feel? You think I don't carry the burden of our love on my shoulders just to keep it from crashing down onto you?"

What I wouldn't give to bear that crash. Couldn't he understand how badly I wanted that? That I could take on anything with him by my side? "I can handle it," I said.

"*I* can't, and I've told you that, but you don't care how hard it's been for me."

"I don't care?" I whispered. I hiccupped, my nose tingling. The threat of my tears only seemed to make him angrier as he thrust a hand in his hair. "How can you say that?" I asked. "You're *all* I care about."

"No, I'm not. You don't care about all the ways I'm dying inside. It kills me to know I've made you sad and that this strains your relationship with your family." He flexed his hands, his fingers curling, then reaching for the ground. "It kills me to know there are a million better men out there for you than me, including Corbin. If you cared, you wouldn't be standing here right now, asking me to pick you when you know, you *know* I can't."

My mouth hung open. He was acting as if I was the selfish one, when all I'd done was love him and do everything in my power to keep it to myself. Or so I'd thought. "Why can't you? Is it because of her? Do you love her?" One rogue tear escaped, sliding over my cheek. "Do you love her . . . more than me?"

He smacked his fist against his chest. "I am not the man for you," he said. "I can't give you the life you deserve."

"You can." I called on all my strength to inhale back my tears and show him he was wrong. "I've never been more sure of anything."

"All right, Lake," he said. "If you're so sure, then tell me how it works."

"What do you mean?"

"You want me to pick you? Fine." He threw up his arms. "To hell with it. I pick you. What happens next?"

I shook my head slowly, my stomach fluttering. "I . . . what?"

He opened his arms, showing me his impressive wingspan. "Tell me what we're going to do. We go back to the bonfire and what? You going to tell Tiffany the wedding's off and I'm leaving her for you, or should I? Then what?"

I swallowed, my heart pounding at just the thought of telling Tiffany, at the pain I'd cause. Was I ready to do it right this instant? No, but I would find the strength—for him. "Then we be together."

"So how exactly does it work? Do we go to your parents' tonight and tell them the good news? Because if we don't, Tiffany will. So we pack up your things and go . . . where?"

"I—I don't know." I could hardly wrap my head around what he was saying, because the details didn't matter. *We* mattered. This love mattered. I burrowed into my cardigan, suddenly freezing cold. "I'll stay home, and you can go to . . ." He couldn't return to Tiffany's. As it was, she'd probably burn his things. "A hotel. Go to Gary's."

"What makes you think your dad won't wring my neck before I walk out the front door? Why the hell do you think he's so happy about this wedding?"

A wave crashed hard, and water slithered up around my ankles. Manning walked backward, up to dry land.

"It's only a few months," I said, pushing my feet through the sand, following him. "Then I'll be in the dorms."

"And me?" He fisted his shirt, right over his heart. "What will I do? I can't live in a dorm."

"We'll find you an apartment in Los Angeles—"

"My parole mandates that I live within county lines."

"Then I'll drive back and forth." I grasped at straws, feeling like I was losing a battle I'd always been so confident I'd win. "I'll come nights, weekends—"

"Between classes, homework, exams—not to mention all the fun shit you're supposed to do in college—you really want to be driving two hours each weekend to stay with your ex-con boyfriend?"

"Yes," I said quietly. My hands began to shake as my dreams sifted through my fingers. I'd been holding on at any cost, but Manning insisted on smashing everything into smaller and smaller pieces until our future was nothing but grains of sand under my feet.

"Even if I could move to L.A.," he said, "I'd have to find a landlord willing to rent to a felon, and then I'd have to come up with first-and-last month, security deposit, and rent each month."

I shook my head hard. "We'll find a way."

"My savings went to the court, to some woman I supposedly traumatized when I was with you," he said. "And your dad has a job for me. A good one, in construction."

"My *dad*?" I asked. "Why are you bringing him into this? Who cares about him?"

"I do. I care, Lake." Up until now, he'd been heated, but suddenly, his voice became grave. "I want the same things for you and Tiffany that he does. He's not my enemy. In fact, he's going to look into wiping my record clean. I want that so much, Lake, you can't understand."

"I can, because *I* want that, maybe even more than you." I touched the base of my neck, my pulse thumping under my fingertips. "You aren't the one who has to live with the guilt of knowing your hands are constantly tied because of decisions I made."

"Exactly. I'm the one with the tied hands. You think he'll do anything for me after this? You think he won't spend every free minute he has scheming to get me out of your life?"

"We don't need him." Even as I said it, guilt panged in my heart. He was my dad. As much as he frustrated me, I loved him, and I cared what he thought. Manning was right—Dad'd never be okay with this. I hadn't really considered that having Manning in my life might mean losing not just Tiffany, but my dad, too. "You'll find another job." My voice weakened. "Another apartment."

"It's not that simple, Lake. I have nowhere to live, no car, no money, my credit is shot and I'm on parole. I'm a criminal. These things matter."

"No, they don't. They're just dumb details—"

"They're life, Lake. Relationships, marriage, they don't run on love alone. I tried to tell you that, I . . ." His throat rippled as he clenched his teeth. "My parents were as different as you and me, and they thought love was enough. My dad loved my mom so intensely, he sometimes hurt her. And us," he added quietly.

My chin shook. He had to know we weren't his parents. *I* did. He was my soul mate. Didn't that mean we'd be together one day, no matter what? Wasn't that the definition of a soul mate? Tiffany would always be able to find someone else. Her soul mate was still out there. But me? Manning? This was it for us. We could fake it all we wanted, but the truth was, there was nobody else out there for me, or for Manning. We needed each other. "You'd never hurt me," I said. "And even if I thought there was a chance you might, I'm still willing to take that risk."

"I'm not." The way his voice broke squeezed my heart, sending more tears down my cheeks. "What can I offer you? How will I take care of us?"

"I'll ask my dad for money," I said. I never had, not in the way Tiffany did, but I could do it for a while.

"No."

"But he gives it to you and Tiffany."

He took a step toward me, seeming to double in size, and to my surprise, I moved back. "That's different, and you fucking know it."

"That isn't fair." I dug my toes into the ground, seeking comfort in the soft sand. "Why would it be any different than him giving you money to take care of Tiffany?"

"Because that's Tiffany and this is *you*." He gritted his teeth, looking up at the sky. "I can't do that with you. I can't expect you to understand, but I need to you to. I need you to understand this is best."

"It's not best, and I don't understand how you can say it is." I laced my hands over my heart. "You asked if I could go up there and tell Tiffany? I could. I would say goodbye to her, to my dad, for you. Don't marry her, Manning. Be a man, and tell her you don't love her."

His neck thickened, veins rising from under his sleeves, cording his forearms. "Don't tell me to be a man," he said, his fists curling. "What do you think I've *been* doing? Why do you think I've been doing it? For you, Lake." His body vibrated as he ran both hands through his hair, pulling. "You don't know what you're asking of me."

"I'm asking you to walk away from all of this." I'd never seen Manning so angry, but I needed him to see I wouldn't break. I wouldn't be pushed away. Instead, I stood taller. "I can be enough for you."

"They'll never forgive you."

I stepped up to him, into the force field of anger pulsating around him. "I don't care."

He looked down his nose at me. "I'm not going to take your family away from you, Lake."

"You'll be my family."

"You should have the world. Fuck the world—you should have the universe, the sky, and every star in it." As close as I was, I could see every fleck of pain in his eyes, the frown lines etched in his skin, the anguish in his tensed muscles and jaw. "I can't give that to you. I'll never be able to. I've seen too much. Had too much taken away. I can't be happy enough to make you happy, and I can't provide for you the way you deserve. You're at the start of your life, on your way up, and I . . ." He inhaled a breath through his nose, wincing like it pained him. "I can only bring you down."

My tears fell faster now, but I wouldn't lose hope. I couldn't. Because there was something he couldn't deny, and if he did, he'd be a liar. "Even if all that's true, you're forgetting one thing. You can love me more than anyone else could. How can you ignore that?"

He hesitated. "It's not enough."

It's not enough. You're not enough. I shook the crushing thoughts out of my head. "It is enough."

"It's not. I've seen it firsthand with my mom and dad—"

I got in his face. "I don't care what you've seen. You're making excuses."

"Why would I?" he asked. "What makes you think I want it this way?"

"So you can be miserable! Because you think *that's* what you deserve." I wasn't sure where it came from. Maybe I stunned us both because for a second, we each went silent. It all boiled down to the simplest equation—Manning thought I was too good for him, and that he was bad, and those two things were enough to keep him away. "You're not bad," I told him. "You are not your father."

He stepped back as if I'd struck him. I hoped I had if it meant pulling him out of this nightmare. "You can't say that," he said. "You don't even know him. You don't know what he did."

"He hurt your sister, your mother, and you. You have never hurt anyone, Manning."

"No? I put my hands on you when you were sixteen. I fantasized about stripping you of your innocence when you were seventeen." His already-dark eyes blackened like the sky. "I'm not sure I would've stopped that night in the truck if it weren't for the cop."

"But you did, even though I begged you not to."

"Maybe next time, I won't be able to. Do you see how worked up I get around you?" He pulled on the front of his t-shirt with a fist. "Do you see my anger, Lake? You're going to tell me I'm not dangerous?"

"You aren't dangerous," I said, trying to keep any trembling from my voice. Like that night in his kitchen, his admissions kicked up my heart rate, but any fear I felt just made my toes curl. If this was a dangerous man, I more than accepted that about him. I wanted it.

"I would've killed that guard if I hadn't been pulled off," he continued. "I went to that same place my dad did. I snapped—and I could snap again."

Something pulled deep in my belly. Manning didn't just believe he was bad. He lived it. I could see it right there in his face, hear it in his words. He and I together would be explosive, and that was why he put distance between us. "Not with me, Manning. You don't scare me, no matter how hard you try to."

"I'm not trying to scare you—I'm trying to *show* you." He began to pace. "I want to be a good man, Lake. I want to help people, not hurt them. I can't do that for you, but I can for Tiffany. Getting lost in you could mean losing my control, too. I could do to you what my dad did to my mom and to—" He stopped and sucked in a breath, unable to say Maddy's name. He didn't need to. She was here between us, her presence strong like it'd been in the truck. "Always, in the back of mind, are all the ways I could hurt you just by loving you," he said to me. "Not only because I come from a violent background, but because I'd be holding you back."

In the distance, my friends hollered and laughed, probably taking beer bongs or fighting over the stereo. "That's not true."

"What can I offer you right now?" he asked.

"Love," I said weakly, but I knew what he'd say.

It wasn't enough.

His eyes darted over my face. "Do you want to keep up the same euphoric highs and crash-and-burn lows we've already put ourselves through the past two years? Because they'd only get more extreme, and that scares me. My greatest fear is becoming my dad. I can't be the one who steals your future . . . or your innocence."

"Yes, you can."

"Okay. Maybe I can." He squinted out toward the black horizon. "But would you let me?"

I opened my mouth to say, not only would I let him, but I'd beg if he wanted. *Take me as I am, and we'll figure out the rest.* But the truth was, I didn't know the rest. I couldn't say with absolute certainty that we'd be okay. In my mind, the two of us were tangled sheets and big love and hours of tracing every part of the bodies we'd fantasized about. Where did school and money and work factor into all that? I realized that whatever guilt I felt when my family turned me out, Manning would blame himself. Whatever problems arose in our relationship, Manning would shoulder them, even though he'd warned me against them. And if we had those blow-out fights, and Manning said or did anything to hurt me, even by accident, he'd convince himself he'd become his dad. Ironically, in the end, it was me who could turn Manning into his father, and Tiffany who'd helped Manning believe he was a good man.

I didn't know what to say but the only thing that made any sense to me. "You're what I want."

"But I can't be what you need. Still, after everything I just said, knowing all the ways it could go wrong, knowing the man it would turn me into to love you and to ruin you . . ." He ran his hand over his face, as if forcing the words out. "If you ask me to choose you, I will—even if it could ultimately destroy me."

I remembered the night we'd almost gotten caught in the truck, how childish I'd felt for how I'd acted. He'd asked me not to do it, but I had. He'd been led away in handcuffs, he'd stunted his future, because I'd wanted something and hadn't considered the consequences.

"You don't care how hard it's been for me," he'd said earlier.

Of course I cared. The only thing I wanted more than my happiness was his. A lump formed in my throat as everything I'd known to be true shifted. These past two years, I thought I'd been brave. Strong. Loved. I'd only been selfish to think Manning wanted me to fight for him, when instead, pushing him only hurt him.

I turned my head and tried in vain to hide the endless stream of tears streaking down my cheeks. My sister stood by the fire, arms curled around her waist, watching us. Tonight, he'd be walking back to her. I covered my face, my world crumbling.

Manning let me stand there and cry into my palms. He didn't comfort me, and I finally understood how it would be unfair of me to ask him to. Through my fingers and the blur of my tears, I noticed my missing anklet. The bracelet I'd made for Manning had fallen off, probably with the licks of the ocean. It was done. *We* were done. Only my pain persisted.

Manning had once told me you couldn't move the stars. I'd thought that meant our love was predestined, written in the night sky, sure as death. Behind my lids, I pictured the two stars and realized for the first time the permanent distance between them. And I accepted that there was, and always had been, a third star.

You can't move the stars.

I had tried, and I had failed.

24
LAKE

Gripping a bouquet of peach and cream garden roses, I peeked around the hotel's archway. Friends and family quietly filtered onto a perfectly manicured lawn, murmuring as they took their seats for the ceremony.

The sun began to set over the Pacific Ocean, fiery orange dipping into cool blue. This morning's cloud cover had given way to an unblemished sky. With everything happening around us, it should've been easy to avoid looking at Manning, but that always had been, and always would be, impossible for me. My gaze lifted above the crowd and down the petal-scattered aisle. Manning stood under the sheer curtains of a gazebo on the edge of a cliff, his back to me as he spoke to the best man. The first time I saw Manning on that construction site, he'd been larger than life. Today, he was so much more. He commanded attention without trying. His shoulders stretched a bespoke suit, and his hands sat loosely in his pockets as if it were any other day.

He turned his head, giving me the pleasure of his profile. Strong jaw, full mouth, thick, black, recently trimmed hair. Even with the scar on his lip and the new, slight curve of his nose, he looked refined, the sum of all my dreams come to life.

Henry spoke to Manning with the air of a father figure, his hand on Manning's shoulder. Manning just listened and rubbed his sinfully smooth jaw as he stared at the ground. Henry paused, as if waiting for an answer or acknowledgement, and his smile faded. He looked to the back of the decorated lawn, through the arches hiding the bridal party. He looked at me. Maybe Manning wasn't as calm as I thought. Maybe he was having second thoughts.

I, on the other hand, had only one thought.

Mine.

The air buzzed, charged with murmured excitement, even in the vastness surrounding us. Water and sky swallowed the horizon. If I'd ever imagined this moment, Tiffany about to walk down the aisle, I would've thought it'd be pure chaos. Knowing how she thought the world revolved around her, and this being the biggest event of her life to date, it would seem inevitable.

That was why her calmness unnerved me. Sarah fixed the train of Tiffany's strapless dress on the grass while Mom hugged her tightly, rubbing her bare shoulders. Surely, as the Maid of Honor, there was something I should've been doing, too, but I couldn't bring myself to move. Nobody was yelling or crying or putting out fires. All I heard was blood rushing through my ears.

In a few minutes, it would all be over. Everything. The last couple years of my life erased with a simple "I do." There were bows tied to aisle chairs and petals on the ground. Somebody had spent the time to do that—peel flowers just so Tiffany could walk on them.

Gary shook Manning's hand, and Manning smiled so widely, it knocked the wind out of me. It wasn't just breathtaking—it was genuine.

The violinists began to play, and the bridal party took their places. My dad kissed Tiffany on the cheek before whispering in her ear. Her eyes lit up as he pulled her into a hug. Mom held a tissue to one corner of her eye and then the other. They were happy. I wasn't. I could still change that . . . if I decided their happiness was worth my own.

I didn't know the right answer. All I knew was my love for Manning. He watched my mom, then Gary head down the aisle, followed by the bridesmaids. I just watched him at the head of it all, hoping for a spared glance in my direction. And suddenly, it was my turn to go, to walk down the aisle to him, but not the way I'd dreamed about.

"Lake," Dad said from behind me after too long had passed. "Go."

I looked back at him and at Tiffany, their arms looped together, and remembered the night months ago on the beach when I'd told Manning I could walk away from them for him. He'd said something about my dad in the heat of the moment that hadn't registered for me until weeks later.

"Why the hell do you think he's so happy about this wedding?"

I'd turned it over and over in my brain until the pieces had finally come together. Dad had hurried this wedding along because he knew that wherever Manning went, I'd follow. Even if it meant leaving my family behind. Even if it meant dropping out of USC. The one way, the only way, I'd never be allowed to love Manning was as Tiffany's husband. The betrayal cut deep, but I'd kept the hurt inside and a smile on my face to make it through all of this.

I took a step, and my heel sank into the grass. I wiggled it out and brought my foot back. "I can't do it," I whispered.

"That's what the stones are for." Tiffany gently pushed me forward. "Use the path. Go ahead."

As if it was easy. As if I wasn't walking toward the most horrific thing I could imagine. I couldn't do it. Tears flooded my eyes as the spikes of my heels dug into soft ground. The guests, turned in their seats, started to murmur. All eyes except Manning's were on me, and the music played on, beautiful, haunting. Despite my protests, my hair had been swept off my bare shoulders, putting my heartbreak on display for everyone to watch like a movie.

I started down the aisle. At rehearsal, I'd been reminded over and over to keep the pace of the music. Time slowed with me, an eerie tranquility coming over me the way I imagined it felt giving in to drowning. Corbin smiled at me, his arm over the back of his mom's chair. Val sat by him, stoic, and I knew her heart beat as hard as mine.

I turned forward again, silently urging Manning to raise his head and look at me. We'd communicated so much that way, glances here and there, our own language. Walking toward him like a bride made my hands sweat around my bouquet. I scraped my thumbnail down a stem, wishing for the prick of a thorn to distract from the pain in my chest. Manning must've been sweating, too, because he wiped his brow, then his hairline, but even as I approached the front and took my spot, he still hadn't looked. Maybe because he knew what he'd see if he did . . . my delicate birdy heart, ripped right down the middle by a great bear.

Through all this, I'd never doubted that he belonged to me. Never wondered if he loved me. He didn't have to say it for me to know it was true. For over two months, I'd done as I was told, smiling through the pain, making plans to start USC next week. But in that moment, overwhelmed by Manning's beauty, by the pain I knew he felt, too, I couldn't remember why I'd stepped back.

Because I was staring at Manning, I didn't even hear the Bridal March begin, didn't see Tiffany come out, but suddenly she was there, passing me her bouquet, moving in front of Manning, her back to me.

"Friends and family," the priest said, "we're gathered here today to witness the union of Tiffany and Manning, and to celebrate their love by joining them in marriage."

My heartbeat thundered in my ears. The priest smiled and said things I couldn't register, things Manning and Tiffany repeated. People laughed. Not Manning. He just stared at Tiffany.

If he'd only glance over, I knew what I'd see in his eyes, because I'd seen it before, in the few raw but powerful moments we'd had the last couple years. I'd see the depth of love that kept him away, the heat that kept him close.

Henry passed Manning the rings. Things were moving too fast. He wouldn't, *couldn't*, put that ring on her finger without sparing me even a glance, I knew it in my gut. On the inside, I screamed for him, convinced he would hear me. He focused on Tiffany so hard as he slid on her ring, he didn't even blink.

Maybe he didn't think love was enough, but it was. I knew it was. If he wasn't going to stop this, I would. For him. I loved him enough to do this on my own. Maybe he'd be mad for a while. Maybe he'd even try to stay away. But eventually, when things had settled, he'd understand why I couldn't let him make this mistake.

I knew what I had to do, and it had to be now.

"Marriage changes you," the priest said. "It betters you. It heals you. It will define you as a couple and deepen your love for one another."

Now. Now. *Now.*

Everyone on the lawn watched, rapt. Mom, Dad, grandparents, toddlers, cousins. Corbin winked at me. Val chewed her thumbnail. Gary and Henry, maybe the only two men who'd ever given Manning a fair chance, stood tall and looked on proudly. I would hurt them, too. Everyone.

"Should anyone in attendance know of any reason why this couple should not be lawfully married, speak now . . . or forever hold your peace."

Two years ago, I dove into a lake at midnight hoping Manning would follow. The world had gone instantly black, deafeningly still, until I'd heard the woozy echo of Manning calling me back. I'd stayed submerged a little too long, punishing him for denying me, wanting him to worry. The silence of this moment was the same. Dizzying. Disorienting. Sluggish but calm. Everything shrunk down to the man in front of me.

Tiffany's veil lifted with a breeze. Beads of sweat had formed on Manning's hairline. He squeezed his eyes shut briefly. Could I do it for him? Ruin a wedding, a marriage before it began, a life? My own sister?

He'd asked me not to. He'd asked me to let this go.

Sarah, behind me, rubbed my back, and I realized it was because I shook with silent sobs. Scalding tears flooded my eyes, warming my cheeks.

Manning finally looked at me, his face pale, his ever-dark brows drawn so tightly that his forehead wrinkled. In his honeyed brown eyes, I saw all the agony the last two years had caused him. Our hot, construction-site afternoons, our cool, starry nights, and all the days he'd lost because of me. He swallowed, maybe holding back his own tears.

My love for him spanned the ocean, the sky over our heads, an infinite universe of stars. I could do this to Tiffany, but I couldn't do it to him. I sealed my words inside along with a great love that somehow fit inside me.

Maybe one day, Manning and I would challenge fate, defy gravity, and move the stars ourselves.

But today was not that day.

BOOK THREE IN THE
SOMETHING IN THE WAY SERIES:

MOVE THE STARS

LEARN MORE AT
WWW.JESSICAHAWKINS.NET/SOMETHINGINTHEWAY

TITLES BY
JESSICA HAWKINS

LEARN MORE AT JESSICAHAWKINS.NET

SLIP OF THE TONGUE
THE FIRST TASTE
YOURS TO BARE

SOMETHING IN THE WAY SERIES
SOMETHING IN THE WAY
SOMEBODY ELSE'S SKY
MOVE THE STARS
LAKE + MANNING

THE CITYSCAPE SERIES
COME UNDONE
COME ALIVE
COME TOGETHER

EXPLICITLY YOURS SERIES
POSSESSION
DOMINATION
PROVOCATION
OBSESSION

ABOUT THE AUTHOR

JESSICA HAWKINS is a *USA Today* bestselling author known for her "emotionally gripping" and "off-the-charts hot" romance. Dubbed "queen of angst" by both peers and readers for her smart and provocative work, she's garnered a cult-like following of fans who love to be torn apart...and put back together.

She writes romance both at home in California and around the world, a coffee shop traveler who bounces from café to café with just a laptop, headphones, and a coffee cup. She loves to keep in close touch with her readers, mostly via Facebook, Instagram, and her mailing list.

CONNECT WITH JESSICA

Stay updated & join the
JESSICA HAWKINS Mailing List
www.JESSICAHAWKINS.net/mailing-list

www.amazon.com/author/jessicahawkins
www.facebook.com/jessicahawkinsauthor
twitter: @jess_hawk

91582753R10227

Made in the USA
San Bernardino, CA
22 October 2018